Keepers of Knowledge and Truth

By

Sandy Kelly

Dedications

This labour of love is dedicated to my four sons: Travis, Spencer, Jason and Adam, who got me started with online gaming many years ago.

To my two daughters, Christina and Tiffany.

And of course, to my patient and supportive husband, Doug.

Acknowledgements

I would like to acknowledge my second cousin, Ginny, for giving me the courage to pursue the dream of authorship. Writing has always been a passion, but it was her kind words that pushed me forward. Thank you, Ginny, much love.

Here's to the memory of Trooper, a lost and then found German Shepherd, who was a loyal friend and a protector of cats and little girls.

I feel that I must also mention my late mother-in-law, who was born and raised in County Durham, England, and helped us all to develop a love for that part of the world.

About the Author

The author started online gaming in the early days, when her four teenage sons would come home from school and disappear for hours. Curious about what they were doing while sequestered in their bedrooms, she began watching them as they played their online games and then she started playing with them.

She was fascinated by the graphics and the storylines.

Many years later, she has shifted to writing, but she still loves the thrill of the games, despite the dangers of entrapment. It's easier to step away and write about them, rather than be trapped in a dungeon raid or an all-nighter.

Chapter One
Reunion

Jesse sat on the shore of Lake O's, admiring the dark blue expanse before him. It had been two months since returning from captivity, and while his physical recovery was progressing, the damage to his heart and soul would never wholly heal until he found Breeze.

"Excuse us, Master Jesse," the young man interrupted Jesse's musings.

Jesse turned to face two young men. He would never wholly understand how this war with Tazeron sped up the development and growth of children in this world.

"Yes, Caleb, what can I do for you?"

Jesse marvelled at how mature this boy was. Just six months had passed since Jim and Sara's youngest son had been rescued from Tazeron. Jesse had last seen Caleb at training the previous week.

"My friend Ammon and I were wondering if you needed any more magicians to assist in the rescue of Ammon's sister, Breeze."

Jesse appraised the eager young men and realised that he might indeed need their help.

"I'm sure we will need your skill in the coming future. I suggest you continue your training. I have heard your names mentioned, and I look forward to your service."

The two were pleased with Jesse's response and smiled, nodding, excusing themselves as they passed a large red rooster on their way back to the village, pausing momentarily to bow to Rambo as they retreated. Jesse smiled as he watched the approach of his friend and mentor.

"Good morning, my friend," Jesse greeted Rambo. "What are you up to today?"

"Zealoc and Beloe have returned from their scouting mission, along with Zealoc's sister, Martha, who is visiting. I thought you would like to hear their report," Rambo informed Jesse after morphing into his smallest dragon form.

"I would indeed. Thank you for letting me know. I'll return to the village at once."

"No need to rush. They were all starving, as they put it, and will be eating for some time. We have time to sit awhile. One of the Toulonians will notify us when Zealoc is ready to give their report."

Toulonians were a previously unknown race of bird people that were recently discovered when Jesse returned to the village with the Raven Bob and his family. They were like harpies in appearance, but without the attitude and feistiness. The Raven discovered them high in the mountains while on a scouting mission. The Toulonians had the head and upper body comparable to elves, but the wings and legs of birds. Their backs and chests were covered in feathers. Standing three feet tall and brightly coloured, each member of the flock was an individual in feather pattern and colour.

It was fascinating to Jesse that these remarkable creatures could camouflage like a chameleon, allowing them to fade into their surroundings. Jesse wondered how they had been previously unknown to the people of Xanthara. He concluded that it was their small numbers, quiet disposition, and vanishing ability that had shielded their existence.

The Toulonians were quickly assimilated into the village and given the distinction of messengers because of their flight speed and excellent memories for details. They seemed pleased with their new rank among the elf people and Xanthara in general. It was also learned that their skill in magic was considerable as well.

Jesse settled himself back down on the log he had been sitting on and gazed once more over the smooth waters of the large lake.

"Rambo, why do you think I can't touch your mind anymore? For that matter, why can't I feel anyone's mind, including the creatures we brought back with us? I didn't have this problem when I was first rescued. I talked to the animals on the island. It seems like everything changed when I returned to my body after I died."

"I'm not sure, Jesse. Perhaps the trauma of what you went through while captured, or the way you discovered the commitment rings and the fate of Breeze. All of that has no doubt caused you much pain, and your brain and essence need time to recover. It might be any number of reasons, my friend. You are healing on so many levels."

Jesse looked down at the twin rings on his left hand, both silent since returning. Even the silver chain he wore, a gift from the white druid, was silent. He wondered if his mind was blocking everything, perhaps a way to protect him from further pain.

"Do you think I'm blocking everything, Rambo?"

Rambo turned to face Jesse. Jesse could feel the warmth, like Rambo was scanning him, but not a single thought.

"I don't think so, Jesse. I don't feel any walls up, but there is something different. It could just be the trauma. Try not to obsess over it, give yourself time. Perhaps Brutus could try cleansing you like he's doing for Tommy. Maybe there's something there that the healers have overlooked. It couldn't hurt. It's an unfortunate thing that all the Dumplumba and Naqisha trees were destroyed."

"Indeed. Perhaps they would help me. Maybe the fire ants have a secret one hidden," he mused. "Rambo, how am I ever going to find Breeze if my mind doesn't clear? I can't even reach the talisman, and it's right here on my shoulder. I feel useless and wasted. All I want to do is rescue her and get on with the fight, and it's being denied me."

He slumped forward, resting his head in his hands.

Rambo wrapped a wing around Jesse in a gesture of comfort. There was a rustling behind them, and they both turned to face an elaborately feathered female Toulonian with a flamboyant arrangement of orange, green, and mauve-coloured feathers. Her bright red eyes and distinct feminine curves were disarming, and both Rambo and Jesse were snapped back to attention by her singsong voice. Jesse was reminded of those ladies that sat on rocks and charmed sailors. What were they called? Sirens, that's it. Or was it Wili, or Vila? Whatever they were called, these Toulonian ladies had the same effect.

"Master Zealoc sends greetings and desires your company at the village centre, sirs. I am Fesha."

"Thank you, Fesha. The message is received gratefully," Jesse answered, impressed that the delivering Toulonian always gave their name at the end of the message, like signing a document. They also wanted to know how the message was received so they could return with honour or so they said at the beginning of their service.

Jesse and Rambo flew back to the village centre at the central campfire and there met with their friends.

"Greetings, Zealoc and Beloe. What news do you bring us?" Jesse asked.

"Young sir, it is indeed good to see you walking around. How goes it with you?"

"Not as fast as I would like, but well. What news do you have for us?" Jesse asked again, anxious.

"It is hard to say, Jesse," Zealoc began. "The game world has changed drastically since we lost you. There are more underground areas and floating cities. There is also an underwater world with caverns and mazes. The only hope of finding Breeze and the others who have been taken are the talismans. The problem with that is Tazeron has figured out a way to block the talisman's sensory abilities.

"The new game master or creator Tazeron has recruited is completely rewriting the game world connected to the online role-playing game Tazeron is bound to. We no longer know what to expect as we did before. All we know is the Shield is still in place and working as designed."

Jesse groaned and slumped onto a bench.

"With your mind-searching abilities, there still might be hope," Beloe added.

"I'm afraid my mind-searching isn't working at the present. I don't know why."

"Not working? I don't understand," Zealoc said, stunned.

"Jesse isn't able to perceive my thoughts or mind search as before his capture. It could be because of trauma, but we don't know," Rambo added.

"There is one other possibility," Zealoc's sister, Martha, spoke up.

"I'm sorry, Jesse and Rambo. This is my sister Martha. Father sent her to me so I could watch out for her," Zealoc grinned at her.

She punched Zealoc in the shoulder, making him yelp.

"Dear brother, our father sent me to watch over *you*," she winked at Zealoc before turning to address Jesse and Rambo. "I'm honoured to meet you," she said, smiling brightly as she gave them a nod.

Jesse smiled back, but then asked what she meant about other possibilities.

"We could enter the game world from the printed side, picking up enchantments that could possibly help your mind-searching, Master Jesse."

"I'm not sure that would work, Martha," Beloe chimed in. "Witches, Frog Princes, and other fairy tale creatures aren't very reliable unless you need a poison apple or really long hair."

"What about using the mind-searching powers of Rambo, Oongo, Molo, and Bob?" she asked.

Jesse's face brightened.

"Excellent idea, Martha. What do you think, Rambo? Is it a possibility? Could you and the others search the world as we travel through, for any sign of the missing ones that might lead us to their location?"

"It's worth a try. I'll contact the cats and apes and explain. I'm sure they'll be eager to assist," Rambo said. "Another possibility could be the Toulonians, with their flying abilities. I know they haven't been involved in this war, but it's in their interest as well. I'll talk to them."

"Jesse, I also have a message for you from Rusty Palmer," Zealoc said. "His physical recovery is progressing very well, and he's enjoying his work with the return groups."

Jesse was pleased to hear that. Rusty was enthusiastic about repairing the damage he might have done when first coming over into the game with Tazeron, before he realised how utterly evil Tazeron was.

Zealoc continued, "As we branch out into the new game world, it's a total redo, including flora and fauna. Nothing is the same as it was. The levels of the mobs have been increased, and their abilities have changed. Jim and Sara said it was like a total makeover expansion."

"Holy cow," Jesse whistled.

"One good thing, and we do not understand why this is, but the immortals can now use their magic. On the other hand, Tazeron can use his magic too."

"What!" Jesse said, shocked.

"Too bad we couldn't get rid of Tazeron before they got their magic back," Ginnea said, approaching the group with Zeela, Cami, Sean, and David beside her.

"Indeed," Jesse nodded in their direction. "I get the impression that things aren't going to get any better if we sit around waiting for something else to happen. I know I'm not completely healed, but

I'm very anxious to get back into the battle and rescue Breeze and the others."

"Jesse, perhaps you should wait," Nexlucimus said, approaching from the shadows. "We all understand why you are anxious to return to the war. However and please don't interrupt," the Elder said, as Jesse opened his mouth to protest, "it would be foolish to re-enter before you are ready."

"I can do it, Master Nexlucimus. I know that I can," Jesse said, pleading.

"Jesse, look inside. What do you see? And remember, I can see also," Rambo told him.

Jesse turned inward and was surprised to see that his red ribbons of fire were not there.

"What happened to me? I had the fire while on the island. Zeela, what has happened? No fire, no mind-searching, no hearing Rambo's thoughts, nothing. I'm worthless to the Keepers, to Breeze... to the cause." His voice broke, and he turned away from the gathering.

"Jesse, when you died, a part of you was lost. You need to find that part. Wolfa can help you with that, she lives here now. I know this will be tough for you, but it must be. We need the whole Jesse, the full, complete, and influential Jesse that we are all aware is in you somewhere. You have been broken, my young friend. You must heal," Zeela consoled.

As hard as it was to hear, Jesse knew it was true. He had forgotten that when you died in the game, even when resurrected, you became a changed being. You had to endure resurrection sickness for a time. He had to rediscover his powers, find himself, and become who he was meant to be. In a sense, he must be born again, not just resurrected.

"Zeela, I have wondered what was wrong with me. What you say rings true. I will stay, even if it isn't my first choice, and work with Wolfa."

"Jesse, when you disappeared," Rambo said, emotion in his voice, "I felt that I had lost a part of my life again, as when Pearl died. I have lost so much. Then I found you but you had to die to become whole physically. Another part of me grieved. Giving you that tonic of renewal was one of the hardest things I have ever had to do, besides saying goodbye to Chaelea. Take care, my friend. Find yourself. We all look forward to your return."

That night, before the group was to leave for the game world, Rambo and Jesse sat on the shore of Lake O's, reminiscing. They thought about life at Gran's, and the lessons she taught. They recalled the flight into the lake near Gran's house, and the ride Rambo gave Gran over the Slaters. The memory caused them to enjoy a hearty laugh.

They called to mind the battles into the Shimmering Mountains and the Castle. They pondered the attack on the twins, the death of Gran, and the subsequent rescue of Caleb. They talked about Jesse's seventeenth birthday a few months ago. They laughed and wept and renewed their bond for each other through their reminiscences.

And when Jesse had trouble staying awake, Rambo flew him back to his room and placed him on his bed like so long ago, when they had first journeyed to Xanthara.

In the mid-morning, when Jesse finally woke up, the group was gone. While his heart was heavy, there was a reason for his remaining, and he went in search of Wolfa, his former teacher.

On his way to Wolfa's, Jesse decided to stop at the healing facility and visit Tommy. It had been many months since Jesse had last seen his friend. At that last visit, the young Elder was lying in a herb-induced coma so he wouldn't damage himself with thrashings. Jesse hoped it would be different this time. He quietly walked into the darkened room.

"Hey, dude, what's up?"

The familiar voice, from the shadows, spoke.

"Tommy?"

"Well... it's not Santa Claus, even if I do look like him, and I feel as old as the myth."

"Can we open a curtain, so I can see you?" Jesse asked.

"Sure, knock yourself out, but I'll warn you to be ready for a shock."

Jesse walked over to an outer wall and pulled back one of the substantial curtains. When he turned around, what he saw did indeed shock him. Sitting on Tommy's bed, sounding every bit like his friend, was a shrivelled up little old man with thinning white hair.

"I believe your grandmother was always telling you to close your mouth and not stare. Am I correct?"

"Tommy... What has happened to you? Did the spider poison do this to you?"

"That and the herbs the healers gave me. Brutus also helped, poor guy. It took a toll on him as well." Tommy pointed to a corner of the room, and Jesse was once again shocked to see a small black dog curled on a pillow, shivering.

Jesse walked over to the little dog and stooped down for a better look. Brutus growled and jumped to his feet.

"Jesse, back away carefully. Don't break eye contact with him, but move away quickly."

Jesse did as he was told, and Brutus settled down again, curling into a trembling ball, keeping an éye on Jesse.

"What has happened to the both of you?"

"The poison that the glass spiders use is a potent neurotoxin affecting the central nervous system. Even a minuscule amount more and I wouldn't be here," Tommy explained. "I basically have no memory of the past months. Now that you're here, perhaps you can fill me in."

"So why do you look like a little old man with the white hair? And what happened to Brutus?"

"The healers did the best they could with what they knew. Brutus helped by pulling the poison out of me into himself. From what I understand, the poison is fast-acting but slow-moving. It comes on fast and leaves slowly, destroying the brain's ability to respond to stimulus. The body starts to age and, with the war and the metabolic changes in elves right now, my system got confused. The healers feel confident that both Brutus and I will return to the way we were before. It will just take time. Brutus, as an animal, will expel the poison faster than I would have, but it's still uncomfortable for him, so he's cranky right now. If he bites you, there might be some transfer of the poison, so stay away from him for a while."

"Wow, that totally sucks."

"Totally." Tommy smiled a toothless grin, and Jesse couldn't help but laugh.

They both laughed until their sides hurt. Brutus growled, but he didn't get off the pillow. Jesse was glad for that.

"So, what's been happening around here, and where is everyone?" Tommy asked. "I heard rumours about you and Breeze and cages and all sorts of craziness. So, I hope you've got time because I've got questions."

Jesse decided that perhaps he'd look for Wolfa tomorrow. This was probably just as important right now.

The rest of the day, except for meals, was spent filling Tommy in on everything that had been happening. The journey through time was both enjoyable and painful. There were beautiful memories and horrible ones. Tommy listened intently about the damage to Xanthara and the capital city, the new world of games, and the traitors to the cause. He was amazed at how things had changed and how powerful his brother, Tazeron, had become. He was distressed at Jesse's suffering while he was in the cage, and that he had to die to become whole again, and that he was struggling now.

"Sounds like we'll both be healing and regaining what we lost over the next while. Perhaps we can do some of it together," Tommy said, sounding hopeful.

"Perhaps. I'm hoping your mother, Wolfa, can help."

"If anyone can, it would be her," Tommy said with confidence.

After an enjoyable visit in which they lost track of time, one of the attendants told Jesse that it was time for Tommy to get some rest, and Jesse, feeling tired himself, left for his own bed.

Chapter Two

New Hope

As the morning sun streamed into Jesse's room, he watched tiny dust specks floating in the light, and an idea struck him. He quickly dressed and headed out the door in search of Mistress Wolfa. Running fast, he rounded a blind corner and nearly toppled Master Nexlucimus, who had stopped to chat with one of the village children.

"Young Jesse, what a pleasure to see you up, and... exercising... so early in the morning."

"I'm sorry, Master Nexlucimus. I need to find Mistress Wolfa, and I'd like to talk to you at the same time, sir."

"Certainly. I believe I saw her near the healing facility. Might I ask what this is about?"

"I had an idea that I want to present to you both. I'm hoping that it will help me solve the problems that I am having."

"I see. That's a splendid idea, Jesse. You continue to Mistress Wolfa's house, and I will meet you there shortly. Is that satisfactory?"

"Yes, sir. Thank you. I will find her and meet you there," Jesse said as he turned and ran off.

"I hope this works... it had better work... Breeze, hang in there. I hope to be coming for you soon."

As Jesse approached the healing facility, he did not see Mistress Wolfa anywhere. He ran inside to ask, when she stepped out of a patient's room. Running down the hall, Jesse skidded to a stop next to Wolfa and made a quick bow.

"Mistress Wolfa, I need to talk to you about the problems I've been having with my mind and magic. I have an idea that might help, but I need to speak with you and Master Nexlucimus. He'll meet us at your home. I hope that's all right with you," Jesse said.

Mistress Wolfa was startled by Jesse's approach, her eyes wide with concern, but she recovered quickly and remained calm.

"Of course, Jesse. I'm done here; we can go there now if you wish."

"I wish, and thank you." Jesse started to run out of the building but was stopped by Mistress Wolfa.

"Jesse, I see that you are anxious, but we must be respectful of the patients in this facility. Walk... at least until we are outside, then we can hurry."

"I'm sorry, you are right. I want to get back to normal so badly that I forgot the needs of others."

"I understand," she said with a smile.

Once they were outside the facility, Wolfa took the lead, and they hurried. Arriving at her home, Wolfa invited Jesse in and directed him to a chair.

"Jesse, wait here. I need to check on the children. I will not take long. The twins should be waking soon, and I want to let Meriloc know that I am back."

"Yes, of course. I don't mean to interrupt your family's routine. I'm sorry." Jesse took a deep breath and tried to quiet his anxiousness.

Mistress Wolfa studied him for a moment, then she turned and left the room.

While Jesse sat waiting, Master Nexlucimus knocked at the door. Jesse stood to answer, but before he could reach it, a curly-headed little girl ran past him with a blue skeedler in hot pursuit. She opened the door and hugged the Elder's knees, while two more babies crawled into the room with their own skeedlers trailing behind.

"Well, my goodness, hello, Chrystalina. How are you today?" Nexlucimus asked, picking the little girl up.

"Hi, Uncle Nexi... do you want to see my wiggle tooth?"

"Certainly. It would be my great honour."

Jesse smiled as he watched the Elder holding his young niece while she showed off her loose tooth.

"Oh good, Nexi, you're here," Wolfa said as she entered the room, scooping up babies as she went. "Jesse is quite anxious to discuss his ideas with us. Chrystal dear, would you take Janessa and Shaemen to Meriloc in the kitchen, please, and then I want all of you children to stay at the back of the house until I say differently. Do you understand?"

"Yes, Mother, I understand. Uncle Nexi, please tell Aunt Zeela about my wiggle tooth when you see her."

"I will indeed," he said as he put her down, and she disappeared into the back of the house with the twins.

"Now, Jesse, have a seat and tell us what has you so excited," Wolfa said, indicating the chair he had been sitting in.

"It might be nothing," Jesse said as he sat down. "But then again, it might be the answer to my problems. That's why I wanted to talk to both of you."

"Anything we can do to help in your healing, Jesse, will be a help to not only you but the quest. Please continue," Nexlucimus said.

"While lying on my bed this morning, I was watching dust flecks falling through the sunbeams streaming into my window, and I remembered something Gran told me when I first started living with her. She said, 'By small things are large things accomplished.' What she meant by that is sometimes, to do something big, you must do a bunch of little things first. I don't think I'm explaining this very well. If you never dusted away any of the dust specks that are always falling from the air, soon everything would be under a blanket of dust, even with the skeedlers."

Both Wolfa and Nexlucimus studied him pensively and then looked at each other.

"Jesse, what does all of this have to do with your situation?" Wolfa asked.

Jesse sighed. "Let me ask you a question first. What does it mean to be dragon-blessed or kissed by the White Druid?"

"Why do you ask this, Jesse?" Wolfa wanted to know.

"Because, Wolfa," Nexlucimus answered, "Jesse has had both."

Wolfa gasped. "You are serious, Nexi?"

"Indeed, I am. Jesse, show Mistress Wolfa the chain you wear and the talisman."

Jesse stepped closer to the pair and pulled up his left sleeve past his shoulder so Wolfa could see the talisman. He then pulled the chain out into the open and let it rest against the satin of his robe.

"How is this possible, Nexi?" Wolfa stammered.

"We aren't sure. Try to touch the chain, Wolfa."

"Master Nexlucimus, are you sure that is wise?" Jesse asked, concerned.

"I feel that Wolfa needs to do this, Jesse. Yes, I am sure."

Wolfa reached for the chain, but it merely passed through her hand, like air, as George had said.

"I am astonished beyond belief, Nexi. I had no idea anything like this was possible. Does this mean that Chaelea is close to us, and possibly returning soon?"

"We do not know, but Rambo is certainly hoping, understandably."

"Poor Rambo. Nexi, what can we reason from this?"

"I believe, in a way, that is Jesse's question as well. Jesse, you have already been told what it means to be dragon-blessed and kissed by Chaelea, have you not? Tell us exactly what you want to know."

"I want to know why, if my mind and magic are supposed to work wherever I am, no matter the circumstances, I no longer have access to them. Especially if no one can take them away from me without my permission. Master Nexlucimus and Mistress Wolfa, I feel like my mind and powers are being buried under a thick blanket of some kind. How is that possible, and can I get a blessing of some sort, like Cami? That is my question."

Both leaders sat for a moment, pondering Jesse's questions. Then Wolfa spoke.

"Jesse, I cannot see a person as you could, but I believe that you know others who can. Almost any animal that you have met, especially Oongo, would see your magic if it were still there. Do I remember correctly? Perhaps he could consider you and find where your magic is being held."

"Oongo is with Rambo, searching for Breeze," Jesse said sadly.

"Jesse, the blessing Cami received came from the gods, and I feel no such directive in this matter. Something else is at work here, and I believe that you might find help among the Toulonians," Nexlucimus said. "I have discovered that they possess great powers of insight. I will talk with their Chief, who recently revealed that they are very skilled in ritual healing magic. In the meantime, Jesse, I suggest that you search yourself. You indeed have a lot of power. Red magic is not something that can be stored away like a pair of shoes, and the mind travel or mind talking that you possess are indeed great blessings."

The head Elder stood and stretched.

"Well, Wolfa, my dear, after I speak to the Toulonian Chief for Jesse, I must make a trip to Braern. I have a need to visit Father. Is there anything you wish me to tell him, or Mother? I will return later this evening by way of warp stone."

"Just send them my love, and let them know about Chrystalina's wiggle tooth," she said with a smile.

"Indeed, I will. I must go now." As he started to leave, he turned to face Jesse.

"Jesse, I know that you are in pain, but we will figure this out, and I feel in my heart that you and Breeze will be reunited. The Toulonian Chief is called De'Larjanian."

Jesse gave Nexlucimus a little bow. "Thank you, Master Nexlucimus. I'm just anxious for things to be the way they were. I miss Breeze so much, and I feel worthless."

"You are not worthless, my friend. Look at all you have done. My feeling is you will once again have the chance to prove your calling and your importance in this battle. Take heart, my young mage. The gods are watching you with pride."

Jesse, having no reply to this, merely bowed as Nexlucimus left.

"Well, Jesse, Heralon is gone for the rest of the day. Would you like to stay with the children and me for our meal during the refreshing, if it comes?"

Jesse was about to thank Wolfa for the invitation and then decline, but he thought better of it.

"You know, Mistress Wolfa, I would enjoy that very much. It's been a while since I've seen Meriloc, and I would enjoy spending some time with you and your family, and perhaps get my thoughts on something else for a while. Thank you, yes, it would be my pleasure."

***

Later, as Jesse was walking toward the healing facility to visit Tommy, Bob the raven flew up to him and cawed.

"Hello, Bob, how have you been?"

Bob cawed again, circling Jesse twice before flying slowly down a different path from the one Jesse walked. When Jesse did not follow him, Bob came back and repeated the process, circling twice and then flying slowly down the other path.

"You want me to follow you?"

Bob landed and bobbed his head twice. Jesse hurried up to him, and the two of them travelled down the path as fast as Jesse could run. At the end of the trail, before it turned into the thick forest, stood a brilliant blue- and red-feathered Toulonian. He was flanked by six other Toulonians, and Jesse could only guess that this was the Toulonian Chief, De'Larjanian. Jesse bowed to the small, feathered man and received a bow in return.

"Chief De'Larjanian, it is with great pleasure that I meet you."

"Young Keeper Jesse, I understand you have a great need of healing for your mind and your soul. I sense that you are dragon-blessed and Chaelea-kissed. I am greatly puzzled as to why you would need our help."

Jesse was surprised. "Did Master Nexlucimus tell you this?"

"No, young Lord, I can see it all over your being. I also saw the red fire that I was told you had lost. I assure you it is not lost, only buried beneath lies and deceit. Who has done this to you?"

Jesse was astonished at this news. "I have no idea. When I look inside myself, I see nothing. It is lost to me. I need your help, sir, to rediscover myself so I can serve Xanthara and her people, as the Keepers strive to destroy the great evil that threatens us all."

"We know nothing of this war and the great evil that you speak of, but I feel its influence here. If it is possible to fool one of Chaelea's children, a prince such as yourself, then perhaps it is time to learn more and join you. The healers that I have with me and I will do all that we can to help you, young Lord, as Master Nexlucimus has requested. Jojodunja, Bjorin and Meajnaka, prepare the ceremony. Young Lord, you will sit in this chair."

Jesse was so astonished at the words of the Chief that if a chair had not been conjured out of thin air, he figured he would be sitting on the ground right now. This was not the first time someone had called him a child of Chaelea, but a prince and a Lord? Jesse had no idea what the Chief was talking about, but Master Nexlucimus would be asked as soon as he saw him again.

After about ten minutes, the ceremony was prepared. Bob and several of his family members were watching from the treetops, and that made Jesse feel relaxed.

Jesse watched as the Chief and his assistants circled a bowl of sweet incense, waving their hands through the smoke, pulling it closer as they breathed it in. The Chief then uttered some chirps as he removed a small flask from the folds of his side feathers. Pouring a thick substance into his hand, he spilled some on the hands of each of his fellows. One by one, they rubbed their hands together, placing a hand on a different part of Jesse's body, each in turn uttering a blessing. The Chief and one other put their hands on Jesse's head.

"We bless your head that your mind will be cleared and free from evil, that you may see and hear the truth."

Two others placed their hands on each of his shoulders and arms. "We bless your shoulders and arms that you may be resilient in your fight against this great evil, lifting others as they may need."

One placed her hands on Jesse's chest. "I bless your heart that it may be healthy and pure as you continue to seek the innocent and free them from bondage."

Two others placed their hands on his legs and feet. "We bless you that you may walk with the gods, knowing your correct path, and run with strength and purpose toward the overthrow of this evil."

When they had said their blessings, they all placed their hands on his head. Jesse peeked out through his lashes, and he could only see bright feathers surrounding him. The scent of their healing balm was sharp in his nose. Chief De'Larjanian began to chant and sing in a quiet melody that soothed and brought comfort to Jesse. He felt himself descending into a trance.

The deeper into the trance Jesse slipped, the more he recalled the details of the last few months. He remembered every aspect of his capture by Tazeron, even the loss of his arm. The trance summoned up the strange dream he had of the laughing madman and how he, Jesse, grabbed a rope and fell. Jesse saw George and how the small goblin had nursed him back to health. He relived the cages and all that happened there. He viewed the animals that helped and the men he met living in the other cages. Jesse thought of discovering his magic again and the destruction of Tazeron's fortress. He cringed at the shock of seeing the two commitment rings and the pain he had felt. Jesse rejoiced at seeing Rambo, and his fear of taking the mixture of renewal. He considered his promise to Tazeron that he would find Breeze. But what he also contemplated was how frightened Tazeron had been of the one-armed man, and how he had run.

"Look inside yourself, young Prince, child of Chaelea. Your essence is healing, and as it heals, all will be restored to you as before, along with other gifts. The gods have decreed it, and this great evil that has been done to you will be removed so that you may perform the task that you were born to do. We restore you, young master, Lord of the Prophecy, and we charge you to never again doubt who you are, or what you can and must do. It is done. So shall it be. Awake now."

When Jesse opened his eyes, he saw as purely as he had when Rambo first blessed him, and he vowed that his sight would never be dimmed again. His mind was back, and as he looked inside, his ribbons of magic were brighter than ever. Considering the situation, Jesse knew exactly where to go. He would find Tazeron and end this war.

As he stood, he felt taller, and he bowed deeply to the Chief and his people who had restored him.

"Young Keeper Jesse, I must tell you that never have we had a healing such as yours. We saw with you what terrible things tormented your essence, and we grieved. Then we saw the greatness of what you must do, and we rejoiced. We will gladly serve with you in this war if you so desire. The blackness and evil that hid your powers were removed completely, but not the evil memory. We then took that memory of the evil from you so that you could be wholly cleansed. We will destroy it. It will not infect you again. We wish you peace in your journey."

"I am grateful beyond words," Jesse said humbly. "Thank you for your kindness to me. I would ask another favour of you. A friend of mine has been grievously injured by glass spider poison. He is still ill in the healing facility, along with a shapeshifter named Brutus who tried to heal him. I would be indebted twice more if you could heal them both."

All the Toulonians bowed to Jesse and said they would visit the healing facility directly.

As Jesse warped back to his sleeping room, he felt, for the first time in months, a familiar presence, and it shocked and gladdened him.

"Jesse, my love, I can feel your presence. For so long you have been lost to me, and I feared for you. Listen to me, Tazeron has greater powers, and he has the keys that he needs to open one of the portals to the mortals, only one. It is possible for you to seal. There is urgency. I must go. Find the way, worry not for me. Discover the way. I love you."

For the first time since his return from capture, Chaelea's chain pulsed with life, warming his whole body and manifesting her love. The commitment rings beamed awake, both glowing brilliant white to match the dragon that was their image. Jesse realised that the change to the red and green colours had been a result of the deep darkness that had possessed his mind and soul. With the Toulonians' blessings, they were now once more pure, as before.

There was still so much to do, and Jesse felt an urgency to join the main body of Keepers.

Chapter Three
Return to Normal

Jesse had never been flattened by Rambo while he was in rooster form, but that was exactly what happened when Jesse warped to the group's position. Rambo was so happy to see him that he charged forward, tackling Jesse flat to the ground. Then, while standing on Jesse's chest, the rooster crowed loud and long.

"I have missed you too, Rambo! Now get off me, Zjordiaasinario Tilopjartelorian!"

Rambo quickly jumped off Jesse, morphing into a small dragon form. He stood there staring at Jesse, shocked.

"You spoke my actual name. How did you know? Where did you learn it? No one has spoken it for these many years." His voice trailed off as he walked a little way away. *"Chaelea..."* he whispered.

"When I saw your face just now, your actual name came to my mind, and I knew how to say it. Rambo, I have had an amazing experience. It will take me some time to understand all the changes, but I can tell you this, my mind is back to normal. It is probably even better, as is my magic, and Breeze has contacted me."

Jesse grinned at Rambo's stunned reaction as the rest of the camp gathered around them. They were also surprised to see Jesse.

"We were scouting when we heard this feathered bolt bucket yelling his lungs out. We thought something was amiss and came running," Jim said.

Sara was at his side in panther form. Two more panthers and an azure elf mage joined them shortly, the Slater children.

"Aye, I nearly wet myself. It startled me that much," Beloe said, laughing.

Jesse looked around at his friends, excited to see them again. "It is so good to see everyone. I have so much to tell you."

"We are glad for your return, Jesse; are you well then?" Zealoc asked.

"Yes, I am well and eager to join you," Jesse said.

In all, there were nineteen members of their party when everyone gathered. Since Jesse was eager to listen to the group's plans and learn what had changed during his absence, the meeting quickly redirected in that direction.

"What has been happening around here, Zealoc?" Jesse asked, looking out to the new world.

"Well, we have needed to become familiar with the new layout, as you can see. Even the plants have changed, so the potion masters have been relearning their skill. Animals and mobs are different, so while Tazeron and his captains have insider information, we do not. It is a total make-over expansion, and during these past weeks, while you have been recovering, we have been exploring and learning.

Mally's group has the job of tracking Tazeron and his supporters. Healamonster has taken charge of Beloe's group so that he, Beloe, can assist us here. Two songsters, or bards as they are more commonly called, were added to Heala's crew by the names of Julia and Ginger, so Heala's troop is ready for anything that comes at them, or they can assist us if needed. Their chief task is to map out the geography of the game so we have a better idea of where things are. It helps that the bards can sing songs of group invisibility and travel."

"I know those two players. I met them at the place of learning during my training," Jesse said. "I need to ask, has anything been done to locate Breeze?"

"I am afraid not, Jesse. Until the talismans work again, she will be tough to find," Zealoc said.

"My talisman works, and not only that, but as I prepared to come here, I received a message from Breeze," Jesse announced, astounding them considerably.

"How is that possible?" David wanted to know.

"I am not entirely sure. It happened after the healing ceremony the Toulonians performed on me."

"What occurred during the healing, Jesse?" Zeela asked.

Jesse related the ceremony of healing that the Toulonian Chief and his core of healers had carried out. He told them about the evil lies and deceits that had been placed deep inside him during his capture, and how they had been purged, leaving him clean and whole. All his tortured memories had been erased from his essence. Everything had become purer.

He conveyed how the Chief had kept calling him 'Chaelea's child' and 'a Prince'. He asked if they knew what was meant by 'the Lord of the Prophecy'; none of them did. Jesse continued.

"When it was over, I knew that I needed to come here. I also understood why my mind, magic, and talisman had not worked. It was a healing procedure assuredly, but also a believing process. Just like when I was in the cage and believed that nothing worked then Oongo pointed out to me that all was intact, and I just needed to look inside and see. Everything changed. This new game expansion has opened many possibilities. We must relearn what is possible and have a more precise vision."

"So, what are we going to do, Jesse, have more definite sight classes?" Beloe snorted.

"Yes, Beloe, that is exactly what we are going to do."

"You are serious, Jesse?" Zealoc asked in disbelief.

"Yes, Zealoc, the only way to do this is if we are all on the same page. It is a raid of truth and action, and everyone needs to understand the mechanics."

"I think we know that, Jesse, but we need to get going. We must stop Tazeron before he passes into the mortal world," David said.

"I know, Dad, and that is precisely why this is important. When Breeze contacted me, she told me that Tazeron knows how to open one of the portals to the mortal world, but only one."

There was shock in the group at this announcement.

"We are to find the way to seal that portal, but before we can do that, we must have all our players fully functional. We cannot do this if I am the only one with a working talisman. We will figure this out, and then we will kick some evil butt."

"It is good to have you back, Jesse. I guess we will find out what the plan is in the morning. Right now, I vote we go eat. It smells like supper is ready," Beloe said.

As the group left for food and to talk about what they had been told, Jesse remained behind to chat with Rambo.

"You have been quiet, my friend. I sense that you are bothered by my using your actual name."

"Indeed, Jesse, but that is not all of it. I am disturbed on so many levels. Have you shared any of this with Nexlucimus?"

Jesse studied his friend for a moment. "I have not, but we can easily enough. We can warp there."

"I believe that would be wise. I will let Zealoc know. We can talk to the group when we return."

They prepared to leave the village, and to Jesse's surprise, Zeela wished to travel with them. Jesse touched Zeela and Rambo, warping all of them to the elf village.

As soon as they landed, the skeedlers were there to greet them. In no time, they were clean and ready to meet with Nexlucimus. Zeela walked ahead to prepare for them. Vendors were setting up their evening meal carts. Jesse grabbed some fruit and bread to eat as they walked to the Elder's home. They strolled in silence, except for Jesse's munching.

"You are a noisy eater, my friend."

"Why did you not grab something to eat? Could you not find any bugs?"

"I did not see any. Did I miss them?"

"I am sure you will find something crawling around later. I will try to eat more quietly."

"Perhaps, but greater things are bothering me than not eating, Jesse."

"I know, and I am sorry about that. I feel as though your worries are my fault."

When they arrived, Nexlucimus was waiting for them, curious about their visit. He invited them into his study, where Zeela was also waiting.

"Before you begin, Jesse, I had a fascinating visit with the Toulonian Chief De'Larjanian concerning your healing. He tells me that never has he felt such power coming from someone, and such evil trapped inside an essence. He said that what they removed from you looked and felt like tar. How do you feel now?"

"I feel fantastic, sir. Everything is back to normal. In fact, much better."

"Master Nexlucimus, I must expand on this somewhat," Rambo said.

"Indeed, proceed, my friend."

"We have felt the hand of Chaelea in this quest almost from the beginning, and now Jesse says the Toulonians called him 'child of Chaelea', 'a Prince', and 'the Lord of the Prophecy'. Another thing troubles me. When we first saw each other after Jesse's return to camp, he was given my actual name and how to say it. This has not happened since Chaelea was taken. I need to understand."

"Before you say anything, Master Nexlucimus, Molo also called me 'child of Chaelea' and, while Oongo called me 'brother of Rambo', he also referred to me as a 'chosen Prince'. I have been curious about these things as well. Only since my healing have I remembered them," Jesse said.

Nexlucimus studied his hands for a moment, then gave a great sigh. "I can only give you my impressions of what these things mean. Rambo, my friend, I know your separation from your dear wife gives you much sorrow. Someday soon I feel that you will be reunited. I do not know why Jesse received your correct name, but I guess that it is a blessing from your wife, to let you know that she misses you also. Jesse, you will not repeat Rambo's correct name again unless you are asked. Do you understand?"

"Yes, sir, that will not be hard. I barely remember it."

"That is good. About the other items of concern for this quest, Jesse, Chaelea and the gods have taken a keen interest in you and your part, and your eyes have been opened by the Toulonians. Now, my young magician, I feel a higher authority has been placed on your shoulders. You must act well on your part. Think of yourself as Chaelea's adopted child, a Prince as you would be if she had given birth to you. Rambo is your brother through his blessing, but as the adopted child of Chaelea, you are his adopted son. The ceremony that the Toulonians performed on you has given you enhanced insight and the right to your expanded station in this war. You are charged with educating the rest of your party and taking leadership.

"Rambo, I am impressed that you must give them all a blessing. As Jesse is now your son, he may assist if you wish. I want you both to know " He paused, gathering his thoughts. Jesse felt something different in the Elder. "This is a directive from the gods. Do not ever doubt who you are, or what is expected of you."

There was a radiance coming from the Elder as he spoke. When he finished, there was silence, and the glow gathered inward and faded.

"Now, my friends, I feel a new life in this quest. I suggest you go and tend to your duties. Zeela, my dear, I need to talk with you."

"Yes, Nexi, I felt a need to speak to you as well. Jesse and Rambo, I will see you later."

After leaving the Elder's home and warping back to camp, Jesse and Rambo walked off a short distance to have a private talk.

"Rambo, I do not know about you, but I am stunned by what Master Nexlucimus said to us. I know in my heart what needs to be done with our group, but the full adoption and Prince thing are startling. What are you thinking?"

"I think I always wanted a son, but I never considered adoption. It explains a lot the fact that you are a Finding and can talk to animals, the high magic you possess, the chain that you wear and the commitment rings that changed to Chaelea's likeness and now glow with her brilliant white. The fact that Tazeron fears you and has tried to blanket you in evil to mask your abilities. There are other things, but those are the important ones. Much of this will be a matter of learning as we go."

"I am sure that you are right about that," Jesse mused. "Something else is bothering me. Rambo, all your life you have been a Prince. I have been a commoner in fact, a loner most of the time. I do not know how to act or what to expect from others. What should I do?"

"You do not need to do anything different, Jesse. Things will fall into place naturally. No one needs to know about the adoption."

"Okay, that makes sense, thank you. So... Dad... or do you prefer Father? How do you give a blessing?"

Rambo laughed, and it felt good. "I prefer Rambo... my son. You can leave the blessing to me if you wish, and I will abandon the teaching to you. This will be a shared kingdom."

"Sounds good to me... Dad," Jesse grinned as Rambo rolled his eyes.

As they walked back to camp, Rambo shoulder-punched Jesse, knocking him sideways.

"What was that for?" Jesse asked, regaining his balance.

"Nothing, I just felt like it," Rambo snickered.

Jesse stopped walking and stared at Rambo. "You know something, Dad, you have a wicked sense of humour, and it is sure good to have you back."

Rambo wrapped a wing around Jesse as they resumed walking. "It is good to have you back too, my son." They both laughed.

Everyone gathered around them as they strolled into the firelight.

"Tell us more about this training you have for us, Jesse," Mr Chambers said.

"Before we get into that, is everyone here?"

"Yes, Jesse," Zealoc said.

"While all of you were eating, Rambo and I made a short trip back to Xanthara to talk to Master Nexlucimus, and he had some advice for us. First, the gods have authorised Rambo to give everyone here a dragon's blessing."

There were gasps of surprise from the group, and the remarkable cats and apes roared in approval.

"Well, it only makes sense," Jesse told them. "Tazeron and his group of losers have their magic back and know the game world inside and out. They have meddled with our talismans and just about everything else with their blanket of evil crud. We need all the help we can get."

Jesse stepped aside, and Rambo approached the group solemnly. "This is not a light thing that I have been asked to do, and you will be well to remember that fact. Please kneel."

As they all knelt, Rambo began to hum, and the air snapped and crackled.

"I bless you to go forth in service to the gods of both worlds. Remember always that you have been gathered as warriors of good and mercy. Use your powers wisely and act well your part. You will forever see clearly, knowing who you are and for what purpose you live. Never again will you be confounded by evil. Your mind will tolerate only truth and honour as you complete this quest and proceed forward. So it is given, so it will be."

As Rambo finished speaking the blessing, there was a loud whoosh of air overhead, and everyone fell back to the ground, looking up. There before their eyes, above their heads, was a magnificent white dragon. Rambo whimpered as he too knelt.

"My dear children, I accept your willingness to serve this noble cause. Be it known that your sacrifice is pleasing to the gods. I have watched from afar and will continue to do so. I pray and intercede with the gods for you, but this is still very much your war. I come now only as a token of support. In time, I will return to assist as you continue with valour, but this is not yet. Be of good cheer, you are equal to the task. Use wisdom, and you will be guided by those chosen to lead. Do not doubt, nor falter. Both the mortal and immortal kingdoms teeter near peril. We are watching. Rambo... soon we will walk together. Jesse Finch, receive your crown."

She waved a wing in Jesse's direction and then disappeared in a flash of light.

Jesse stood next to Rambo and whispered, *"What did she mean by my crown?"*

"Jesse," David said in awe, "you are wearing a circlet of light."

Jesse reached to touch his head but could not feel anything. "Does anyone have a mirror?"

Cami had a small one, but Jesse saw nothing when he looked at it.

"It's fading now," Martha said. "I guess it would be hard to wear a crown into battle."

"Hey, can everyone else see things better than before?" Beloe asked the group. They all stated that they could, and that they felt lighter and more powerful, both in strength and magic.

"I can even see into the dark," Cami stated, and others said they could also. There would obviously be a period of discovery and learning their new abilities.

Oongo, Purja, and Molo came forward and bowed before Rambo and Jesse. "We are in your service for the justice of all the innocents, and we freely accept your leadership."

Although Jesse and Rambo were the only ones who heard the creatures, everyone in the group stepped forward, bowed, and likewise expressed a similar vow.

Then, two chuckles from the back of the group, there were a couple of soft pops separated by a mere second of time.

"Whoa... they're working again... sweet!" Jim and David had decided to test their talismans and warped to Xanthara and back, bringing with them a dozen pizzas and a bucket of fruit drinks, losing almost no time in the process.

"We figured a celebration was in order," David grinned sheepishly.

"We hit Xanthara so fast even the skeedlers didn't see us," Jim laughed.

"What, my hog rat stew wasn't good enough for you two? I thought you said you were full," Ginnea said, her hands on her hips and a smile playing on her beautiful face.

"Sorry, Ginnea, my dear, your stew was delicious. We just needed a snack," David grinned and winked at her.

Jesse did a double take and watched his dad brush Ginnea's arm as he passed, giving her a peck on the cheek.

"Do we have another blossoming romance, Rambo?"

"Maybe..."

"Yeah, yeah, I see how you are," Ginnea said, taking a huge bite of pizza as she softly bumped against David with her hip, teasing him.

"It's sure looking that way, who would have thought?"

"Love can happen in very unusual ways", Rambo smiled.

"True... I guess you and I have many things in common. We are both separated from the ones we love, and it's this war that has done it to us. I don't know how you have managed it for so long. At least you saw her tonight, and now you have the promise that she will be returning soon."

Rambo was silent for a long time. Jesse began to worry, but then Rambo spoke. "It gladdens my heart to think that she and I will once again walk together. When she returns to me, I want this to be a better world, a safer place. Where we can raise many more children, and it would be a pleasure if you and Breeze could share that world with us."

"Rambo, my brother, that is pleasing to me as well. We will most assuredly make this a better, safer place for our future families. Now, my friend, I need to get some sleep. It's been a very long day."

"Agreed, it has indeed."

Chapter Four
A New World

Before the morning began to lighten the mist of darkness that was still night, Jesse had his secret weapon, Rambo, step forward and explain what he had in mind to start the day.

Rambo snickered as he morphed into his rooster form. Taking a deep breath, he reached deep inside himself and released the most eloquent and very loud rooster rendition of morning taps. It was glorious and brought back many youthful memories for Jesse of living on base with his mother and father.

Jesse and Rambo stepped back and watched as the camp stumbled out of their tent shelters and staggered out to meet them.

"What's up, Jesse? Is there an emergency? I feel like I was transported through time to my time on base." David yawned big as Ginnea joined him, shivering in the chilled air. David put an arm around her.

"Yes... There is an emergency. We are at war, and it's time to get on with it. No more laziness will be tolerated."

More of the raid group joined them, looking like they'd been yanked out of bed with hangovers after a night of partying.

"A pathetic bunch of warriors we have here, sir. What do you suggest we do with this ragtag group?" Rambo, now in small dragon form, clicked his tongue.

Jesse pretended to ponder the situation as he paced in front of the company. "Stockades. We will place all of them in the stockades, while they think on their insubordination and slothful behavior."

"Aye, sir. Excellent idea. It will be as you have said."

"What's going on, Jesse? We don't have stockades. What are you talking about? Is this a joke?" Zealoc wanted to know, but before he could finish, cages like the ones Jesse had spent months in materialized around each of them. Shock and indignation swept through the group. Only the magnificent cats and apes were spared. Jesse sent the animals a mental picture of what was happening, and they seemed to understand, quietly slipping out of camp. Zeela, still with Nexlucimus, was also excused.

There were many shouts of outrage, but Rambo sent a spell of silence, and the camp fell quiet.

"I am sure you are wondering what this is about," Jesse began. "When I was imprisoned, I had time to think about the war and why we were fighting it. I thought about all of you and the battles you were fighting while I could do nothing but sit in filth and starve. I was denied my family, my friends, and my betrothed. I was ridiculed, threatened, deprived of privacy and basic humanitarian comforts. Still, I had faith in my fellow fighters. I started opening the camp, getting other prisoners to share themselves with me, and their companions in confinement. It worked. We became one in purpose and friendship."

"The purpose of this exercise is to test your ability to work together. Be grateful this is only a test and not real imprisonment. We will release half of you to use only the talents granted by the game to free everyone else. No help from me, Rambo, the cats, or the apes. If you are not successful within four hours, you will change places with those still caged and start again. No food, no water, no bathrooms. Your talisman will not work. You will not speak to Rambo or me. We will explain when you finish your task. You are freed."

Jesse waved his arm, and every second cage vanished, releasing the occupant and lifting the silence spell. Quietly, the freed members gathered to plan. A startled yelp came from one of the caged mages as the back of his enclosure exploded out. Cheers erupted as other mages followed suit, tearing open their cages.

But then the first swarm of large flies descended, biting and drawing blood. Rambo and Jesse shared a secret smile. Hog rats soon appeared, chasing the freed players up onto the cages. Plans shifted, strategies formed, and each time they solved a problem, a new one emerged.

Three and a half hours later, Jesse and Rambo, pleased with their teamwork, decided to let them finish. The final cage opened to a mighty cheer, and the players dashed for the restrooms. David and Jim, with permission this time, warped to Xanthara for food, taking Ginnea along to carry supplies. The flies and hog rats vanished.

"I think that went surprisingly well, don't you, Rambo?" Jesse asked.

"I do. I believe it was very successful but we will see after everyone eats and we have a chance to discuss the lesson. I think you are a master teacher, just like your grandmother, Jesse. She would be proud."

"Thank you, Rambo. I hope so."

After the meal, Jesse called the group together. He was surprised when Zealoc led them in a cheer.

"Jesse, we have all agreed that after our initial shock of being put in those small enclosures, we each have a greater appreciation of what you went through while in captivity. We salute you, sir."

They saluted, then knelt on one knee, pledging loyalty to him and their cause. Jesse was so taken aback he was speechless.

"Did I not tell you to not worry about your authority? You are indeed a real Prince," Rambo said quietly.

Jesse bowed and saluted, grinning with pride. "You are amazing. No matter what Rambo and I threw at you, you overcame it. We knew this would be unlike anything you'd experienced. It was necessary to break walls of pride and stubbornness to get you to work more as a team in uncharted areas. You did not disappoint. This will be your only lesson of clear thought and practice. Well done, team well done."

I will now tell you how your lesson was set up and accomplished. Each of us has been gifted individual abilities from the changes in the game, Rambo's blessing, and the blessing we received from the White Druid. I have had talents given to me for my leadership position. Do you remember the crown of light? Each of you will find that enhancements have been placed on you and your abilities. These are skills for your own stewardship. I invite you to experiment, and just like the mages found out today, you are stronger than you thought before.

Later tonight, we will have a raid meeting, as both Healamonster's and Mally's groups will be arriving soon. We will have a reunion and feast, but I warn you not to stay up too late. When you wake up in the morning, be ready to take on the day. We will start early. You are dismissed now to prepare for the arrival of our guests.

As everyone left, Jesse found himself facing his mortal father, David.

"What has happened to you, Jesse? I almost don't recognise you anymore."

"Many things have happened to me, Dad, most I can't talk about. Just know that you will always be my mortal father. I will always love you, but I no longer belong to you in the same way. When this atrocity is over, I will be more at liberty to talk about things. In the meantime, do as Rambo blessed you. Know who you are, and your importance to this cause, act well on your part. By the way, I noticed that you and Ginnea are becoming a couple. I want you to know that I very much approve."

"Thank you, Jesse. She's a wonderful person, and we are indeed becoming close. If we had commitment rings, we would be wearing them. We feel like you and Breeze; we cannot marry while Tazeron is still in the world. I need to go now. I am so proud of you, Jesse. I am honoured to serve with you." David gave a little bow and turned to leave.

"It's my honour, Dad. I love you," Jesse whispered as he watched David return to the rest of the camp.

"Growing up is a hard thing, Jesse, but you are handling it well," Rambo said.

"It is indeed, thanks to you, my friend," Jesse answered.

Within an hour, people began to arrive. When they were all assembled, a total of forty people crowded the camp. There was much laughing, harmless pranks, lots of shouting, games of competition, and a few duels. It was good to see their entire raid group together in one place. Jesse realised that there were other invasion assemblies across the game world working toward the same goal, but he was eager to be the group that brought Tazeron down.

As Rambo called the assembly to attention, there was much to discuss. Jesse had each team leader give an account of their assignment. Healamonster was the first to report.

"In our effort to patrol the new game world and map the different areas, we found it tough at first because the talismans were malfunctioning, but then yesterday, they began working fine. Because we had discovered most of the regions, it was easy to warp to them and map the vicinity. There are four new floating cities, two of which are friendly, one is not friendly, and one is neutral. There is an underground cave system with several sunken tunnels that are full of water and many serpents. We could determine no mortal or immortal life forms, just non-player characters, or NPCs as we call them in the game. One area is a desert that is devoid of oxygen. You need a never-ending breath amulet or spell to go there. Of course, you knew that. All the plants, mobs, and animals were different. There is even a fish that walks on dry ground. We never could determine its purpose.

"Frankly, we were amazed that there aren't more unfriendly areas, considering that the new game master Tazeron has employed is a big reason that there are so many changes. Apparently, the mortal world still has more say in what happens to the game world than Tazeron was hoping for. He doesn't have as much control as he wanted. It seems that specific rules of the world still apply. They did get the mob levels raised and the spawn rate shortened. They also appear to have more magic at their disposal.

"I'm sorry to say that we couldn't find the missing council members, or your lady, Jesse."

"Thank you, Heala, that information is all beneficial. Mally, could we have your report, please?"

"Of course, Jesse," Mally said, as she stepped forward and faced the gathering. "Our assignment was to track Tazeron and his close followers. What we found was that while he still has many followers, there seem to be fewer than before the expansion. The bad news is that they are more powerful. Tazeron, as you know, was and still is a mighty magician of the gold order. They are exceedingly rare.

"He discovered that if he takes blood collected from prisoners and mixes it with his own blood, he can open a portal to the mortal world. He can only do this once every full moon, and it takes him a full day to recover. He has sent several people into the mortal world, but he doesn't know how to get them back. They all seem to be so anxious to get there that they don't care about that little detail. After they go over, there is no contact with them. The plan is that those who cross over will get in touch with the mortal anti-gods and form a partnership. Tazeron wants to take control of that connection. We don't see that ever happening, but stranger things have occurred.

"Another thing we discovered is the council members that seem to be floating in a kind of limbo. We could only see them after the talismans started working again, and with a true sight spell that our Necromancer, Pumpkin, conjured. It usually only works on undead, but for some reason, it worked on the council members. They were not dead, just frozen or something we were not sure. And Jesse, we also could not find any signs of Breeze. We are so sorry."

"Thank you, Mally. Do you have any suggestions as to how we should move forward now?" Jesse asked.

"I do have one idea, Jesse, but I would like to talk to you and Rambo in private, if I might."

"Of course. I want to thank all of you for coming tonight. Now please go get something to eat and enjoy the evening. We will start early tomorrow. Heala, would you and Mally please meet with us here after you get food and drink, say in thirty minutes, please."

Both team leaders agreed to meet back and then left to eat.

"Well, Rambo, what do you think?"

"I'm not sure. I'm surprised at how easily Tazeron gained access to the mortal world. That puzzles me."

"Something that he said to me while I was captured seems important now. He said that my blood would help him as much as any of the others and that Breeze would complete what he needed. It didn't make sense at the time, but maybe it does now. I don't know."

"Perhaps I can shed some light on that, Jesse," Zeela said, as she approached from the shadows, making Jesse jump.

"Dang it, Zeela, you need to wear a bell or something. That stealth of yours is scary."

"I'm sorry, Jesse. I'll be noisier around you," Zeela chuckled.

"Don't worry about it, Zeela. Your stealth keeps me on my toes. What's your news?"

"While I was visiting with Nexi, he received a communication from one of his aides. Apparently, there was more information about the formula needed to open the portals. Certain combinations of blood opened specific portals. To open all the portals required pure mixed blood from someone like one of Jim and Sara's children. Blood from someone like you, Jesse, mixed with someone such as Breeze or Tazeron, would still open a portal, but only one.

"Once that portal was opened, it would be the only portal they could use. They would be locked into it, and it would have a timer so that they could only use it for one day once a new moon. Since we have two moons, that gives them two days. It takes an incredible amount of magic, even for a gold mage, to stir the potion. Tazeron has a magic timer that drains all his power for a full day."

There was a knock on a tent pole at the command quarters, and Malleesa and Healamonster entered the meeting.

"Welcome," Jesse said. "Zeela was just telling us some new information about the portal formula."

"That's what I wanted to communicate to you, but I didn't want to say anything in the open meeting. There might be a spy."

"Why do you think this?" Rambo wanted to know.

"Just little things really, but enough that we are cautious. I don't know you, Heala, but since our suspicions centred on my group, I believe you are fine."

"Gee... thanks. If you doubt me, I don't really need to be here. In fact, I think I'll go grab another sandwich and get to bed early. It's been a long couple of days. Goodnight."

"I'm sorry, Heala, I didn't mean to insult you."

"No offence, fair lady. I'm just exhausted. Goodnight."

"Goodnight, Heala, see you tomorrow," Jesse said. "Mally, what do you know about the portal potion?"

"I don't know what Zeela told you, but I'm sure it's close to what we discovered. Tazeron can open only one portal every full moon. What we also discovered is that he needs to send someone, preferably a pureblood who is heir to both worlds, through the portal so that they can return. If they don't, they will be trapped over there and eventually lose their bodies, because the timer works that way also.

"I'm not sure how that is supposed to work or what is meant by the 'heir to both worlds'. That confuses me. As far as I know, only the Slater children are heirs to both worlds. If that is true, then their blood would hold the portal open. Your blood or that of the other Keepers would also allow the portal to be opened, however, some kind of timer would close it."

"That is indeed a scary thought, and Zeela's report was similar. No wonder Tazeron is desperately trying to get the Slater children," Jesse said. "Something Breeze told me when she contacted me. Yes, Mally, I have heard from her and that we needed to seal the portal, and to hurry."

Everyone sat there, lost for a moment in their own thoughts.

"We still need to stop Tazeron either by distraction or destruction, until we can figure out where the portal is and how to seal it. And, as much as ever, the Slater children are still in great danger," Rambo said.

"We need to let the children know what we found out, so they can be aware. At least they are no longer babies. The twins are trained druids, and Caleb is an accomplished magician now," Zeela said.

Chapter Five
Deception

The morning came faster than anyone wanted it to. With all the reunions, games, dancing and food, people had stayed up too late, even though they had been warned. It is hard not to stay up late when you see friends who have been kept from you by war. But the morning comes, no matter how tired you are. Such was the case with Heala and Beloe.

Despite Heala's resolve to get to bed early, Beloe convinced him to stay and have another pint of mead while they talked. It was great fun and a much-needed break from all the tedious work of the last few months. Heala just wished his head felt as happy about the distraction as the mind it carried around. That is how it happened, or so they guessed later.

He had gone to the river to wash his face in some fresh water when a sharp sting in his neck sent him running back to camp. He never made it, and since his body was carefully covered with brush and magic, it was not discovered for a couple of days.

"A tragedy," Jesse said to the gathering. They honoured Heala with a quick funeral that left all of them thinking about the possibility of traitors in their group. It was not a good feeling, and nerves were on edge.

So, when three more deaths, Shosho, Tonic and Sheela occurred in the following week, Nexlucimus decided to come and interview all the players under a spell of truth. The questioning was proceeding smoothly when Malleesa made a shocking discovery. A note had been placed on her bed along with one of her darts of searching. She went immediately to the location of the inquisition. Unable to speak because of her emotions, she handed the note and dart to Jesse. He read it to the small gathering of leaders.

"My dear sister, it would be impossible for me to convince you of my reasons for siding with Tazeron. It has nothing to do with money or power and everything to do with principle. I resent our lives being invaded by these mortals. They are inferior to us in every way, and when I think of how they are destroying each other and all that the gods have given them, it makes me angry. Tazeron may not win this war. I can see that the gods are not with him but I still believe in his purpose. I may die, but in my mind, I die with honour. I used your darts, Malleesa, so in a way, your hand helped Tazeron's cause. I am still your loving brother, Faber.

Jesse crumpled the piece of parchment and stood with his head bowed. His face was grave when he looked up.

"Mally, I can't tell you how sorry I am. I want you to know that none of this is your fault."

With tears in her eyes, Mally faced the group. "You are wrong, Master Jesse. I was his leader, his older sister and his friend. I should have seen this coming. I have had feelings, little clues, but nothing substantial. Now I realise that I should have been more diligent about following through with my instincts. Master Nexlucimus, I believe that the questioning should continue. We must know if there are any other sympathisers to Tazeron among us. There must be no more deaths from within."

Shock spread through the camp as word circulated about Faber. Master Nexlucimus continued the enquiry, and two more were eliminated from the raid, not because they sympathised with Tazeron, but because they understood why Faber had. The possibility of problems was there, and so Toos and Rose were sent to Clay for careful watching. They would be under house arrest but not imprisoned.

Later that night, Jesse held a meeting with all the raid members who were left. Master Nexlucimus stayed to attend.

"You are all aware of why this meeting was called. We have lost seven excellent people in the last week and a half, and it is a sad commentary on the situation facing our two worlds. Four people, Heala, Shosho, Sheela and Tonic lost their lives because they were mortal. Even though they were in character, they cannot be resurrected within the game because of the way they died. The darts used were dipped in a potion of never-ending death for a reason. Faber wanted them to stay dead.

"The evil that Tazeron has inflicted on this world runs deep and powerful, as witnessed by us losing Rose and Toos because they felt sympathy for the way Faber felt. It does not matter if we completely understand why Faber, Rose and Toos felt the way they did. What is important is that we end this as quickly as possible, with no more decent people dying or being misled by the whispering of the evil that surrounds us."

"Master Jesse," Julia raised her hand.

"Yes, Julia, you have a question?" Jesse asked her.

"Yes, sir. How is it possible, with the blessing of Rambo and the White Druid, for this to happen? I don't understand."

"Perhaps I could answer that, Jesse," Nexlucimus stood. Jesse bowed to the Elder and stepped aside.

"Even with a blessing from the gods, respectable people still have their free will and make their own choices. All through history and even before that, there have been those who have gone against the powers of good and righteousness for the sake of rebellion or stubbornness. We see Tazeron in our world, and you can see the anti-gods of the mortal world as examples of this. Good people make poor choices and do bad things all the time.

"The difference is this: evil tries to force, entice or fool people into submission, offering them glory, greed and power, often using hatred as a pathway. Righteousness loves and teaches through example and guides people through free will to compassion, charity and service. The operative words are submission and free will. That is the difference. One is a loss of self for glory, greed and power, and the other is making a difference through service. Does that make sense?"

"I think so, sir. Thank you," Julia said, looking pensive.

"Are there any more questions?" Jesse asked.

There were no more questions, and the meeting was adjourned. Nexlucimus bid them all farewell and was transported back to the forest with a hearthstone.

An unnatural quiet blanketed the camp as everyone drifted back to their areas. The evening meal was prepared by the assigned group, and only minimal chatter could be heard as the food was eaten and then cleaned up. People retired to their beds early, and gloom settled over them.

During the night, a mighty roar rattled everyone out of their beds. Torches of magic were lit and shouts erupted throughout the camp as people scrambled around, unorganised.

"Stop and listen to me!" Jesse yelled, as he sent a vast bubble of glowing energy above the camp, encircling them all. Gradually, everyone settled down and gathered to Jesse, who was standing next to Rambo and Zeela in the centre of the gathering. While they stood there, Oongo and Purja walked into the light with Molo. People backed away, giving the large animals their space. Oongo spoke to Jesse's mind.

"Young Prince, while we patrolled the parameters of the encampment, it came to our mind that there was a feeling of doom

settling here. This camp must be moved. You have been here too long, and there are those who would do you harm if you remained. Already, there is a small army marching to this point, led by the traitor Faber. They will arrive within the hour."

"Oongo, we will break camp this instant. Would you lead us to a safe place?"

"We will do as you command. Molo has found a group of caves in the hills that will work well."

"Excellent… we will follow you, Molo."

"Listen up, people, the great cat Oongo has informed me that there is a small army marching this way. They will arrive within the hour. Molo and his clan will lead us into the hills, where there is a group of caves. We leave in ten minutes or less."

Everyone hustled to break camp, and they were ready to move in less than the allotted time. Molo and the other animals guided them, as Jesse provided a light that did not shine beyond their members. No one on the outside would be able to see it. Caleb and Ammon used their magic to erase any trace of the group's travelling. Even moving fast, it took them over an hour to reach the caves, but they found them comfortable and secure. They could be easily defended and made an appropriate place to base their camp. Despite having thirty-three people still in the group, the caves were spacious. There was a freshwater spring that ran through the back of the caverns, and the flying mounts shared a smaller cave nearby.

Jesse called a meeting once they were settled.

"There has been a depletion to our raid. If we were back home playing the game, we would just put out a request and fill our empty slots with pickups, but not being home, cancelling because we are short on members is not an option. We must finish this, and while there are other groups of raiders out there, we have no way of knowing how they are doing or if they are having the same problems. So, as of this minute, our period of mourning and licking our wounds is over. Tomorrow, we fly into battle and start kicking Tazeron's evil butt. Now get some sleep."

"Jesse, come with me, my son."

"OK, is there a problem? Am I in trouble... Father?"

Jesse felt more than he heard Rambo's soft chuckle as he was helped onto Rambo's back. "No, just some quality father and son time."

"Uh-oh... what did I do this time?"

Now Jesse could hear Rambo's laughter as they flew off into the cold night air.

"You worry too much, a sure sign that you are carrying a heavy load."

"What choice do I have? This raid is a big responsibility and so much rests on its success."

"Delegate more of that responsibility, let others share the leadership. There are many excellent people in the camp. There are

also some accomplished great cats and apes that are eager to serve. Tomorrow, we will go to battle not knowing what we will face. Let others help, they are anxious to do so."

"Rambo, I would love nothing more than to do just that, I'm just not sure how. You know what I wish for?"

"What is that, Jesse?"

"I wish I was back home with Gran enjoying my senior year of high school, and that Breeze was a girl at school, and I could take her to the movies or a football game. Some parts of my life here are truly amazing, like flying on the back of my best friend who happens to be a dragon and my adopted father. I love cuddling with Breeze while we watch a refreshing and eat pizza conjured from thin air. I hate that Gran died and that many more people will die before this stupid war is finished. We have lost so much, and I'm afraid it's far from over. We have got to find that portal and seal it. We must end this so everyone's life can return to normal, whatever that is."

"I agree, so are you going to divide up the raid and delegate out the responsibilities as a respectable leader, son?"

Jesse laughed *"I will try, sir. Will you help me?"*

"I will indeed. Shall we return to camp, or do you want to fly some more?"

"I would love to fly all night, but we should get some sleep. Let's head back."

"As you wish, my friend."

The camp was quiet when they landed. Jesse saw the great cats patrolling the parameters, and he waved to them as he walked towards his sleeping area. He saw Rambo become a rooster and walk out to them. He noticed the cats bow to Rambo as he approached.

Crawling into his bedroll, Jesse said goodnight to Breeze as he always did, but this time she answered him.

"Jesse, it is nice to touch your mind. I heard of your camp's tragedies. There was much bragging and loud laughing here. I am pleased that more did not die before the perpetrator was discovered. Tazeron is sure that more of the people of Xanthara will join him as he convinces them of the wasteful and destructive nature of the mortals."

"Breeze, where are you being held? Is it like Cami's capture, or are you allowed more freedom? Are they treating you well? What are the possibilities of a rescue?" Jesse asked.

"I am well, Jesse. Don't come for me, seal the portal. I love you; I must go."

It was so frustrating to only have pieces of conversation. Breeze never gave him much information except to seal the portal and that she was well. Perhaps Rambo was right. Tomorrow, he would turn the raid over to his captains, and he would concentrate on figuring out how to seal the open portal. In the meantime, sleep was what he needed.

Rambo, in rooster form, crowed everyone awake at daybreak. Breakfast was a simple meal of fruit, bread, and leftover stew from the night before.

"As of today," Jesse announced to the gathering after breakfast, "I will be turning the main body of the raid over to Zealoc and Mally. Sean, Peter, and Ginnea will be sub-captains. I will be trying to locate the open portal with the help of Rambo, Zeela, and Cami. Our friends, the Cats and Apes, will assist in a plan to distract and frustrate. We might need to return to this place, but I'm guessing that we are through with this location. I wish you well, my friends. We will be in constant contact as we move forward.

"Jim, my friend, guard your children well. I fear Tazeron will have his sights on them even more as we get closer to sealing the open portal."

"I understand, Jesse, and we wish you success in your goal. Farewell."

Jesse and Cami mounted Rambo as Zeela led the way to the place that Healamonster's group had said Tazeron's camp was located. They flew south-southwest as the morning sun filled the crisp air. It was a beautiful day in the game, and it seemed peaceful, but that, like so much, was an illusion.

"Everyone, invisible now. Something or someone is tracking us. Can you feel it?" Jesse asked the group.

"I feel it now," Zeela said. "Strange, my wings feel like I am flying through water."

"Indeed, Zeela, I am also feeling that way," Rambo said.

"It is an illusion. I can see into it. Here, let me show you." Jesse pulled out a pinch of pure sight dust and blew it into the air, which shimmered and then cleared, revealing a purple mist.

Zeela and Rambo stopped their flight, hovering in place as they studied the mist.

"It is to confuse us. I detect nothing that will harm us," Zeela announced, and then she flew into the mist, disappearing from their sight.

"Zeela..." Jesse called. "Are you OK?" There was no answer, but then she flew out of the mist, followed by ten tiny glowing bubbles.

"Whoa... what are those?" Jesse asked. They did not seem to be dangerous, but they could be a signal of some kind.

"I have no idea, Jesse, but there are tons of them in the mist, all sizes, shapes and colours."

Jesse tried to touch one of them, but it quickly moved away. "You know, they remind me of the direction balls on Xanthara. Can you talk to us?" he asked one of the balls. Nothing happened. "Guess not."

Then, out of the mist, came a giant snake, hissing and curling around the bubbles. The reptile shot a lightning bolt at Jesse that missed him only because Rambo moved quickly.

Cami screamed and pointed at the mist as a dozen more snakes erupted from the cloud and raced in their direction.

"Go, go, go!" Jesse yelled.

The snakes only chased them a short distance, apparently satisfied that they were leaving. Dodging lightning bolts was not on Jesse's plan for the day.

"Heala never mentioned purple mist and lightning-spitting snakes in his report," Rambo said.

"It seems things have changed," Cami said.

"Cami, please send a report to all the members with talismans, letting them know about these snakes and the mist," Jesse said.

"I will do that," Cami said.

"So much for feeling confident about our danger level. Rambo, try flying higher to see if we can get above this mist and how big it is."

"Jesse, I was wondering, do you think that we created the cloud and the snakes by using the sight powder?" Zeela asked.

"That is an intriguing idea, Zeela. Let me try something." Jesse waved his hand, removing the sight powder, and the mist and snakes disappeared, but the feeling of flying through water returned.

"That must be why we felt no danger because we created it ourselves. Cami..."

"Already on it, Jesse, I will let everyone know."

Travelling was slow due to the thick air, but they were still able to cover a reasonable distance. Before long, a valley with a lake in its centre came into view, giving Jesse an intense feeling that he had been here before.

"Do any of you remember being in a place like this before?" Jesse asked them, but none of them had.

Flying around, they discovered the entrance to several underwater caves and the remains of a floating city that seemed to have been destroyed.

"What do you think happened here?" Cami asked.

"Zeela, was that one of the friendly or unfriendly floating cities?"

"Unfriendly, according to Heala's map," Zeela said.

"Looks like the other raid groups have been busy. Let's turn north toward the airless desert. No sense following behind another group."

Chapter Six

All messed up

When they reached the airless desert, Rambo cast a bubble around Jesse and Cami while Zeela activated one of her amulets. The area was surprisingly green with many flowers, but when they got close, the flowers tried to grab them.

"Not as friendly as you would think. So much for trying to smell one," Cami said.

After flying around for a few hours, they decided nothing was there and started to leave when Zeela noticed something. Off in a remote corner, there was a momentous stone carved with ancient looking ciphers.

"It appears to be a warp stone," Jesse said. "Like what we would use when summoning members to a raid."

While they were examining the rock, the runes on its surface began to glow blue.

"Take us up, Rambo, out of sight, but so we can still watch."

From their viewpoint, they were surprised to see several elves walk out of the stone.

"Zeela, what elves are these, friendly or unfriendly?" Jesse asked.

"I don't know, Jesse. Should I try to find out?"

"What do you think, Rambo?"

"Let's watch a minute first, Jesse."

As they watched, a troll and an ogre joined the elves, appearing out of a previously unseen hole in the ground. They had an animated conversation in a language unknown, even to Rambo. Suddenly, one of the elves stopped talking and looked up toward the hovering dragon. Pointing, he sprouted wings and flew closer to Rambo.

"Peace, adventurers," the elf addressed the group, speaking in common elvish. "We see that you are strangers, and we wonder if you have come here of your own determination?"

"Our own purpose," Jesse answered. "Who are you? Who do you serve? Who is your leader?"

"We are free citizens and serve no master. Do you come in peace, or are you here to kill and destroy our world like the others?" The little man became agitated, and Jesse started feeling alarmed.

"We come in peace. We are here to track and rid this world of evil. We are Keepers of the Shield that protects."

With a smile, the elf heaved an expression of relief. "Welcome, then. It's so hard to know any more who is here in peace and who comes to destroy."

"Tell me, friend, do you have a village? And have you noticed any unusual portal activity?" Jesse asked.

"Our villages were destroyed when the world changed, we are wanderers. We have not seen any unusual activity, but we have heard rumours from our friends down below. We cannot leave this area except by warp stone. The air is too dense for us to breathe. Come, talk to them." He flew down and invited Rambo to land.

"What do you think, Rambo? Do we trust them?"

"Let's give it a try. You can always warp us out with the Talisman."

"OK, let's go down."

When Rambo landed, his feet sank into the soft sand, and he became trapped in underground roots.

"What is the meaning of this, elf? Do you cause us harm?" Rambo asked.

"No, good sir, we have no knowledge of your sinking."

"Jesse, warp me out of this stuff."

"I don't think so, dragon..." the troll said as he targeted Rambo with a Dart of Searching.

"Jesse, now would be appropriate," Rambo said. In a flash, they were back at their camp in the cave.

"Since when did trolls get the ability to use the darts of searching?" Jesse asked.

"I have no idea, Jesse," Zeela said. "This new expansion has everything all messed up."

"Cami, have you heard back from the other raid members?"

"Not since I told them about the mist."

"Zeela, as you look at the map Heala left, what do you think is the best possible location for Tazeron's portal?"

"It could be anywhere, Jesse; I have no idea."

"OK, do you think we could learn anything by going into the mortal world and getting on the game?"

"I doubt it, Jesse," Cami said. "There are many games, and the portal could be hidden in any one of them."

"So, what do we do? Give up? Waste another day exploring?" While he was talking, Jesse had a thought. "Zeela, let me see that map." She handed the map to Jesse, and he spread it out on a large flat boulder. Placing one hand on the page and the other on the chain he wore, Jesse asked his Talisman to take him to the breached portal. He was transported. Luckily, there was no one there, and Jesse quickly warped back to the cave.

"Wow... that was amazing!" Jesse yelled as he punched both fists into the air. "We've got this now... AWESOME!"

"Jesse... what just happened?" Cami asked. They all wanted to know. Jesse explained what transpired, much to their astonishment.

"I know how to win this war now!" He performed his best Zealoc jig and war cry. "That's for you, Gran, time to give them hell!" He could feel her smiling at him.

"Are you ready to seal off a portal?" Jesse asked the group. They all laughed and said yes. "Then let's go kick some evil butts."

Jesse and Cami climbed on Rambo, and Zeela landed between them. Jesse wasn't sure if he needed the map, but he held it anyway. Jesse was sure all he needed was the talisman and perhaps the chain. Jesse sent his mind to the amulet, and since they were all touching, they were all transported. This time, when they landed, there were three blood fairies and a pygmy troll standing nearby.

"Rambo, your turn, my friend."

As the blood fairies loaded their darts, Rambo blasted them and the troll into fine dust. "Excellent work!"

"My pleasure, Jesse, now what do you plan on doing with this portal?"

"Let me show you," Jesse said with a wink. Jesse bowed his head and placed his right hand on the portal. With his left hand, he held the chain and touched his talisman with his mind, picturing the portal sealing itself. In a puff of green and dark red magic, the portal folded in on itself, becoming a small clear stone that Jesse picked up and placed in one of his hidden pockets.

They all stared at him with their mouths open.

"Oh, come on, guys, didn't you learn anything when Gran was with us? Close your mouths and stop staring, it's rude." He chuckled at their shocked expressions.

"How did you know what to do?" Cami asked.

"It was a feeling more than knowledge. I remembered something Gran told me when I died. She said that the talisman would help me find Breeze. I figured that if it would help me find Breeze, maybe it could help me locate the portal. And it worked. Now I have another idea. Cami, it's time to call the troops, but not here. Tell them to meet us in that huge valley with the lake. We're going to make Tazeron think he's been infested with fleas."

They warped to the Valley of Giants, as they called it, because it was so vast, and began making camp. After greeting the other members of their raid, they all settled in and enjoyed an evening meal of vendor food (no one felt like cooking). While they ate, Rambo told them the story of how the portal was destroyed. There were yips of joy and encouragement, since they had found no luck in discovering where Tazeron and his minions were hiding. Jesse explained his idea of using the talismans and, with renewed hope, they went to their beds eager for the new day. Oongo, Purja, and Molo patrolled the perimeter, while groups of three and four people patrolled the inner camp area.

In the morning, they broke camp and paired up for *Operation Flea Jump.* The plan was to pair those who had talismans with those who did not. The talisman bearers would warp their partners into Tazeron's camp. Once in the field, they would stir up trouble by killing mobs, stealing equipment, kidnapping mortals they found and sending them to Clay for prison time, along with any other disruptive activities they could devise. Since there were seventeen people with talismans out of the thirty-two raid members, it was almost an even split. Everyone was excited to finally be doing something that felt useful. Even the great cats and apes said they could find ways to cause trouble.

They targeted supply lines, food preparation, healing facilities, laundry, bunk rooms, and flying mount stables. They even graffitied buildings with words of discouragement and offers of amnesty to defectors. They would simply pop in, make their mischief, and pop out. It was quick, easy, and worked amazingly well. Tazeron's troops abandoned their posts with startling speed. With low food supplies, lack of sleep, missing equipment and flying mounts, many surrendered. Those who turned themselves over to the raid were transferred to Clay for holding until after the war. There was even a rumour that one of Tazeron's game masters was quitting, though that was likely only speculation. The raid showed no sign of faltering. In fact, they saw indications that the game masters were increasing the challenge in their own way. Spawn rates increased, food was conjured at a faster pace and granted better stats. Mobs and mortals no longer needed to sleep or recover their magic mana.

Jesse's raid soon began receiving offers of help from members of other raid groups. Even though the largest raid groups in the game were capped at forty, no such restriction applied here. Three other raid leaders met with Jesse and his captains to discuss the possibility of joining forces. That would bring their total number of raid members to over a hundred and sixty. Such numbers were unheard of or even impossible in the game for many reasons. Severe computer lag would have been the biggest problem, but just the mechanics themselves would have been unmanageable. Here, however, those issues were irrelevant. This was a real war, with numbers to match.

The number of talismans in these other raid groups was close to the same ratio as Jesse's, meaning they could continue *Operation Flea Jump*. Yet with so many people, it might be better to simply storm the castle, or wherever Tazeron was hiding. To Jesse's delight, some of the Keepers who had been prisoners with him on the island were part of the joining groups. Jesse also learned that many of the gamers, not Keepers, like Rusty, had gone to help the teams find children pulled into the game and send them home.

After a brief reunion, and as they were preparing to set up the mechanics of the history-making raid, everyone in Jesse's original group received a disturbing message. The talismans told them that there had been another tragedy: the Slater twins were missing and presumed dead. The entire raid was devastated. Even the new groups felt the intense pain of Jesse's team. How could this happen when things had been going so well?

Jesse related the history of the riddle to the other leaders, and how the Slater children were an essential part of it. Since one portal had already been destroyed and the pressure was mounting on Tazeron and his group, it had only been a matter of time before another strike on the Slaters occurred. Had they been negligent? Had they let down their guard while revelling in their successes? These were questions they asked themselves as they grieved.

"This war has cost us so much, I can't bear any more heartache," Jim said. "Sara has taken this very hard; I fear for her health."

"I know, Jim. We have all lost a part of our lives through this. Your children are very special to all of us. Tell us how this happened," Jesse asked.

Jim studied his hands before speaking. "Mary and Jason have always hated being a burden on the community. They often talked about going out on their own. Just last night they wanted to do more and use their druid talents to flush out Tazeron and his minions. I wouldn't hear of it; it was foolish. But always headstrong, they left us a note saying they were leaving. We followed their trail and found..." Jim's voice faltered. "We found a clearing with signs of a fight. Jesse, there was panther fur, druid feathers, and blue blood splattered around the area."

Mr Chambers finished for Jim.

"Jim, would you like us to send Caleb to Clay for his protection?" Zeela asked.

"No. As much as I would protect him, he is a man now and must decide for himself. I'm afraid Sara would not agree with me, but we can't control him any more than we could the twins."

"We will do all that we can, Jim. I promise you that," Rambo said.

"Jim, we have enough people in our company now that we can form a search party for the twins. I would let you take charge of that, and perhaps Sara would feel more at ease if she were to join you. We have several hunters now who are excellent trackers, and with a small party of people skilled in tracking and stealth, you should have no problem finding out what happened to the twins. I suggest you leave at once, and be careful not to engage. Make sure that Sara and Caleb, if he joins you, understand that. Send us another message when you find them, and we can warp people to your position," Jesse advised.

"Agreed, Jesse, we will leave at once, and I am sure that Caleb would be interested in helping as well," Jim said, the determination in his voice palpable. "I will organise a search party, and we will leave immediately."

As Jesse and Rambo left the Slater tent, Jesse looked out over the valley of giants and realised why this place was so important. It was in one of his dreams, the one directly from the gods. It was the beginning of this quest, where Master Nexlucimus had said that he, Jesse, had control of who the players would be. How could that be, when he had no idea who would be there or how all of it would unfold?

"Rambo," Jesse said as he looked out over the camp and the large gathering. "This place, it was in the dream that Breeze gave me. How am I ever going to lead a group this big?"

"Jesse, you forget that Breeze gave that same dream to me. That was the first time that you saw me in full battle size and form, like this."

Jesse looked over at his friend, his mentor, and his adopted father as Rambo changed into his full battle size. The whole camp of over one hundred and sixty souls saw. They stood at attention and shouted a cry of power and solemnity. They were ready to follow these two warlords into whatever was required.

"Do not doubt. Remember who you are, and all the right people who are down there to support you and our quest. Jesse, you are young, only seventeen, and a terrible responsibility has been put on your shoulders. But you were chosen for this, and you are not alone."

"Rambo, you are correct. I do feel overwhelmed. Breeze is missing, the Slater twins are stolen and possibly dead, and Tazeron's influence has disrupted everything, including the scattering of the council. At times like this, I have no idea what to do next. But with you and all these incredible people," he motioned towards the gathering, "we will make it through."

Just then, there was another shout as heads turned towards the east. There in the sky was a brilliant white bird. Only it was not a bird. It was a snow-white griffin with a golden rider on its back.

"Could it be, Rambo? Is it possible?" Jesse whimpered.

"Yes, my son, it is possible. Let us go and meet them."

Rambo helped Jesse onto his back, and the giant dragon took off with his Prince to meet the griffin from the east, in the valley of giants.

Chapter Seven

Returned

Jesse watched the snow-white griffin land on the small island in the middle of the lake, in the valley of giants. Rambo headed in that direction while all eyes on the ground watched. When they landed, Jesse dismounted and approached the pair with Rambo at his side.

The golden rider removed his helm, and for the first time in almost a year, Jesse faced his friend as he had been before the glass spider's insidious attack. Jesse's joy overcame him, and he stumbled. Tommy rushed forward and caught Jesse before he could fall.

"Tommy," Jesse whispered, "you and Brutus are whole. What miracle caused this to happen?"

"We had a couple of visits from some friends of yours," Tommy said solemnly. "Toulonians, I believe they called themselves. I will recount the incident later, Jesse. For now, we have some serious problems I must tell you and the other leaders. Please introduce me to this distinguished gathering of raiders."

Jesse turned to the gathering and, with the help of magic, he addressed the people of the raid.

"Fellow Keepers, we have gathered in this place to continue our great quest. We thank all of you for your sacrifices in fighting this war with Tazeron and his minions. We all know the seriousness of this endeavour, and at this final hour, before we go to battle, we are joined by a member of the governing authority of Xanthara. May I present to you Prince Tomitobias Silverrod, first in command over the city and this world."

Jesse started at his own words as a loud cheer filled the valley. He stared at his friend as Tommy nodded pensively towards the gathering, raising a hand in greeting.

"Rambo, what does this mean? The words just came out of me. I had no control."

"I am afraid," Rambo said, "that it means Nexlucimus has disappeared, along with all the other remaining council. Tomitobias is all that is left of the ruling members. This is most grievous."

"Come, Jesse," Tommy said gravely as he mounted Brutus. "We need to call a meeting of the leaders."

As they prepared to call the raid leaders to a place that Tommy had chosen, an intense wind began to blow. Jesse watched in horror as people were hurled high into the air, flung about, and then dropped to the ground. There were many injuries. Jesse used his mind to search the area and discovered an alternate plane of existence just below their feet, and three people off in the distance whom he did not know.

Jesse sent a message to all the Keepers with a talisman, instructing them to gather those without a talisman to themselves and form an interlocking group. After some time, all the members of the raid, including the injured, were collected close to Jesse and Tommy. This was no small task considering their number.

With the help of his talisman and the chain around his neck, Jesse opened a portal to the other plane, and everyone escaped into it, away from the destructive winds. Right before entering the sanctuary himself, Jesse noticed a piece of the sky flapping strangely, and as he studied it, he was shocked to see a figure flopping there like a sleeping marionette dancing behind a torn curtain.

He tried to comprehend what he saw as Tommy came back to his side. Jesse pointed to the image before their eyes. As he did so, he remembered the dream that Breeze had given to himself and Rambo long ago.

"We must get below, Tommy. Come quickly."

Without hesitation, Tommy followed.

Once below the howling gale, Tommy called to the assembly, gaining their attention.

"Friends, there has been a serious breach of authority in the capital city. I alone have survived a coup d'état that was led by various community leaders who wished for power."

There was horror expressed at this news and much talking, as many worried about family and friends.

"These community leaders believed Tazeron's cunning words, his lies. I alone survived because I was concealed in the healing facility. The Toulonians, seeing the mischief, diverted the evildoers' attention from me."

Jesse and Rambo explained who the Toulonians were to those unfamiliar with them.

"The Toulonians brought me word of the outcome. Zeela, Nexlucimus is safe for the moment, but in hiding with the elves for his safety, so be at peace with that knowledge. We are not sure about all the others, but we do know that they are all incapacitated in some way. The Toulonians have told me this. We are aware of our duty, mission, and path. We must not lose sight of these things. We will press forward. We will succeed."

Jesse then addressed them while the healers continued their work caring for the injured. There was a subdued mood among the members of the large group.

"Because this world keeps changing and the stakes are always shifting, we are using much of our valuable time and resources just adjusting to the problems we seem to encounter. While Tazeron presses forward, we fall behind. I have seen this place, this gathering, in a dream. My Shadow Dream showed it to me long ago, and I only just now remembered it.

"Tazeron is doing to us what we were doing to him. He is throwing fleas at us with this storm. I saw three strangers on the island, but I did not recognise them. I believe they are responsible for the wind and these injuries. Despite this setback, we must stop Tazeron. Zeela, my friend, are you all right?"

"Yes, Jesse, I am."

That was the only time Jesse could remember Zeela with tears in her eyes. She stood off by herself, subdued, unlike her usual self. She seemed in shock.

"Watching this windstorm and the three strangers, I noticed a strange sight. I thought I saw someone caught in the wind like a marionette, and I realised something. I believe I know where the missing council and many of the other people might be."

There was a shocked response from the group.

"Then why are we standing here? Let us go and rescue them," Zealoc stated fiercely.

"No, Zealoc. I also know that we cannot recover any of them. In my dream, we tried to rescue them, but the harder we tried, the more they were moved away from us. They will have to save themselves while we rescue this quest. They were a distraction."

Total silence followed this announcement.

"But Jesse…" Zealoc began to disagree.

"Jesse speaks the truth," Tommy interjected. "We must remember our path. This is a war, and we must do what is necessary, no matter the pain it causes us. For the greater good, we must abandon the few," Tommy added with much discomfort.

"Truly spoken, Milord," Rambo said as he entered the room. "Sorry I arrived late, but I was watching the wind, and I made a discovery. I invite the raid leaders to come and see what I found. They will report back to the rest of you."

Still stunned by the words of Jesse and Tommy, the leaders followed Rambo outside. They were amazed to see calmness and a now clear sky. There was a tiny shack with an old woman sitting in a rocking chair a short distance away.

"Where did she come from?" Beloe asked no one in particular.

"No idea," Rambo said. "She wasn't there when I came in just now. I was going to point out a bright oval in the distance just west of us, over there." He pointed in the direction he spoke of. There was indeed something that looked like a new portal, and no sign of the three strangers that Jesse had seen just moments before.

"I feel like I need to find out what's going on here. This woman, whoever she is, is a clue," Jesse stated. "Come with me, Rambo, you too, Tommy. The rest of you, please remain here."

The three of them walked the short distance to the old woman and her shack.

"Hello, young Keepers, are you having a good day or a bad day?"

They were dumbfounded not only by what she said but by what she was doing. She was carving a baby out of a blue stone as though it were the softest wood or a bar of soap.

"Why do you bring trouble to my world?" she asked, continuing to shape the baby. "Why do you not give respect to others' property? What must an old woman do to have peace and quiet?"

"Who are you, Mother?" Jesse asked. "How can we help you? What must we do to restore your property, and the peace and quiet of your world?" Jesse did not know where the words came from, but they seemed to be what he needed to say.

The old woman smiled at him and then forcefully threw down the baby she had been carving. It bounced a couple of times, then lay silent in the dirt. They watched it for a moment or two, thinking it would change into something, but it did not.

The old woman took another piece of blue stone from a box and started carving another baby. She was surprisingly fast, and as they watched, she whittled and threw down several more infants into the dirt.

"Mother, I am confused," Jesse said. "What can we do to help you?"

Again, the old woman only smiled silently and kept at her work. She now had many babies lying in the dirt at her feet and began fashioning another.

At last, she spoke. "I am Matilda, and it is I who will help you, young Keepers."

Both Rambo and Tommy sucked in their breath and released it in a low, soft whistle, confusing Jesse even more.

"Jesse, be careful with what you say. Do not speak back to me. She is one of the Ancients," Rambo warned.

Matilda turned to Rambo and winked at him, giving him a radiant smile. "I hear all, young Prince, including your pain."

This stunned Rambo, and he bowed to her.

She continued, "Take this army that I have formed. They will help you confuse and defeat the evil that is destroying the peace of this world, and has brought trouble and disrespect for the Elders and young alike. These soldiers will teach what only those with eyes to see and ears to hear will understand.

"Use them wisely, Prince Jesse, Prince Tomitobias, and Prince Rambo. Give one to each of your chief captains and the others to those you choose. They will give the power to escape any harm or destroy an enemy. Use them once for need, use them twice for greed, use them thrice for sorrow.

"Be kind to your elders at all times, respect them, give them honour as you have this day done to me, and your goal will not elude you for long."

She paused for a moment, surveying their surroundings.

"Now I tell you a mystery," Matilda said, as she stood and motioned with her hand out over the vista where the vast army was gathered, watching. "While it might seem strange to you, after collecting such an outstanding complement of soldiers who are willing to serve and even die for the quest, I tell you, they are not needed."

This surprised Jesse and the others very much, and Jesse was about to say so, but then Rambo spoke to his mind.

"Jesse, I saw you stiffen at her words just now. Do not interrupt her, only listen."

Jesse chanced a glance at Rambo and then at Matilda. He noticed that Matilda was smiling.

"You have a wise friend, Jesse," Matilda said to him. "Yes, I know you and all of these." She looked out over the valley.

"This quest is about to change and surprise you exceedingly. Listen to wisdom, remember the past, and honour the future. Send the others back to where they came from. They will not question. They will soon be needed elsewhere, and you of this company will understand."

With those words, the old woman and her shack vanished, leaving the three friends with twenty-five blue babies all lying in the dirt and now crying.

"Man, I thought I was past being surprised," Jesse said, as he walked over to the babies and started picking them up.

"I have lived a long time and have seen many things, but this is a first. I am astonished," Tommy agreed, as he bent over to help Jesse pick up the crying infants.

"An Ancient… Chaelea, what are we supposed to do with all these little ones?" Rambo said aloud, as he watched the other two and then conjured a bubble. "Put them in this, we can float them back to camp."

As soon as the babies were all placed in the bubble and it was sealed, the crying and squirming stopped. They seemed to fall asleep, rocked by the motion.

"You know, I remember my mum telling me once that the only way she could get me to sleep sometimes, when I was a baby, was to take me for a car ride. I guess it works here too. How are we going to feed these kids? Are they going to need nappies that we must change? What is going on here?"

"I have no idea," Tommy said, shaking his head, and Rambo agreed.

By the time they arrived back at the camp, they had many questions and no answers, except that the Ancients were now involved, and they needed to figure out how and why things had changed to include them.

Walking in with a bubble full of blue babies was a huge topic of discussion, and as they related the story, everyone was amazed. Only one person in the group could offer a possible answer, Mr Chambers.

"So, no one here has ever seen or heard of anything like this before?" Mr Chambers said to the gathering. "Well, I have an idea that could be the answer. All you gamers, have you ever been in a dungeon where there was a character who was part of the game and gave blessings or cast spells of enhancement? Maybe you found a cauldron or box that contained equipment or supplies that fed you and increased your stats?

"Maybe that old lady was just such a random character the game generated. Her only purpose, perhaps, was to gift a player who spoke to her. I suggest that if you see any other senior citizens you treat them as she said, and perhaps there will be more gifts for the raid. I don't have any clues as to how to use these kiddos, however. Someone else will need to work on that."

"When we first went out to her and Jesse began speaking, I was strongly impressed that she was an Ancient," Rambo stated.

There was shocked surprise from the immortals in the group.

"How can that be?" both Zeela and Zealoc asked in unison, and many others murmured in agreement.

"I have heard stories of the Ancients, but never in my lifetime have I ever met one, or anyone who had. What does this mean?" Zealoc asked.

"What I know of the Ancients," said Rambo, "is that they helped form the worlds in the time before time and became as the gods. At least, that is what the legends say. I have no idea what this encounter means, or why it is happening now. I suggest that we pass along the message she gave, about having respect for elders and treating them kindly. We do not want to offend them, especially if they are indeed part of the godhead."

"Before we do any of that," Jesse said, gaining everyone's attention, "we were told by this Ancient, Matilda, that we were to send all of you not of our company back to where you came from so that you can continue your duties there. She said that this quest will soon change again and that you will be needed elsewhere. So please prepare to leave. Use your talismans and be safe, our friends. We thank you for responding the way you did, and for your willingness to serve. I am sure that we will be learning more and may perhaps have further directions for you shortly."

The extra troops not part of Jesse's original raid were dismissed, and after gathering their equipment, they warped out. They left without a single question or concern, just as Matilda had said they would.

"I am sure that if we could talk to Nexi, he would have more answers," Zeela said, and immediately muffled a sob. She asked to be excused.

"Of course, Zeela," Jesse said, concerned, as they watched her leave.

It seemed so quiet without all the hustle and bustle of the added soldiers. Their group of raiders had been reduced from one hundred and sixty to forty-five, and they wondered what was next. How could they possibly continue with so few Keepers? They would once again call another meeting to reorganise.

Jesse, Rambo, and Tommy stepped into another cave to have a rest while they waited for the remainder of the leaders to grab something to eat and join them. David and Ginnea had been busy cooking up a pot of something that smelled delicious. Cami promised to bring them back some so that they too could eat.

"Jesse," Zeela approached excitedly, with no sign of her tears. "Have you checked the babies lately?"

"No, what's up?"

"I stepped into their room, and… come and see! You will not believe this."

Curious about what Zeela was so excited about, Jesse and Rambo hurried to where the babies were sleeping. What they saw astounded them, for they were no longer infants. They were full-grown azure elves who looked precisely like Jim and Sara's twins. There were even a few who resembled Caleb.

"Whoa! What have we here?" Rambo exclaimed.

"Master Jesse, Matilda has placed us here to assist you. How may we serve?" one of the now full-grown elves said.

"What is going on, Jesse?" Cami asked as she walked into the room with a steaming bowl of something that smelled wonderful. Sean, Beloe, Zealoc, and the other leaders were on their way.

"I have no idea. Let's find out. Who are you, and what can you do to help us? What are your talents?" Jesse asked.

Another of the young men stepped forward and made a deep bow. "We are moon soldiers, carved out of blue moonstone. We have one season of life in which to serve the assigned. We can be or do any task once. We can be or do any task twice, if necessary. We can be or do any task thrice, for the price of a life. We cannot kill or maim. We do not require food, drink, shelter, or sleep."

This revelation stunned all of them, and there was a moment of silence before anyone could speak.

"Amazing," Jesse said. "Zealoc, as the main raid leader, would you take these soldiers? I am sure that they have special abilities that we will discover."

"Sure. I have no idea what to do with them, but I will figure it out," Zealoc said, eyeing the blue soldiers cautiously.

"Moon soldiers, would you follow Zealoc here while we decide how best to use your talents?"

"Yes, Master Jesse, we will go with Zealoc. Since Matilda chose you as our first commander, we will also support you, no matter whom you assign us to."

"Jesse, might I suggest that Cami and I warp over to Tazeron's base camp? We could go cloaked with invisibility and scout out the situation there," Tommy suggested. "Perhaps we could learn something about the Slater twins at the same time."

As expected, Mr Chambers objected, but then he was invited to go with them.

"I am for that idea, Tommy," Jesse said. "And I think you should leave immediately. I would suggest that you consider taking Zeela and Beloe also."

Chapter Eight
Moon Soldiers

After the meeting, Jesse decided to take a walk outside the cave for some fresh air. Rambo went with him.

"You have contact with Breeze, correct?" Rambo asked Jesse.

"Not too often. She has been quiet lately."

"Have you told her about Matilda and the moon soldiers?"

"Not yet. Perhaps now is a good time while it's quiet."

"Have you noticed that they resemble the Slater children?"

"I have. Here goes. *Breeze? Are you there?*"

"Yes, Jesse."

"What do you know about Matilda and the moon soldiers?"

"Only what is contained in our traditions. Why?"

"Well, she paid us a little visit this night, and we now have twenty-five of her moon soldiers."

Silence.

Silence.

"She's not responding, Rambo. It's like she"

"JESSE! Come to me quickly! Bring Rambo and four of the moon soldiers. This is what I've been waiting for. Hurry! Combine the powers of the talismans, you must find me. Come under Rambo's invisibility cloaking. See you soon, my love."

Jesse was so startled by the enthusiasm of Breeze's response that it took him a moment to form his words and relay her message.

"She wants us to go to her. She was very excited at the mention of Matilda and the moon soldiers. She wants us to bring four soldiers with us."

"I guess we had better get going then," Rambo replied.

Breeze's excitement infected Jesse. He missed her so much, and to know that he was going to her now sent his energy level soaring. Before they left, however, they needed to call a meeting with Zealoc, who was the senior raid leader now that Tommy was gone. David, Ginnea and Martha were also included, since they would help with the assault organisation. Jesse explained what he and Rambo were going to do and where Tommy and his group had gone. After securing four of the soldiers, Jesse turned the troops over to Zealoc's command, knowing that they were in good hands.

After the meeting, Jesse and Rambo prepared to depart with their moon soldiers as Breeze had requested. There was a slight problem. Gathering the four moon soldiers, Rambo and their gear was the simple part. Getting everyone into one spot so that he could have contact with them was more complicated. One of the soldiers mentioned that they could collapse together into one place. Jesse did not understand what the soldier meant, so the soldier demonstrated. All of them could stand in the same location at the same time, thus reducing the space they occupied. Instead of having four of them, it appeared there was only one. The soldier also mentioned that while they were united in one spot, all their strength, spell power and other abilities would be combined into one soldier, multiplied by four in this case.

The young moon soldier cautioned that if they were connected in that way, one talent would be taken from each. Since each soldier only had two skills to begin with, that would be a substantial cost. While the increased abilities sounded attractive, Jesse and Rambo would have to decide if it was worth the price when the time came. Jesse had a thought regarding the idea.

Speaking to the moon soldiers, he asked, "What can we call you? Do you have names?"

The soldiers looked confused.

"What does Mistress Matilda say to you when she needs you to do something for her?"

"She never needs us, sir."

"Okay then, what do I say to you so that you know I'm talking to you?" He tapped one of the soldiers on the chest. "And not him." He tapped one of the others.

"We understand now, sir. You call us by our appearance, or you give us a label when you provide us with an assignment."

Jesse was getting frustrated. "Okay, if I say, 'Hey baldy, come here,' you go bald?"

To Jesse's surprise, all the soldiers became bald. Jesse smiled, an idea hitting him.

"Blue beetle bugs collapse."

All the soldiers became blue bugs and stacked on top of each other. Jesse then told them to become soldiers again and form a line.

"I'm hoping that I'm not wasting you by experimenting with this exercise."

"No, sir. Shapeshifting does not apply."

"Excellent. Soldier one, purple donkey." The soldier he pointed to obeyed.

"Soldier two, brown mouse." Again, compliance.

"Soldier three, troll. Soldier four, small Rambo."

They all did as instructed, but soldier three was so fat he nearly squashed everyone else in the cave. Jesse had him change into a book. Soldier four did not turn into Rambo the small dragon or the chicken; he transformed into the actor from the old film, in miniature.

"Wow, soldier four… small Tazeron."

The soldier changed into a small Tazeron, who just stood there, waiting for further instructions.

"Ooh, my heck! Rambo, are you thinking what I'm thinking?"

"Sorry, Jesse, I was watching the results of your experiment and missed what you were thinking."

Jesse showed Rambo his thoughts, and there was a sharp intake of breath from his friend.

"Jesse, it might work. Let's go talk to Zealoc."

"Soldiers, as you were. Wait here for us."

"Yes, sir," they replied, returning to their original form.

In Zealoc's tent, Jesse explained what had just happened with the moon soldiers. They had Zealoc bring one of his men so that he could see for himself what was possible. Jesse explained that shapeshifting did not classify as a trait that could be used up. While they were having the soldier change into various forms, Jesse had another thought.

"Soldier, can you become more than one? If so, how many?"

"Yes, sir. Just like we can all stand in one spot, we can become many."

"What do you mean by many?"

The soldier looked confused. "Until we are no more, sir."

"Explain."

"Each time we split, a piece of us is used to create the new soldier."

"So how many soldiers are inside each of you? Can you tell when you are almost no more?"

"I do not know, sir. Would you like me to try?"

"No, not at this time. It is enough to know that it is a possibility. Thank you, soldier, you are dismissed."

Jesse watched the soldier leave and then turned to the others, grinning.

"Holy cow! We have just made an amazing discovery! Zealoc, I will not tell you how to use these soldiers, but you at least know some of the potential. There may be other qualities with this gift from Matilda that we have not yet discovered. Use the twenty-one soldiers wisely, my friend. Have one of the wearers of the talisman contact me with updates as you proceed and while we are away looking for Breeze. Be safe."

"You too, Jesse. Be safe," Zealoc responded.

Jesse and Rambo packed up for their trip, and with their soldier entourage, they set off on their quest to find Breeze. Jesse had their soldiers change into eagles and follow behind while he rode on Rambo's back.

They had not been on the trail very long when Rambo noticed something. A softly glowing oval ring.

"Jesse, do you see what I see up ahead?"

"Yes. What do you think it is? A portal? If it were the middle of the afternoon instead of evening, we probably would have missed it. Soldier number one, come here."

"Yes, sir?"

"If I asked you to fly into that glowing circle and then return, would that be one of your talents?"

"No, sir."

"Would you do it then, and report back to me with what you find?"

"Yes, sir."

At that, the moon soldier in eagle form flew into the glowing circle and disappeared.

"Jesse, what did Breeze mean when she told you to use the talisman to find her?"

"I think it's like the power when the portal was destroyed, but I have to be careful. I need a map. Hey! I wonder if one of the soldiers could become a map?"

Just then, an enormous red flame exploded from the glowing circle, and a very charred soldier staggered out of the opening, falling face down in the dirt. They ran to him and turned him over. He began to speak.

"Portal, trap, run, they are coming. You will lose your lady if you destroy the portal." The soldier gave a shudder and died.

"Jesse, destroy the portal, quickly! Jesse! Now!"

Jesse was in shock. He heard Rambo as if from far away.

"Jesse! Do it now!"

Jesse stumbled toward the portal. Placing his left hand on the frame, he grasped the chain around his neck. Power pulsated through him as he released the magic, and the portal shimmered and its light went out, just as a big ugly demon head pushed its way into the opening and growled at them. With the closing of the portal and subsequent shattering of the circle, the demon head popped off its owner's body and rolled a few feet down the slight hill.

"That was too close. Let's get out of here," Rambo said, then stopped as he looked closely at his friend. "Jesse, what's the matter?"

"Did I just lose Breeze when I destroyed that portal?"

"No, at least I don't think so. You know how controlling Tazeron and his minions are. It's my feeling that Breeze isn't anywhere close to here. I bet they told the soldier to say that in the hope of scaring you. Try reaching her."

"Breeze, Breeze, can you hear me?"

Silence.

Silence.

"Breeze, answer me. Please answer me…" Jesse slumped to his knees, holding his face and sobbing. "I can't lose her again, Rambo."

"Jesse, stop this. You haven't lost her. Look inside yourself and believe, never doubting. Remember, you need to focus."

"I completely understand that Breeze and I will see this battle to its close. I must fight these feelings. But what if it's true?"

"Then we still finish this war, and you will see her after it's over. She is immortal, and even if she isn't in this world anymore, she can never die. She has served the gods faithfully for millennia, and they take care of their own. You are needed here and now. Don't you dare give up! Both of our worlds need you, and if nothing else, I will not abandon you or this quest. It means too much for all of us. Now get up and let's keep going. Call one of the soldiers and get a map. *Breeze is somewhere waiting for us.*" He finished the last part speaking directly to Jesse's mind.

"Thank you, Rambo."

To Jesse's surprise, someone else spoke into his mind. *"Jesse, listen to him and don't doubt. Besides, I understand that you made Tazeron a promise, and we must always keep our pledges."*

"Breeze?"

"Yes, I am still here, waiting for you. There is much to tell when you arrive, but hurry."

Wiping his face and feeling somewhat foolish, Jesse stood. *"I can't stand the thought of losing you again, Breeze. Where are you, and how do we find you?"*

"I am in a water cave in the Red Mountains. Be careful, glass spiders are guarding the place. And Jesse, remember neither of us can truly die. So, as Rambo said, if not in this life, then in the next, we will be together. We are bonded. I love you, never forget that. Now use one of the soldiers for a map and make sure he labels himself. See you soon. Rambo, use your invisibility."

"Rambo, am I ever going to grow into my place here? I turn to mush far too easily."

"Indeed, you do, and yes, you will. You have already grown much." Rambo punched Jesse's shoulder lightly and smiled his toothy dragon grin. "You must remember the gifts you have and the blessings that you have been given. Now call a soldier, let's get going. Your wife is waiting, and it's never a good idea to keep them waiting."

Jesse laughed. "So, I am learning."

Chapter Nine

Spider Webs and Mysteries

"Soldiers, to me," Jesse called. All the moonstone soldiers gathered to him.

"Tiny beetles, collapse."

All the soldiers became small blue bugs stacked tightly together. Jesse picked up the stack and placed it in a hidden pocket in his robes.

"I'm impressed. That is much easier than full-sized soldiers or flying eagles. Great idea, Jesse."

"It does simplify things. Now I just have to transport myself and a pit bull wannabe."

"What do you mean, 'wannabe'? Remember what Matilda said, 'Be respectful to your elders, so get it straight… son.' By the way, weren't you going to have one of the soldiers become a map?"

"Oh yeah… geez, now I'm getting forgetful." Jesse removed the stack of beetles and placed it on the ground. "Top soldier, become a map of the area. Label the Red Mountains and its caves. Also, I want the map to glow so we can read it in the dark. The rest of you, stay collapsed."

Jesse placed the remaining blue beetles back in his pocket while Rambo unfolded the map.

"Jesse, look at this. There are several water caves under the Red Mountains. The Red Mountain range seems to run the entire length of this valley, which appears to be many leagues long. By the way, it was a good idea to make the map glow, since the moons don't give much light."

Jesse groaned. "Breeze, this is going to take a while. The mountain range is very long, and there are many water caves underneath it. Do you have any directions for us?"

"Yes. Fly to the range and then mind-search for me. I will try to stay in contact with you. I know that there are many dangers in these caves. I am currently trapped in a small cave that is guarded by glass spiders and sealed with a silencing spell, so I can use no magic. Jesse, I am sure that there are traps set for you. They captured me in the hope of catching you. I have heard them talk about it. Be careful."

"We will be careful. For now, while we fly to the mountains, we will remain silent with Rambo's invisibility. Take care, Breeze. I can't wait to see you."

After studying the map, they launched into the sky, taking directions from the stars. Rambo put the bubble around Jesse. It would not take long with his speed. Jesse lay back to watch the stars. Suddenly, the bubble was attacked by huge bats.

"Rambo, what's happening? Are you ok out there?"

"I am fine, Jesse. Bats don't see the same way other animals do. Their sonar alerted them to us. I don't know if they are servants of Tazeron or just looking for a meal. I won't shoot them down. It would let every mob in the area know we are here. I'm sure that there will be traps, as Breeze warned us. They can do us no harm. We are close now. Prepare for other dangers."

"Should I try contact?"

"Not yet. Let me fly the range first. We might see something helpful."

As Rambo flew, he seemed to pass through an area that reminded him of their experience with the purple mist. The air felt thicker, heavy. Then, without warning, he was tangled in webs. He was still moving, but slower with the added weight.

"Jesse, warp us out to a safe place."

"You got it," Jesse said in response. He warped them back to the forest of elves. What they saw surprised them. The buildings were deserted, and many had been burnt.

"What happened here, do you think, Rambo?"

"More importantly, I am wondering where the people are," Rambo said, as they flew through the village. Then, as if in answer, Bob appeared and circled Rambo's head, begging him to follow.

"Bob seems anxious that we follow him, Jesse. Perhaps this will give us the answers we need."

They followed Bob into the forest and then up a steep mountain pathway. The higher they went, the more severe the weather became. Thick snow covered the ground, hiding the path and the shrubs and bushes. Some of the trees were entirely encased.

"What is happening here, Rambo? I didn't know that Xanthara got snow."

"It doesn't. This is because of Tazeron and his infection. Of that, I am sure. Look, up ahead, a cave. Bob just flew into it."

As they landed and entered the cave, they were greeted by an army of Skeedlers. It seemed that the snow did not deter them from their duties. After their cleaning, which in Rambo's case was very welcome because of all the spider webs, they were greeted by the Toulonians. There were other surprises as well.

"Prince Rambo, Prince Jesse, we are honoured by this visit. As you can see, we have been forced into exile, along with these others. The world as we know it is changing. Might we offer you some refreshment?" the chief offered.

Rambo and Jesse were stunned by what greeted them. Along with the Toulonians were a few of the primitive peoples, trolls and ogres. They all seemed to be in a pathetic condition. The once sleek feathers of the Toulonians were battered but clean. The trolls and ogres were either juveniles or pygmy versions, for they were slight for their kind. The Ravens were among the collection of refugees. Also, there was a scattering of elves, including, to their amazement, Mary and Jason.

"We are stunned by this greeting, sir," Jesse said, and Rambo agreed. "I am almost beyond words. What has happened? Mary, Jason, I don't understand. We thought you were dead. Please, tell us what happened."

"Master Jesse," Mary started, but then thought better of it and stepped aside as the chief came forward.

"Honoured Princes, please have a seat and accept our hospitality while we tell you of our trials."

"Excuse me a moment, sir. Before you begin, I must make a couple of contacts. I will return shortly," Jesse said. With that, he stepped outside to contact Breeze, the raid, and Jim and Sara.

"Breeze, are you there?"

"Yes, Jesse. Is everything ok? I expected you to be here by now."

"We are fine. We were attacked by huge bats, and then Rambo got tangled in spider webs. He told me to warp to a safe place, and the first thought that came to my mind was the forest of elves." Jesse then explained what they found and how they found it. Breeze was astounded.

"But it never snows on Xanthara, and there are no pygmy trolls and ogres in that area. Mary and Jason! Jesse, what is happening to our world? I fear that it is more than just Tazeron and his infection. Don't worry, my love, I am fine, but missing you terribly. Find out all that you can. There are clues in this meeting. Gather them and let me know later. I love you."

"I will. And Breeze, I am missing you too."

After contacting Breeze, Jesse sent a message to Zealoc via David, telling them what they had discovered. They had questions, but Jesse had no answers. He promised to contact them again later and asked them to pass the word on to Tommy and his group. Jim and Sara were ecstatic about Mary and Jason. They were satisfied knowing that they seemed well and that Jesse would contact them when he had more news. Jesse then returned to the meeting.

"I apologise for that delay. I needed to report our location. Now, sir, tell us of your trials."

The chief stood before them, and with reservation in his tone, he related what had happened to them and the forest of elves.

"After Prince Tomitobias left here, the village was attacked in earnest. The elves attempted to run to their underground sanctuaries, but they were blocked. I did not see what happened to them after that, because those of us that could fly left for this cave. Later, we were joined by these children," he motioned toward the trolls and ogres. "They told us a brave tale that I will allow them to repeat to you now."

One of the troll children, who was much larger than the rest, stood. She was very uncomfortable standing before this group to speak.

"Sirs, I am Samalla of the Dark Rock clan. I am a keeper of children for the tribe. Many seasons have passed since an evil presence came to our village. My father, JoJoleek, was chief, a braver leader we have never seen. He fought against the scourge. He believed the brave man Zealoc, who came to tell our people of this wickedness. My father was taken and tortured until he died. They hung his body for all to see, to scare us."

She shuddered, and tears filled her eyes, which she tried to hide.

"I hid the children and myself, but we were found by my mother. She told me to follow the evil or die. Some of the children wanted to return to their parents. I could not keep them. I ran away with these few, and the ogre children you see here too. The same thing happened to their people. When we got to the forest of elves, we were afraid because their village was in ruin. The big black bird saw us and led us here to this place. We wish to stay here. We do not like the evil that killed our families and changed our ways."

Mary stood and embraced the girl. They sat down together. Mary stroked the young troll's hair as she hid her face and sobbed. Jesse was stunned not just by the sadness, but by the bravery of the child.

"You were very brave, Samalla. For not only running away from evil but helping these others to escape as well," Jesse told her. "We are all proud of you. Mary or Jason, could you tell us your story?"

Since Mary was still comforting the child, Jason stood, bowing to the chief and then to Jesse and Rambo.

"We were unwise. We decided to leave and try to find Tazeron. We did find him, but when we saw how many followers he had, we knew we were foolish. We also knew that we would die if discovered. We came to the forest of elves. It was our home, the only home we have known. It was still burning when we first got here, and the villagers were running to their underground sanctuary. We hid and witnessed a strange thing happen. A bright white light covered the village. When it was gone, so were the people. The few evil people that were still here burning buildings were dead. As we watched, their bodies crumbled to dust. We do not know if everyone died or if it was just the evil ones."

"Rambo, do you think it was Chaelea? Do you think she transported the elves to a safe place?"

"I do not know. This keeps getting stranger and stranger. Jesse, I think I would like to go to Clay when we are done here. What say you?"

"I was thinking the same thing, my friend."

"I am confused," Jesse said to Jason and Mary. "We were told that you were in a fight. Evidence was found: panther fur, druid feathers, and blue blood. What can you say about that?"

Jason and Mary seemed confused by this disclosure.

"We know nothing of this, Master Jesse. We were never injured. Frightened, yes, but there was no fight. Like we said, survival for us would have been impossible had there been an encounter."

"This is another mystery. I hope soon we have answers," Jesse said.

The Toulonian chief stood before them. "We are safe for now. The evil does not know that we are here. This is a big cave with water, fish in the water, and water plants. We will do well here. The children of the trolls and ogres are safe with us. We will care for them, but the elf children must go with you. We feel this strongly. They match the stones in your pocket, and this too is a sign."

Jesse and Rambo were stunned, since no one knew of the soldiers that Jesse carried.

"How do you know of the stones?" Jesse asked.

"What stones?" Mary wanted to know.

Jesse removed the beetle stones and asked them to return to their soldier forms. This they did. There was a shock in the room. The soldiers bowed to Mary and Jason before collapsing back into their stacked beetle form. Jesse returned them to his pocket.

"The Ancients have spoken to me," the chief said. "These young elves can help end the evil of this world, along with the Keepers who are at this moment fighting. I will do one more thing before you leave. I will give you all a blessing. This is from the gods of both worlds. I knew you would be coming here on this day. That is why I had Bob come down to meet you. You are being watched, and those who watch are smiling on you. They desire to show you the path. Be faithful. Remember who you serve, and focus on your talents. Now kneel. You too, Prince Rambo."

Jesse, Rambo, Mary, and Jason knelt before the Toulonian chief. He touched each one of them with his hand, calling them by name.

"Jesse, Rambo, Mary, and Jason, by the power of the gods of both worlds, I bless you to know who you are and why you are here. You will lead, and you will serve. Many will follow. If you die, not one moment will pass before you are returned to your body, never to die again. I bless you with strength, wisdom, and understanding. Go now, act well your part."

As they got ready to leave, the troll girl came up to Mary and hugged her once again, thanking her for her comfort and kindness. Mary, in turn, thanked the girl for her example of bravery and for not surrendering to the evil that had invaded their world.

Jesse told the twins that they were making a short trip to Clay to solve a mystery about the missing elves. The twins were excited to find out about their friends. Rambo put a bubble around them even though they would warp.

The first thing that Jesse noticed when they got to Clay was how beautiful the city was becoming. It was remarkable to see the progress that they had made.

"Jesse, my young friend, it is pleasing to see you. How is Breeze doing?" Master Osuweep asked.

It saddened Jesse to have to tell the Elder that Breeze was a captive of Tazeron. He was surprised when Master Osuweep laughed at the message. Jesse could not understand how the Elder could find humour in this.

"Master Osuweep, I mean no offence, but how can you laugh at Breeze being imprisoned?"

"Jesse, my boy, no prison can hold Breeze. No silencing spell can stop her magic, and no evil can hide her voice against it. She is part of the legions of Shadow Dreams. As a reward for her service, she is immune to those things. The gods have decreed it. Please excuse me for a moment, I seem to be needed by one of my council members."

Jesse was stunned. What did that mean?

"Rambo, what does this mean? I am shocked."

"I too am shocked, Jesse. We must find the answer to this. It is a serious question that needs answering."

While Rambo and Jesse were speaking with the Elder, Mary and Jason visited others in the city and discovered that the lost elves were not on Clay. Where could they be? Where were Wolfa and the children, and all the others, including Breeze's parents, who had finally moved there?

The twins shared their findings with Jesse and Rambo. The news left them all with an empty, hollow feeling. What was happening?

Jesse had an idea, perhaps even a way to solve some of the mysteries. He resolved to present his concept to Master Osuweep when the Elder returned.

Chapter Ten
More Questions

"Master Osuweep, we have a mystery. There is a chance that the Breeze I have been speaking to is not the real Breeze. We have no idea who this counterfeit Breeze might be. I have a favour to ask of you. If you were to question Breeze and ask her one question that only she would know, what would that question be? I do not want you to answer aloud. I want you to write it on a piece of paper. Do not tell me what the question is, or the answer. Please write the answers on a separate piece of paper. I do not want to see either. I will have the children here hold them. Perhaps it would be a good idea to have two questions and answers. Can you do that for me?"

"Certainly, Jesse. So much strangeness in today's world. I will have those ready for you shortly. The questions and answers are straightforward, and the real Breeze would have no problem answering them."

"Thank you, sir. I have another question for you that is troubling for all of us. The elves from the forest of elves on Xanthara have vanished. We were hoping that they had been brought here for safety by the White Druid, but Mary and Jason have searched while we were talking, and they can find no sign of them here. Is there any chance that you might know where they could be?"

Again, the Elder surprised Jesse and Rambo exceedingly.

"Yes, Jesse, I know exactly where they are. And you were right in your assumption that the White Druid was involved. They were placed in the new world below us. They are helping the young mortals down there while we prepare to assist them from up here. It is a different arrangement from all the other worlds. The humans that will be born into that world are very particular. I cannot tell you any more than that."

"I was wondering, by chance, is Master Nexlucimus here as well, sir? And would it be possible to go down there and visit with the ones that we know?"

"Um… I am not sure about that, my young friend. I really have no knowledge of who was transported below. Nexlucimus could be there, I suppose, but I doubt it, because of the nature of that world. I would also be amazed if you could visit. In the meantime, my young friend, I believe you have a mystery to solve, and I have a couple of important questions to write. I will return shortly. Have the children ready."

"Yes, sir."

Jesse was disappointed that there was no new information concerning Nexlucimus or the others who had been placed in the mortal world, but he would take what good news he had back to base camp. They would simply have to assume that everyone was safe until further disclosure was received.

Jesse had the children ready for the Elder to hand his undisclosed questions, along with the answers. After they had said their goodbyes, the four of them returned to Xanthara. Mary and Jason were saddened that the elven village had been destroyed, but relieved to learn that the elves were safe. The twins, like Jesse and Rambo, hoped to see them returned to their homes someday. It was a journey of sadness because of all the destruction, but also a story of joy. There was much to tell. Rambo placed a bubble around them, and Jesse warped them back to meet up with the rest of the raid.

Once back, and the twins reunited with their family, Jesse and Rambo called a meeting of all the leaders to tell of their journey to Xanthara. There was shock and sadness among them, but also gladness to learn of the involvement of the White Druid and delight in the safety of the elves. After the meeting, the leaders left to share with the rest of the troops what they had learned, and news of the twins' return.

Jesse went to find Zeela, who had been absent from the meeting, while Rambo wandered off into the surroundings to scratch up a snack.

Jesse found Zeela sitting by the lake, staring out over the water. Though it was not as large as Lake O's, it was still peaceful and calming to a troubled soul.

"Zeela, my friend, how are you doing?"

"I am dealing as well as I can, Jesse. I heard that you had called a meeting. Please forgive me for not attending. I would be most interested in hearing what you related to the others."

"Zeela, I am saddened by what we found when we warped to the forest," Jesse said, as he recounted his and Rambo's trip to Xanthara. He told her all that they had discovered, including the burning of the village and the disappearance of the elves. She was understandably shaken by this news and what it might mean for Nexlucimus, the rest of their friends and family, and the others who were missing. She was glad that the twins were safe and that they had made the trip to Clay and learned of the elves. It added to her grief that there was no further knowledge of Nexlucimus and the others who were missing.

"Thank you, Jesse," Zeela said with sadness. "Is there anything else?"

"Zeela, I wish there was more to tell you."

"Thank you. I know that this is a heavy burden for you as well. Now, if you will excuse me, I think I will remain here for a time and enjoy the solitude."

"Of course, Zeela, but before I go there is one other thing. While we visited Master Osuweep, I mentioned that Breeze was a captive of Tazeron. He laughed at the idea. I was shocked. Then he told me that because she had been a Shadow Dream, it was impossible. No prison could hold her. No silencing spell could stop her magic, and she could not be prevented from speaking against evil. He said it was a gift to her from the gods, for her service. What do you think of this?"

"I seem to remember something of this, but the best one to ask would be Tomitobias. He has more knowledge of Shadow Dreams than I do, especially now that he is the head Elder of Xanthara," Zeela's voice broke as she said this. "He has a direct line to that realm."

"Oh my gosh, that's right. How could I have forgotten? Thank you, Zeela, and please be at peace. I feel in my heart that Master Nexlucimus is well, wherever he is."

"Thank you, Jesse, I pray that you are correct," Zeela said, as she turned back to the lake.

Jesse ran towards Tommy's tent and skidded to a stop in front, knocking on the tent post.

"Hey Tommy, you home?"

"Jesse, welcome back. When did you arrive? Come on in."

"First, how come you weren't at the meeting of all the leaders?" Jesse said as he walked into Tommy's tent. "We missed you."

"I didn't know about the meeting. I must have been preoccupied or something. What's up?"

"Is it possible for an ex-Shadow Dream to be put in prison, lose their magic to silencing spells, or have their mouths shut to condemning evil?"

"Nope, why, what's up?"

"I've been mind-talking to Breeze, or I thought it was Breeze. But then I found out that she is claiming all the above. Locked in a cave, and a silence spell blocking her magic. It sounds like Breeze, acts like Breeze, but the fact is, according to you and Master Osuweep, it's not possible. What do you think is happening?"

Tommy sat there silently for a while, watching Jesse. "What do you think is happening, Jesse?"

"What?"

"What do you think is happening?"

"I have no idea, that's why I came to you."

"Let me ask you another question. How many times have you had your magic blocked, or your mind closed, and been left unbelieving since we started this quest to stop Tazeron?"

"Why do you ask that, Tommy? Do you think I'm creating something here? Denying something? What's going on?"

"I'm not sure, but something isn't the way it should be. It could be you, or it could be her, but I doubt that. I don't know."

Jesse was pensive. He had to figure this out. "One more thing," Jesse hesitated. "Rambo and I made an impromptu trip to the forest of elves where we found the missing Slater twins in a cave with the Toulonians. Apparently, after you left the village," Jesse said in a cautious tone, "it was attacked and destroyed."

"Attacked? Destroyed? By whom?" Tommy asked, jumping to his feet, fearful.

"The twins told us," Jesse continued, "that as they watched from a distance, a bright white light covered the area and the elven people vanished. The ones destroying the village were turned to dust."

Tommy, ashen-faced, collapsed into his chair. "My family? All the people? What happened to them?"

Jesse continued, "Rambo and I made a trip to Clay with the twins before coming back here. Master Osuweep told us that the elves were transported to the new mortal world by the White Druid to help there. Your family is safe. We don't know any more than that, Tommy. I am sorry."

"Strange, so strange, but at least they will be safe. Thank you, my friend, for telling me. All the ups and downs of this war keep me spinning. Now I feel the weight of my station even more. Jesse, I am so thankful that you brought this news to me, even though it saddens my heart that the village was destroyed. I wish you well figuring out this other problem. So many unanswered questions," Tommy said miserably. "Did you learn anything else about my uncle and the Council?"

"I'm afraid not. Master Osuweep had no knowledge of him or the others. I believe that they are well, wherever they are. We are just going to have to assume that they are safe. I can't think of it any other way. My head can't handle any more right now. I think I need some alone time. I'll talk to you later, Tommy."

Tommy watched as Jesse walked away from the camp. There was just too much going on. He, like Jesse, needed peace and quiet.

"How many blessings have I had?" Jesse asked himself as he walked. "And how long do they last? How do I sort this all out? Who can I talk to that can give me answers? What is going on? Doubt, always doubt. Doubt not. How many times must I hear that before I start doing it? Doubt not, doubt not, doubt not, doubt not…"

"Breeze, are you there?"

"Yes, Jesse. I am here. How did the trip to the forest of elves go? Did you find the answers you were searching for?"

"Some things were answered, but more questions were presented."

"What questions?"

"Why are you being held prisoner? How can a silence spell block your magic, and can you speak against evil?"

Silence.

Silence.

"I have another question for you, two actually. Both are from Master Osuweep. Will you answer them for me?"

Silence.

Silence.

Jesse felt impressed to try something he had never done before. He looped the chain he wore around his neck through the commitment ring that was Breeze's, with its strange green colour, and then touched the talisman with his mind.

A scream like none Jesse had ever heard before erupted in his mind. His knees buckled, his heart started pounding, and he began to shake uncontrollably.

"Little fool, do you not know who the king is here?" said a female voice. *"Why are you so slow to grasp the truth? You are so easy to control. Is that not proof?"*

Jesse focused his magic, all that he could, and sent it to the voice in his head, the one that the talisman contacted. The one that spoke to him now. The block was broken, but the scream, that terrible cry, continued. He did it again and again and again until he had no more energy left, and the screams were destroyed.

The ribbons of red magic were robust, pure, and clean, as new as after each of his blessings. Both rings felt warm, as did the chain. The ring that was Breeze's didn't glow her soft white, but it wasn't green anymore either. That must have been the link to the game master. Her magic must have been green and imbued into the ring. Jesse felt violated with the thought, but she was gone now. Forever.

"Doubt not, FEAR not, doubt not, FEAR not, doubt not, FEAR not. There is no king here. Be gone, you evil bastard. I will never give up until I find her, and your black heart is vaporised into outer darkness. This is the second time that I have promised you this, Tazeron."

Silence.

Silence.

Jesse heard nothing, and he felt nothing. He was strangely at peace, believing what Rambo had said and even, remarkably, the truth that the false Breeze had spoken. If Breeze was dead, or if he, Jesse, died, even then, they would be together, because their eternal essences could not perish. They were bonded. Someday, they would be together, if not in this life, then in the next.

He was at peace with that. It was time to take Tazeron the evil out of circulation. Jesse realised that missing Breeze so much, and concentrating on finding her, had been distracting him from the purpose of the quest. The world of fantasy would be made whole again once Tazeron was eliminated, and he, Jesse, would find all his answers. He couldn't allow himself to be distracted. Never again.

Jesse stood, brushed himself off, and walked back towards the camp. He would call a meeting with his captains and hear their reports. Then they would form a plan, one having no room for failure, weakness, or doubt. His flaws would become his strengths. He was chosen for this quest. It was finally time to put aside all distractions and childish fears and take the helm that was his.

"Rambo, would you call a meeting of all the captains? We will meet in front of Tommy's tent."

"Sure, Jesse. What's up?"

"I just got some answers, and I want to tell everyone. We will draw up a plan of action. This war is about to turn around, of that I am sure."

Jesse walked down to Tommy's tent, knocked on the tent post, and walked in. Tommy was taking a nap.

"Wake up, you slacker!" Jesse said, kicking the frame of Tommy's camp cot. "Time to go to work. There will be a meeting of all the captains in five minutes. You will be there." With that, he walked out and waited.

Jesse heard Rambo call a meeting of the captains as he waited. Zealoc was the first, after Tommy, to arrive.

"What's up, Jesse?" Zealoc asked.

"Well, a few interesting things have developed that the captains need to be aware of, and I want a report of the camp in my absence. We will put it all together and make plans for our next move on Tazeron."

Chapter Eleven

Undivided

It did not take long for the captains to gather at the front of Tommy's tent. There were many questions and concerns, but first, Jesse wanted answers.

"Zealoc, what happened while I was gone?"

"I sent a patrol out, and they returned with no new information," Zealoc reported.

Jesse was disappointed with that report, but he said nothing.

"Tommy, what did you find at Tazeron's camp?"

"Tazeron has another game master-creator. Even with stealth and invisible spells, we could not get close enough to determine what she is capable of, without detection. We suspect that she can manipulate the vibrations of the air, creating confusion in communication. She seems to be able to control thoughts like the 'Mind Control' that Pearl always talked about. We found that the closer we got to their camp, the more confused our thoughts became. Some were more sensitive than others."

Jesse was not surprised by this account, not with what he had just experienced. It could explain a lot. Jesse noticed Tommy watching him carefully, and he could not suppress a smile. Tommy looked confused. There was no way to mention the elimination of another game master at this point without referring to the chain, and that was forbidden.

"Master Jesse," the timid voice of Caleb spoke up. "May I say something, sir?"

"Yes, Caleb, what is on your mind?"

"Ammon and I have an idea, sir, one that I am sure would work."

Everyone's attention turned to the young mage, his face bright with youthful optimism.

"We know that Tazeron has been desperate to get to me and my older brother and sister. What if we gave him what he wanted? What if we opened the doors for him to go over to the other side?"

There was outrage at this. Everyone objected to the suggestion. Everyone that is, except Jesse. Without thinking about what he was doing, Jesse's hand flew to his throat, where the chain lay hidden beneath his robes. It burned with Caleb's words; it was not merely warm. It burned.

"I… I," Jesse choked, then cleared his throat and spoke. "Caleb, this is such an outrageous idea. Where did it come from?"

"Might we speak in private?" Caleb asked.

Jesse studied the young mage for a moment. "Very well, Caleb. Is it okay if Rambo and Tommy attend also?"

Caleb seemed to hesitate, then nodded in agreement.

"Everyone go get something to eat. Rest. We will close this meeting for now. Come, Caleb, let us hear what you have to say."

The rest of the leaders left to get some food. There was much mumbling, confusion and concern.

"Master Jesse, I will bring my friend Ammon as well. This concerns him also."

"Of course. Shall we get something to eat first?"

After a brief meal, the named group met in Jesse's tent.

"Master Jesse, Ammon, my friend, confided in me last night that he had important information to share with you. We were wondering how and when to do this. I will let him explain."

Their attention turned to the young man, so like his sister, with his pale green skin, dark brown eyes, golden wings and shoulder-length golden hair.

"Ammon, feel free to speak as you wish," Jesse told him.

"Master Jesse, I was forbidden to talk to you about this before now. I have just recently received permission from Breeze to do so."

"Breeze?" Jesse questioned. "How is that possible? Where is she? Why does she not talk to me?"

"I will explain all to you," Ammon said. "It seems so long ago that Breeze was lost. We all know the story, but now you will learn the truth. Breeze was trapped and taken by Tazeron. I do not know how, but she was rescued. She will relate the circumstances later if she wishes. I will say this: all that you have thought to this point is a lie."

Rambo and Tommy both started to object, but Jesse stopped them. "Continue, Ammon. Rambo and Tommy, my friends, we will hear him."

"Breeze was snatched from the hands of death because Tazeron foolishly thought her blood would open the portals he wishes to create. As he raised the cursed knife to sacrifice her, the White Druid intervened. The commitment ring was left behind; Tazeron already had it in his collection. When the Toulonians blessed you and removed the evil from your mind, the person who spoke to you shortly after was not Breeze. It was a new threat, a game master coached by Tazeron who knows Breeze well. Breeze cannot talk to you now because of her. She is safe and protected. I have no idea where she is; she could not reveal it. She speaks to me through our blood and because of our service as Shadow Dreams. I too was one."

This was a surprise to all, but it explained Ammon's connection.

"Ammon, we had no idea that you were a Shadow Dream. I did not know that your blood link connected you in such a way," Jesse mused. "Can you talk to her at any time?"

"Indeed, sir. However, there must be a good cause, like the talisman that is on your arm."

"She is safe and protected," Jesse smiled, feeling relief. "And even though I wish I could communicate with her, that knowledge will have to be enough for now. Thank you, Ammon. This helps me understand many things. I have just discovered on my own that the voice I was hearing was not Breeze; I was confused about who it was. Before this meeting, I took a walk, and while I did, the fake Breeze spoke to me. I asked some questions that she refused to answer. As you say, Ammon, it was a lie. I discovered during that encounter who has been counterfeiting her. It was Tazeron and his game master. There is only one thing that is still a mystery, and that is who has been talking to Rambo. Any ideas?"

"Perhaps I can answer that, Jesse," Rambo said. "I have wondered myself as I listened to Ammon. I only heard her when she talked to you, and if I was addressed or mentioned. At first, I thought the person I heard was Breeze. It sounded like her, but different somehow. Distant, divided. It must have been the new game master. Jesse, we both have been fooled. Our grief has made us vulnerable to deception. Our focus must once again be undivided, my friend. I question how another mortal, even with Tazeron's help, could mind talk."

"We may never know for sure, but the fact that Tommy said this game master could mind control and manipulate the vibrations of the air might have something to do with it. It is hard to imagine. *Rambo, I may have eliminated that game master with the help of the chain and Breeze's commitment ring. I will explain more to you later.*"

"Jesse, I am shocked. Say nothing of this now. Let us hear what Ammon and Caleb have to say," Rambo implored.

"Indeed, Rambo," Jesse said. "Ammon, Caleb mentioned helping Tazeron get through the portal. What was that about?" Jesse

asked, turning his and Rambo's attention back to the two young Keepers.

"This is hard to explain," Ammon said. "Breeze told me to remind you of your orientation, and the memories of Nexlucimus. She said the answer to Tazeron was contained in those memories. I am not sure what she meant by that, but she said it would make sense to you as you watched them again."

This surprised Jesse. He had no idea what Breeze was talking about, but he felt the burn of the chain, and he knew that what Ammon was saying was true. An idea occurred to him.

"Tommy, as a member of the council, would you have access to the memories of Nexlucimus? I assume that they were recorded."

"The orientation? I believe so. What do you have in mind?"

"If the answer to Tazeron is contained in those memories, then I want to watch them again. There is much that I do not remember, and I want as many people connected to Tazeron as possible to watch with me. I want Ginnea, my dad, you, Rambo, Zeela, Jim and Sara, Mr Chambers, Cami, and of course Ammon and Caleb. I also want Zealoc, his sister Martha, and his cousin Beloe. The more eyes and ears we have to watch, the greater our chance of figuring out what Breeze was referring to."

"When should we do this? And what of the others here?" Tommy asked.

"We will leave them here. We will put others in charge temporarily, with instructions to keep searching for ways to abolish Tazeron and those who follow him. Rambo, would you call a meeting of those we will take back to Rodashu while I address the remaining ones?"

"I will do as you ask, Jesse," Rambo said.

Jesse went in search of Rykan, Savana, and Jamison. He explained briefly that he, Jesse, and some of the others would be making a quick trip back to Rodashu. He instructed them to continue gathering information but, unless necessary, not to engage in any battles. They were to organise into small teams and scour the surrounding area beyond what they had done with Zealoc. Jesse was expressly interested in finding any possible portals left behind by mortals. He then addressed the remaining troops.

"My friends, it is necessary for me and some of the other captains to return to Rodashu for a short time. I am leaving these leaders that you see here in charge. I have given specific orders that they will explain to you. Follow their lead, and we will return soon, hopefully with the key to all of this."

After giving the assignments and his message to the gathering of Keepers, Jesse returned to Tommy's tent, where Rambo had the others waiting.

"What is going on, Jesse?" Zealoc wanted to know. "Rambo would not tell us anything other than that you had requested another meeting."

"We are going back to Rodashu, where we will watch the orientation that the other Keepers and I were given at the start of this quest. All I can say right now to all of you is that we have been given instructions that could give us the advantage over Tazeron and his minions."

"Does this have anything to do with what Caleb said earlier, about giving Tazeron what he wanted?" David asked.

"We do not know, but I will tell you this. Ammon here, as you know, is Breeze's brother. What you do not know, and what Rambo, Tommy, and I just learned, is that he was also a Shadow Dream, and he has been shown that Tazeron has a weakness that the orientation and memories of Nexlucimus can help us discover. I want to watch those memories again. All of you have either been involved from the beginning or are personally acquainted with Tazeron. I am hoping that you, my friends, can help me see, or perhaps hear, what I might be missing."

"Jesse, will we be able to get into the council chambers with the occupation going on?" Cami asked.

"We will not know that until we get there, Cami. I am hopeful. It would be best for us to go under the shield of invisibility, I am sure."

Since there were so many in the group with talismans, arriving at the council chambers was fast and easy. They were glad that they had come cloaked with invisibility because the hallways were being patrolled by trolls. Jesse wished for Breeze's talents at controlling them, but they discovered that the trolls would not go past the fairies that hid on the chamber doors.

"I could have talked to them if needed," Ammon told them, "but the fairy guards had them pretty much under control."

Once they were in the council chambers, Tommy took the head chair at the smaller table and invited everyone else to take a seat. The comfortable chairs seemed delighted to once again provide seating for an important meeting. Tommy brought up the lighted panel that Jesse had missed on his first visit, the one that Nexlucimus had called his assistant on.

"Hey Tommy, is Clocks still around, or did he leave when the city was abandoned?" Jesse asked.

"Clocks left with the last of the copied records, Jesse. Why do you ask?"

"I was wondering because Nexlucimus had him bring the most amazing pepperoni pizza to that first meeting."

"Sorry, Jesse, no pizza this time," Tommy smiled at Jesse's disappointed face. "Besides, did you not just eat a while ago?"

"Always room for pizza, my friend. Will it take long to bring up the orientation?"

"Almost ready, just one more thing, and off we go."

The monitor came down, and when Tommy waved his hand, the lights in the room dimmed, and the voice of Nexlucimus was heard by all. Jesse heard Zeela give a muffled whimper.

"Zeela," he asked softly, "are you okay?"

"Yes, Jesse, I am well," she replied, but Jesse noticed that she reclined back and was wrapped by the chair in a comforting embrace. Jesse remembered the feeling of peace that he had felt in the arms of the cushioned seat so long ago. He smiled at the thought as his attention focused on the screen and what they were seeing.

Chapter Twelve

Enlightened

Jesse had a jaw-dropping moment once again as the documentary of the orientation began. He felt as though he was seeing it for the first time. To his amazement, Tommy paused the scene as if it were a DVD player.

"Jesse, as we watch this, I want you to know that it is possible to halt the proceedings so we can discuss what we have seen."

"Nexlucimus never did that. Is this something new?"

"I am sure my uncle did not mention that fact because he was under time constraints to get you back to the mortal world."

"I am sure the rest of us who have seen this film, or whatever these memories are, would like to view it a bit slower," Mr Chambers said. "I know I do not remember very much because I was so impressed by the newness of the material being presented."

"These are my uncle's real memories, recorded in his mind as they happened. Some are the memories of our family. Just like everything that you have ever seen, done, heard, or said, they are recorded in your mind. The difference is that Nexlucimus, and others of his ability, can recall and record their memories for others to see. Someday, each of us will have all our thoughts and activities displayed for all to see, unless, of course, we petition our gods to release them. I believe you mortals call that repentance. We immortals can do the same thing with our gods. Shall we proceed?"

"Yes, please."

"My friends," the voice of Nexlucimus addressed them, "as you see, each time a world is created by mortals, a world of fantasy is created by the immortals' gods to accompany it. This is necessary. Because of their innocence, and lack of knowledge or training, mortals needed teachers. We immortals have been given that great responsibility. We cannot directly interfere with humans, but we can bless them with imagination and dreams. Through these thoughts and imaginations, we can suggest things that will be of help to them in their growth and development. They are free to accept or reject these promptings. In addition to our influence, the mortals are often given directions through chosen mortal men and women."

Tommy paused the memories. "Are there any questions?"

There were none.

"Okay, if not, I believe we can move past the development of this mortal world to the parts of my uncle's memories and those of my family where Tazeron is involved."

The next thing that Jesse saw were scenes of a very young Tazeron as he ran around with his Skeedler. There were sections showing him playing with his siblings. They saw Tazeron on family outings and as a student with his mother, learning the magic of a magician. As he grew, the scenes changed, and Jesse saw him more through the eyes of Nexlucimus as they ventured into the mortal world. Nexlucimus was instructing Tazeron on their duties and some of the projects they were involved with. This was a much younger world with primitive buildings and horse carts.

As Tazeron grew and history advanced, there was a noticeable change in his willingness to fulfil his duties by helping. He was upset that humans became disinterested in the magic arts as their experience increased and their knowledge of science grew. He saw them destroying their beautiful world with poisons and pollution. They disrespected each other and the gods. They became suspicious of magic users and refused further instruction in the use of magic, even punishing those who used it.

"Wait a minute," Jesse said. "Pause this, Tommy, please."

"Yes, Jesse. You have a question?"

"Does anyone else remember this part? Or did I just sleep through it before?"

"I do not remember this part either," Cami and David both said.

"It is possible that Nexlucimus did not show all of his memories, I guess," Tommy stated.

"Tell us, Tommy. What exactly is Tazeron trying to do with the mortals in our time when he gets into the world? I understand him not liking the poisoning and pollution parts because that is still a problem, but why would the mortals not liking or believing in magic anymore be such a big deal to him and his followers?"

"Tommy, could I answer that for Jesse?" Zeela asked.

"Yes, Zeela. Go ahead."

"Jesse, as I watch these memories, I am reminded of Tazeron's increasing need for power. Since he is a magic user, that is a form of power familiar to him. In the mortal world, magic was necessary for many eons of time. Their history is full of examples of magic use. The immortals who first interacted with men and women of your world were given deep respect. They were honoured as gods in some civilizations. Tazeron enjoyed that reverence and affection. As they matured in their development, they replaced magic with science.

Most of the immortals changed their focus at that point. Indeed, many were split off and sent to a different world. As with other worlds, when the mortals reached a point in their development where they could freewill their own dreams and imaginations, most of the immortals left them. The Internet is an excellent example of this; nowhere else can you find such a development. We plant ideas, and where they go surprises even us. I have heard my husband say this many times.

Tazeron was stuck in a way. He did not want to move forward, and he could not go back. He became bitter and saw the answer to this dilemma as taking control. He wanted to force the mortals to remain in the past. If he had his way, there would be no more advancement. Even though now he seems to live for it in the game world, it is because of magic. He sees himself as an absolute ruler.

He is a tyrant who wants total control. He would like to eliminate free will for the mortals. This was unacceptable to the gods. When he and his followers were told to no longer pursue their plans, they refused and escaped into the world of stories and games."

"Zeela, how long, in mortal time, has it been that Tazeron and his followers have been in this stage of rebellion?" Jesse wanted to know.

"That is hard to say, Jesse. They were quiet at first, in the printed world of stories and games. When the Internet took off and MMORPGs came into being, their efforts increased. It was, excuse the pun, a game changer for them when they realised that they could pull mortals into the games."

"Holy cow! For some reason, I thought Tazeron was a new player in the games. I did not realise that he had escaped into the game world many years ago. So, it is only since the Internet that he and his followers have been a problem?"

"Yes," Tommy said. "Before the Internet, they had no way of interacting with the mortal world. They were trapped there."

"Mr Chambers, how long would you say advanced maths and science have been the popular way of solving problems? I am trying to understand how long Tazeron has been locked in the world of stories and games," Jesse asked.

"Developing countries and civilizations have been using maths and science for a very long time, Jesse, hundreds of years. Some cultures, such as the Chinese, were inventing stories and experimenting with maths and science for thousands of years. Other civilizations…"

"Whoa… wait a minute. Does anyone else see what I grasp in this scenario?"

"I am starting to realise a problem for Tazeron if that is what you are talking about, Jesse," Cami said.

"Exactly!" Jesse said, grinning broadly.

Everyone stared at Jesse and Cami, wondering what they were talking about.

"What are you and Cami seeing, son, that the rest of us seem to be missing?" David asked.

"If Tazeron left the mortal world hundreds of years ago, and all he knows since then is what the game world can give him," Cami started to say.

"He does not know what the modern world is really like," Jesse finished for her.

"Of course," Mr Chambers said, a grin spreading across his face. "If he thought the mortals of eons ago were stubborn, pollution-producing knuckleheads, what would he think of them today? Even if he has hopes of engaging the anti-gods of that world, I believe he will be very disappointed, because even the tactics of the mortal anti-gods have advanced."

"So, if we do what Caleb and Ammon were suggesting…" Zealoc started to say.

"Could we save lives, time, and energy?" Beloe asked.

"I wonder if that would work?" Martha asked.

"One other question just came to my mind," Jim said. "What about our children? How can he do it without our kids sacrificing themselves?"

"He would not need them, Jim," Jesse said.

"Wait a minute, son. That poem thingy, what about that?" David asked.

"The moon soldiers!" Rambo and Zealoc said together.

"Exactly," said Jesse and Tommy in unison.

"Another thing," said Zeela, her face shining with excitement. "Once Tazeron is gone from the game world, his evil influence will be gone from Xanthara too, and the captured ones will no longer be trapped by this evil. I will have Nexi back." A tear of joy rolled down her glowing cheek.

"We need a plan. We cannot just charge into the game and hand over the moon soldiers. I think I need to visit my dear ex-wife and her new husband. It is dream time," David said, with a grin.

"I had the same thought, Dad. I wonder what they would think if I showed up on their doorstep with a dragon?" Jesse hooted with laughter.

"I am going with you, Jesse," Tommy said.

As the chatter rose and the possibilities of what this meant were explored, they all stood and converged into a tight circle to discuss the option. There was such a feeling of real joy and energy in the room that they did not notice the door of the chamber open and two others enter. When they finally observed them, absolute silence filled the room, and everyone knelt.

"Chaelea…" Rambo gasped.

"Yes, my love. The gods have released me and Breeze so that we might join this final battle. Please, my friends, rise and never bow to me again. I am once again one of you."

"Milady," Zeela said with reverence, "I see that you are still in your dragon form, as is Rambo. Will that change?"

"We will retain these forms most of the time until Tazeron is completely destroyed, but we can also change into our elven forms as needed," Chaelea said. Rambo was amazed at this.

"And no, Jesse, I will not become a hen chicken. I can see your thoughts, my son, for you truly are our son," she said, startling him. "It is a joyful tale, one that I will share at another time." There was astonishment around the room at this disclosure.

"For now, however, we must make plans to send Tazeron into the world of the mortals one final time. There he will seal his fate along with that of his followers. Breeze, go to your husband. I think he needs your stability."

With that final pronouncement, the White Druid waved her arm, and the refreshing once again began. "Go, my friends, refresh yourselves. Enjoy the moment, because there is much work to be done. After refreshing, we will meet in this room again, but for now, I will visit with my husband. Each of you will spend this time as you please within the adjoining rooms of this chamber."

In their state of stunned joy, the assembly quietly adjourned for some peaceful contemplation.

Chapter Thirteen

Unexpected

Jesse was so astonished at the turn of events that he had a hard time getting his mouth to work, but his mind was all over the place.

"Breeze… I am in shock, I think. So many questions are in my head right now. I am having a hard time deciding what to ask first. What just happened? Where have you been?"

"I think it is best if we take it slowly, Jesse. You have been through so much. First, however, I would like my commitment ring back. I have missed the comfort it gave me and the connection to you."

"Yes, of course. I have gotten used to wearing both."

Jesse carefully removed the ring from his pinky finger and placed it once again on Breeze's ring finger. As he did so, the ring glowed white again, the colour of Breeze's magic. He then kissed her, gently at first and then with more feeling. So many emotions, so much pain and sorrow, and now so much happiness and hope. They spent the refreshing just holding each other, quietly visiting and enjoying the warmth of their reunion.

Rambo was as shocked as Jesse, but he had no such problem with his mouth and releasing his feelings.

"Chaelea, it has been so long. So much has happened, I hardly know what to say except that I feel so blessed to be your husband

and to once again stand in your presence. I wanted you to come back when we could resume our life in a world that was at peace. I want to begin again, to rediscover our bond and our love."

"My husband, I have missed you as much. I am so proud of you and all that you have accomplished in your service to the gods in my memory. I too am blessed with the knowledge that we now stand together as one. We have a beautiful daughter, now grown, and I want to renew our acquaintance with her and our many grandchildren. We were denied the raising of her and the joy of other children, but I promise you that when this grave situation with Tazeron is over, we will have many more children. We will once again walk together in this life, surrounded by the sound of happy laughter."

"Oh, my dear, I so look forward to that life of peace and happiness. I am curious about something, Chaelea. When you first saw Jesse, you said that he was our son. What is meant by that?"

"Have you not felt a special bond to the boy, now a leader among these men? Has he not been called a prince, a lord of the prophecy, and others could see my kiss on him?"

"Indeed, we have wondered about this. Can you explain?"

"I can, but you must promise not to tell anyone until this conflict with Tazeron is over. Can you promise?"

"I can, my dear, indeed I will."

They spent the last moments of the refreshing in quiet conversation, during which time Rambo was once again amazed at the gods' involvement with the young man he considered his friend and much more.

After the refreshing had ended, they gathered in the main council chambers from the many antechambers that branched off. They felt the joy and the promise of the end of the conflict with Tazeron. They were anxious to discuss what they had discovered in the memories and how to proceed. Breeze suggested that they have some refreshment, but Jesse suggested that they all warp back to their main camp and tell the whole company of the return of the White Druid and Breeze, and what they had discovered. He also mentioned that if they did that, his father would be able to enjoy the meal with them. David smiled at Jesse in appreciation. Chaelea said that she would come separately with Rambo, but that the idea was a good one. It was agreed, and they warped back to their camp.

Arriving at the camp, Jesse had Tommy call a meeting of all the leaders. Some of the troops were still out on their surveying missions but were expected back soon. The leaders reported that no skirmishes had happened during their absence. They also learned that Tazeron and his minions had gathered at the south end of the valley, next to the Red Mountains. The game-master creator that Tazeron employed was indeed an expert in the game mechanics. They had had many unusual experiences, including wild storms that made communications impossible. Jesse wondered about this other game-master they mentioned and how many of them Tazeron had at his command. Obviously, there was no shortage.

As the Keepers and others returned, they were surprised to see Breeze. She was warmly welcomed by them. The return of the White Druid was not announced, as Chaelea had requested.

The camp was very interested to know what Jesse and the others had learned on their journey to Rodashu. Jesse and the others who had gone with him explained to the gathering what they had learned and what it meant to the Keepers' quest. There were concerns about releasing Tazeron and his followers into the mortal world and just how that would be accomplished. Jesse explained to the group that there were still details to be worked out, but that the leaders would keep everyone informed as plans were made. It was hard to consider releasing Tazeron, but the company trusted their captains and decided to wait until the details were formalised. The groups that had stayed behind and searched the area while Jesse and the others were gone made their reports. Not much was new, and in fact it seemed as if the Keepers, Tazeron, and his minions were at a standstill.

"This idea to send Tazeron and his followers into the mortal world will change things up for all of us," Jesse said. "Tazeron knows nothing of the mortal world except for what he has been told. We will have the advantage there. I, for one, am excited for the possibilities and am anxious to get started on the preparations. Now,

I do not know about the rest of you, but my stomach is telling me that it is time to eat, and I do not feel like cooking," Jesse concluded.

David, Ginnea, and Mr Chambers volunteered to warp out to bring back the food and drink. Zealoc, Martha, and several others volunteered to go with them, making sure that there were plenty of hands to carry it back. It was requested that they not have a meal of pizza, but that it include more of the foods that the Xantharaians were used to, such as fruits and vegetables, roasted meats, and bread. David did order one pepperoni pizza just for himself.

It did not take them very long to warp out, get the food, and travel back. The group was just starting to enjoy the meal when someone noticed a couple walking towards the camp from the southern end of the valley. Everyone was on high alert, poised to defend the site when Zeela squealed with delight and rushed to greet the strangers. Zealoc, Martha, Beloe, and a few others, including Breeze, Ammon, and Tommy, stood staring in disbelief.

"Come," Breeze said to a confused Jesse, taking his hand and leading him in their direction. He was sure that he had no idea who these strangers were and why they would be walking towards the camp from the southern end of the valley, the exact known location of Tazeron and his minions. They could be part of the enemies. They could be a trap.

As they walked towards the two, they could see Zeela talking animatedly and laughing. If Zeela approved of these two, then they must be okay. Perhaps they were defectors, maybe spies returned, or perhaps they were something else altogether.

When they reached the strangers, apparently elves, Breeze bowed and then turned to Jesse.

"Jesse, my love, permit me to introduce you to Prince Rambo and his wife, Queen Chaelea." Jesse thought he might faint from shock.

"I believe, Jesse, that Pearl was always reminding you to close your loosely hinged jaw. I see that some things never change, do they?" Rambo, in his elf form, laughed as he approached the faltering boy, who looked like he might fall over from astonishment.

"Rambo? How could this be? What happened to your dragon? I liked your dragon."

Rambo changed into his small dragon form. "Is this better?"

"At least now I know for sure it is you. I am surprised by this change; I never saw it coming." Jesse studied his friend and mentor, with whom he had shared so many experiences of joy, adventure, fear, and heartaches. He struggled to control his emotions and did not know why.

Rambo reverted to his elf form and gathered Jesse into his strong arms, holding him tight. After a moment or two, when Jesse recovered from the surprise, he stepped back and stared into the soft brown eyes of his friend, this time with his mouth closed and his emotions under control.

"I always wondered what it would be like to meet you in your real form, but I find that I am missing the Rambo I have always known. This will make meeting my mum and stepfather much easier, but not nearly as much fun," Jesse said, with a teasing grin.

"I can always transform if it pleases you and if it serves a useful purpose," Rambo said, smiling just as broadly. It was strange to see a natural smile without the toothy grin of a dragon. Jesse figured he would adjust… someday… maybe.

As the shock of having the White Druid once again in their presence began to wane, the group relaxed and enjoyed their meal. The visit was enjoyable, leading naturally to the discussion of their findings in Rodashu. It was time to plan the overthrow and destruction of Tazeron and his minions. There was much optimism within the group. After all this time, which felt like years to Jesse, it was exciting to think that they were finally on their way to the end.

Chaelea was the only one who saw the seer ball floating invisibly nearby, and it made her smile. She whispered to Jesse in his mind, *"My son, do you see what I see?" She shared the sight with him.*

"Yes, Mother, I do." He was not sure why calling Chaelea 'Mother' felt right, but it did. He looked to Rambo, only to see him smiling and giving Jesse a wink.

"My son, watch this and then follow with your mind to where this object goes. Rambo, I want you to follow it as well. I will remove

all traces of your presence. No one with magic will be able to detect you."

After she had said that, and much to the surprise of the gathering, Chaelea transformed into her full White Dragon form and advanced towards the seer ball. The results were humorous to those who could see. The ball backed up so fast that it temporarily lost its direction and spun in circles before racing off towards the Red Mountains. Jesse and Rambo had no problem following the object as it dove into a cave and through one of the underground waterways. They followed it into Tazeron's lair, where he and his captains were hiding. The seer ball sought out its master, who was in a trance as she controlled the ball. She abruptly woke and shared her findings with Tazeron and those gathered. Tazeron's face drained of all colour, and he started yelling at his minions. What he was saying, Jesse and Rambo could not hear, but they could tell that he was very agitated and either planning to move out or attack.

"Mother, do you see what we see?" Jesse asked.

"Yes, return to your bodies and let us plan how we can use this to our advantage," she replied.

After Jesse and Rambo had returned from their mind-searching trip into Tazeron's lair, Chaelea addressed the group.

"My children, Tazeron knows that I am here and that he is close to losing this battle. He is desperate, and we all know that desperate people do reckless things. We must act quickly if we are to send him into the mortal world. Jesse, Rambo, and Tommy, I want you to travel to the human world and the home of Jesse's mother and stepfather. Jesse, make your peace with them, then talk to them about our needs. David, it is night there. Give a dream to them both, one that will make them receptive to the quest and the arrival of Jesse, Rambo, and Tommy.

Remember, Jesse, and all of you gathered here, we must do this thing undivided, united in our goal. I cannot do this alone, and neither can any of you. This is, after all, a test for us all from our different gods. It was necessary from the start that we use our talents and help each other. Now go, do your part, and peace to us all."

David warped back to Rodashu and reverted to his essence, then with the talisman, he travelled to the home of Sally and Bill Robinson. He had been there many times before, but this time he felt nervous. It was that important. He began the process of dream giving. It was like what the Shadow Dreams did; the difference was that David was known to his audience. This made having them believe what he was saying more likely. First, David introduced himself to Bill and explained what was going on with Jesse and the quest. He let him know that they would be making a visit in the morning to explain. They would be asking for help in any way possible.

Next, David talked to Sally about their son, Jesse, and how much he had grown and how proud he was of him. He explained that Jesse was a leader among men and that he was leading a quest to save the world from a very evil man. Then he talked to them together, explaining that what he said was the truth and not merely a dream. Jesse and his friends would be there in the morning, and they should welcome them and listen to what they said.

"I still love you, Sally, I always will, but Bill is the man that you need now. Take care, and someday, if the gods agree, we shall see each other again in the next life."

After his message had been delivered, David left the sleeping couple. He hoped that they would be receptive to their three visitors in the morning. David chuckled; for some weird reason it made him think of Ebenezer Scrooge and the three ghosts of Christmas.

"Good luck, Jesse. At least you are not dealing with a Scrooge."

Chapter Fourteen
Return of the Prodigal

Of all the times that Jesse thought of visiting his mum and Bill, it did not feel like it would ever happen. Deep down, he wanted it to happen, and yet the idea terrified him. Jesse had left in a hateful mood. He had made his mum cry. Why would she listen to him now, and what about Bill? Jesse was so nervous that he felt sick to his stomach.

"Jesse, my son, this will go well. Have peace. They will be looking forward to your visit, and there will be a strong desire to understand and help in this quest. I can feel it," Rambo spoke to Jesse's mind.

"Thank you, my friend."

Jesse took a deep breath as they landed on the Robinsons' doorstep in Hutschenhausen, Germany. The home was close to the base where both his mum and Bill worked. His mum was a civilian medical worker, and Bill was a medic, specialising in evacuation and M.A.S.H. operations. He was also a top emergency assistant. Jesse was not exactly sure what they could do to help, but for whatever reason, they were relevant to the quest on this side of the shield.

As Jesse raised his hand to knock on the door, it was suddenly thrown open, and Sally Robinson leapt into her prodigal son's arms, hugging the stuffing out of him.

"Mum, I can't breathe. Have you been lifting weights?"

To his surprise, she did not cry or yell, nor did she call for Bill, who was standing behind her, grinning like the Cheshire cat, to chase them away. She quietly laughed and then invited them all into her home.

"Please come in, Jesse, and bring your friends. Rambo and Tommy, I'm so glad to meet you. It is a relief to know that Jesse has some excellent company to help him in this quest."

Jesse forgot all of Gran's hard work, and his chin hit his chest. Rambo gently pushed his jaw closed as they walked over the threshold.

"We're so glad to meet you, Mrs Robinson," Rambo and Tommy both said. Neither of them bothered to conceal the fact that they were elves, and Sally and Bill did not seem to notice.

"Mortals only see what I want them to see," Rambo had once told Jesse, and it seemed true now.

"Mum, I'm so sorry for the way I acted the last time we saw each other, and Bill, I apologise to you too. I'm really…"

"It is all forgotten, Jesse," Sally said, interrupting him. "We understand better now. We were too strict with a boy that was missing his father. We did not give you a chance to adjust. See how much you have grown. This war really suits you, Jesse."

Jesse was speechless. He had no comeback to what his mum had just said. Tommy filled in the uneasy space of time that followed.

"Jesse is a natural at leading the men and women in our quest, Mrs Robinson. We knew from the moment we met him that he had talents that no mere mortal possessed."

"Indeed, Mrs Robinson, Jesse excels in every possible way, far beyond what is needed for this quest. We are amazed by his abilities every day," Rambo added.

Jesse had to say something, or they would have him walking on water in no time.

"Honestly, Mum, if it were not for the people that surround me, I would be running away screaming like a scared little… Well, you get the idea. A captain is only as good as the people he or she works with, and I have the very best that anyone could imagine. Therefore, we have come to you and Bill. I am not sure right now what you are supposed to do. All I know is that you are crucial to the quest on this side of the shield. Perhaps I should explain all that better."

"No need, Jesse," Bill spoke up. "Your grandmother, Pearl, came to us the other night and explained the whole quest line, and David came last night. Would you believe that we completely understand the whole thing? You see, Jesse, we have a support group here on the base for soldiers addicted to the games and other things."

Jesse could not help it. His jaw was going to need duct tape. It just was not going to stay shut no matter what he did. This was just too much to take in. Unbelievable, in fact.

"Are you serious, Bill?"

"Oh, absolutely. You see, the military encouraged soldiers to play the games to unwind from duty at first. It was better than going out and getting into trouble in other ways, especially in foreign countries, and even back home in the States. They found that soldiers who have Xbox experience make great drone pilots, and those that play MMORPGs have abilities relating to focus and people skills. The problem we have is some of them become so involved that they spend their time playing even when they need to sleep. They are often so tired that they fall asleep when they are supposed to be on duty. Instead of charging highly trained specialists with a grave dereliction of duty, we have started support groups. The soldiers help each other under supervision. It is working very well, and if they work and progress within the program, nothing is recorded on their record.

Because of the visits from Pearl and David, we finally understand what was happening to the soldiers who have gone 'missing'. Now, instead of being AWOL, they are considered MIA until this thing with Tazeron can be ended. I oversee the programme on this base. I have also been training others to go out to other bases, and they, in turn, educate others. We have civilian workers as well, and we are always looking for others. I arrange the meetings and the specialists. This, Jesse, is why your mother and I were so against you playing the games. We could see where they could lead. As it turns out, you were destined to be involved in a way we never could have imagined, and never would we have permitted. Now you will help millions recover their lives and help save the world while you are at it."

Jesse was in shock; he could not process what he was hearing. Never could he have imagined that things would turn out this way. All the time that they had tried to run Tazeron down had been wasted effort, energy, and lives. If he had only followed through with coming here when he first thought of it, maybe Gran, Heala, and so many others would still be alive.

"Jesse, my son, do not beat yourself up over this. It is unfolding as it should," Rambo spoke to Jesse's mind. *"If Pearl had not died, she could not have helped with this programme the way she is now. The same is true of your mortal father. More lives would have been ruined if Pearl had lived than since she died. Their help and sacrifice will not go unnoticed, nor unrewarded. Think about this too: you needed to grow into your position, your manhood. If you had come sooner than this, the groundwork would not have been laid. Nothing is by chance, nothing. All things are in the hands of the gods, and you, my friend, are a pivotal player in all of this, as Nexlucimus told you so long ago."*

It was true, Jesse knew it, but that did not take away the sting, the guilt, the grief, and the pain that he and so many others had to endure. The word must get out about Tazeron and the evil he can spread. Every man, woman, and child who plays these games must know of this evil. Once Tazeron is eliminated, then, and only then, can they be safe again, if the games are played in moderation.

"Bill, if what I hear from you is the case, and I have no reason to doubt you, then the mechanics of what we need are already in place. We have a plan to release Tazeron into this mortal world. By doing this, we will cleanse the immortal world of his infection. Once we cleanse that world, they can help us cleanse this one. People on the games, and now the public, are aware of the 'missing ones'. It should not be hard to teach them about the bug and that Tazeron is a real threat. This world is very different from what he remembers. Once he crosses over with his minions, we believe that he will be very disappointed that he cannot control this world as he thought he could. He will be trapped here, and when he is, we will have the advantage and a way to destroy him. Will you help us spread the word and engage your people in this quest?"

"Yes, Jesse, we will do this. Now go, do what you were meant to do."

"Jesse, we are so proud of you. Please come to visit often, and bring Breeze with you next time. I want to meet my future daughter-in-law," Sally said, hugging her son tightly.

All Jesse could do as Rambo and Tommy led him out was smile, nod, and wonder with absolute amazement at this remarkable visit that he had feared. The gods truly were in control, even with weak mortals and immortals at the helm. Thank goodness.

When they warped back to camp, Breeze ran to meet Jesse as Chaelea greeted Rambo.

"After so long, I will need time to get used to this," Rambo grinned at Jesse.

"Indeed. I guess the dirt baths and bug eating are a thing of the past?" Jesse laughed.

"The dust baths, for sure," Chaelea said with a giggle. *"But he can still eat the bugs if he wants. I have not prepared meals in a long time. He may prefer the bugs. And I doubt, husband, that it will take that long for you to adjust."*

"I need to learn how to listen in on the mind talking," Breeze said, watching them.

"Once you and Jesse are married, it will become easier," Chaelea said.

"Yep, no privacy anymore," Rambo laughed as he snuggled closer to his wife. "Oh, how I have missed having you in my mind, my dear," he added.

Chaelea smiled up at Rambo and then pulled him off in a different direction from the camp.

"I am so glad that she is back," Jesse said, smiling down at Breeze. "Rambo has been so lonely without her. I understand now how awful that feeling is. After Chaelea rescued you, she took you to Clay? I was so close and did not even know it. Did Master Osuweep know you were there?"

"No one did. I was slipped in under the cover of being invisible. The only contact I had was with my brother, Ammon."

"By the way, I had no idea that he was a Shadow Dream. Are there any others in your family?" Jesse asked.

"Yes, my mother, several cousins, a couple of aunts, and one uncle, I believe. The ability is high in some families. I bet some of our children will be called into that service since I was one, and you have so many unusual talents for a mortal, but we shall see."

As they approached the camp, there was some scuffling and loud shouting. Jesse and Breeze ran to see what the commotion was all about. What they found was a deafening game of stone throwing called Grubbily Bub. Like Bacha Ball, it was intense, loud, and often involved wrestling to throw off opponents. Jesse and Breeze watched for a while and then, laughing, they walked away for some alone time.

In a few short hours, they would complete their plans. Let the Keepers and their Xantharaian companions have some fun while they can.

Chapter Fifteen
Making Plans

It was time to make plans. For this, they needed the moon soldiers. Zealoc gathered the ones he had been given and never used. Jesse brought his collapsed beetles and returned them to their warrior form. Minus one soldier, they had twenty-four.

Chaelea addressed them. "Young ones, we have need of your services. Are you willing?"

The soldiers all stood at attention before her. In unison, they confirmed that they were ready to do whatever Jesse, or anyone of his choosing, directed them to do.

"Soldiers, I direct you to follow the orders of Chaelea. Do you agree?"

"Yes, young Prince, we will do as you ask," their response surprised Jesse, giving him a jolt once again. He noticed Rambo smiling at him.

"Okay, one of these days real soon, you and Chaelea are going to have to tell me what is going on here," Jesse said, and he could not conceal the touch of irritation in his voice.

"Answers to all your questions will be given when this conflict is over, when we have peace once again, and when there is time. Meanwhile, enjoy the respect and act well your part, my son," Chaelea told him.

Why did he feel like a naughty little boy? He would try to have patience, but that was not something he was good at. Okay, he would act his part. *"Yes, Mother, as you wish. I will try to remember. Please remind me if I forget."* Now he felt like he was acting in a play, part of a story. He had a weird thought: what if he really was? It made him smile at the absurdity.

"Oh, I will," Chaelea said sweetly, smiling at him. For some reason, this made him feel edgy.

"Moon soldiers," she called to them. "We need three of you to become the Slater children. We need you to have their blood and behave as if you were them in every way. Do you understand?"

Three of the soldiers stepped forward. "Milady, we understand," they said.

"Number one," she pointed to the first in line. "Tell us what you must do to have their blood and become them in every way."

"One drop of their blood will prepare us as you have asked. Our bodies will accept the one drop, and it will fill us with their blood. We will resemble their appearance in every way. Our minds will become theirs."

"Very well," Chaelea said, surprise in her voice. "You are dismissed until we are prepared." The three soldiers joined the others in line.

"Could it really be that easy?" Jesse asked.

"Apparently," Chaelea answered softly, amazed at the simplicity. "I have never seen moon soldiers in action before. This is a first for me too. I know the myth as told in our legends, but that is the extent of my knowledge. All Xantharaians are taught the stories of the old ones, the Ancients. In the beginning, the time before time, moon soldiers were created by the Ancients to assist them as they began the eternities. No one knows exactly where the Ancients came from or much about the moon soldiers and the services they were capable of."

"Will the moon soldiers be able to go into the mortal world?"

"I do not know, Jesse, but I doubt it. Come, we must gather the rest and plan our strategy."

Chaelea had Zealoc call the entire company of forty-five together to explain what had happened. The rest of the army had been sent to locate other units and assist them until further instructions were given. She wanted them to know of this significant change of events and to receive instructions before their return to Earth.

Chaelea placed a bubble of protection around the gathering to keep prying eyes and ears from learning of their plans. She also cast a spell of truth which would expose anyone who might harbour deceitful thoughts of betrayal. She then addressed them with Jesse at her side.

"My friends, we are about to release Tazeron into the mortal world." There were gasps and murmurs of shock from those who had not heard of this idea.

"It has been discovered that Tazeron might not be able to accomplish his evil plan as we first suspected and as he imagines. The mortal world has matured beyond his understanding, having been separated from it these many years. Before we do this, however, we must plan our strategy. Jesse will explain what we have thought so far. We called this meeting of you Keepers and Xantharaians together so that you might give us your thoughts… Jesse."

"My friends, before I tell you about our plan, I want to say how honoured I have been to know each of you. You have worked hard to overthrow Tazeron. We have all felt much disappointment as he has escaped our efforts, and the sadness we have felt as we lost friends and family," Jesse's voice broke briefly. "We now have a glimmer of hope in our quest for Tazeron's destruction. We have twenty-four moon soldiers at our service."

There was excited chatter from the Xantharaians at this disclosure.

"Not too long ago, one of the Ancients, Matilda, carved them for us to use."

"You saw one of the old ones?" Mally asked, shock evident in her voice.

"Yes, Mally, we did. So much has happened since then. At first, we were not sure how to use them. Now, however, we understand. As you know, Tazeron thinks he can create portals to the mortal world with the help of his game-masters and humans that he pulls into the game. He has discovered that to make these portals work, he needs blood to keep them open for all his followers. The only blood that works this way is a blend of this world and the mortal world. This means the Slater children."

"Whoa, wait a minute. You said that he would not need my children," Jim said, as an ashen-faced Sara clung to his arm.

"Father, listen to all of it and…" Caleb pleaded.

"No! I will not! You, our children, will not be used for sacrifice." Jim grabbed Sara and started to leave.

Chaelea changed into her White Dragon form and flew to meet them. "You will listen, Jim and Sara Slater. It is not as you are thinking."

"But he…"

"Silence," she said softly, but all heard it as a shout, especially Jim and Sara. Sara began to cry.

"Peace, Sara. I know of your pain and your trauma. I have felt it all, as you have suffered." She changed back into her elf form. "We do need your children. Do not interrupt. The moon soldiers will become your children. They will take their place. But they need one drop of blood from each of them. That is all. No more will be required. The soldiers will look like, act like, and think like your children, and the children's blood will flow through their bodies from that one drop. You as their parents will not be able to tell the difference."

"How is that possible?" Jim asked quietly.

"It is a gift from the Ancients," Rambo answered, joining his wife.

"When the old Mother, Matilda, gave us the moon soldiers, she said they would confuse and help defeat our enemies. There are many advantages to them. They not only can take the form of someone or something, but they can also replicate themselves many times. There may be other abilities that we do not know. These soldiers have not been seen since the old ones roamed the worlds," Jesse told them.

"I am sorry," Sara whispered, "we have endured so much with these children, and because of them, dear friends have died. I just do not want anything else to happen to them, or anyone else." Sara faltered, tears in her eyes. This was the most Jesse had heard Sara say in a long time.

"I am embarrassed at my outburst. It is just that this whole quest seems to be centred around our children," Jim added. "Even though they are grown now, we have not had them very long, and their short lives have been a constant struggle."

"I do not mean to sound insensitive, but I have an idea how to use the moon soldiers," Zealoc said, addressing the group.

"That is what we are here for, Zealoc. Go ahead," Tommy encouraged.

"First, I believe that we should have a few of the moon soldiers replicate themselves. From our legends, the moon soldiers could do all that they did because of the magic they were imbued with.

"The plan that I propose is to have the replicated soldiers go into Xanthara. We would round up all those that are causing trouble there, such as the traitor council members and others who might have sympathy, such as Faber. The soldiers should be able to detect the traitors. They would have the power to expose and contain them.

"Because of Tazeron's evil infection and these traitors, Xanthara has been polluted. I believe that once we remove that influence, the trolls and other primitive tribes will return to the peaceful people they once were. I also think that, with the help of the Toulonians, these same tribes could be further advanced positively.

"The traitors could be sent to either Clay or another world, where they could be given a chance to realise their mistakes. If that is not possible, or they refuse to change, as Tazeron's minions did in the beginning, then they too would be cast out with him."

"I believe that this could be a good way to start, Zealoc," Jesse hesitated. "My fear is that these traitors could fake their repentance."

"I do not think that would be a problem," Tommy stated. "There are ways of exposing real feelings. It is hard to live a lie for very long. The truth will always prevail. The immortals were an honest, peace-loving people before Tazeron. I am sure this plan of Zealoc's could work, and perhaps something similar should be done here."

"I trust that what my brother has said could be the beginning," Martha observed. "After Xanthara has been freed from this vile scourge, there would be a greater chance of our assisting in the mortal world. I also agree with Tommy. It would be a good idea to use the soldiers to remove the game world of the odorous stench of the traitors here too, at least the Xantharaian ones."

"I think that if we reduce Tazeron's minions down to just the truly evil game-master creators and the greedy mortal slimes that he has attracted," Beloe interjected, "his chances of influence would be nothing."

"I just want to be sure that all the mortals who were influenced by Tazeron are given the opportunity to regret their involvement," Zeela shared. "The immortals really have no excuse for their participation and should be punished as Tazeron."

"If we start collecting all the Xantharaian traitors so that the only ones Tazeron crosses over with are the mortals, I think his chances of influence will be reduced even more. The game-masters will have nothing to manipulate as they do here. Can you just picture that poor pathetic game-master we sent to Clay being any trouble? When she was stripped of her powers and large Troll character form, she was a puny little nothing. This would happen to them all. Plus, I am not convinced Tazeron has totally revealed all his reasons for going over to the mortal world," David told them. Ginnea stood by his side, nodding at what he was saying.

"My friends, it is possible to entirely strip Tazeron of all his supporters, but is that what we really want to do?" Chaelea asked.

"What are you thinking, my dear?" Rambo wanted to know.

"I am thinking that opening the portals and allowing all his supporters in the game world to follow him is precisely what we should do. That will be the only way we can be sure that we know their real intent. The mortals will revert to their human forms, and the Xantharaians will have limited magic for their use. There is no reason to eliminate them all here. I suggest that we have the soldiers act as supporters, replicating the appearance of strength. Have them show up as a large group of rebels. Possibly, they can be the ones that deliver the fake children to Tazeron. They should be able to convince the traitors and Tazeron that they are part of the rebellion, and then maintain that deception in the mortal world if indeed they can go there. Then, if they can cross over, they can become spies for us. Once they are called into our service, they have a short life, but they will always be loyal to Jesse, or whoever he declares as his successor. Right now, that is me," Chaelea said.

The gathering became quiet as they all considered the options that had been presented.

"Would we still clean out the filth that is polluting Xanthara, Milady?" Zealoc asked.

"Yes, it would serve no purpose not to do so. After Xanthara is cleansed and evil removed from that world, we will request the return of the elves. With the return of the elves and the help of the Toulonians, we can rest in peace knowing that healing has begun.

"The Keepers would all be recalled from their duties in this world. They would be sent back to their mortal homes. There they will assist us in the cleansing of Tazeron from the human world. Those of you who received my mark will retain your magical abilities and communication with each other. The rest will be given telewaves and shown how to use them. You will maintain limited magical abilities. Some of you will receive Xantharaian companions."

"Like what Pearl had," Rambo explained to Jesse.

"Excellent," Jesse said. "So, will there be a bunch of wannabe pit bulls looking like roosters? Or griffons masquerading as tiny dogs?"

Rambo did not even bother to answer. He just smacked Jesse on the back of his head. They both started laughing until Chaelea stared them down.

"This is serious, and you two are acting like children."

Jesse looked over at Rambo, causing them to laugh in earnest.

"Honestly, you two. What is so funny? Please share it with the rest of us," Cami wanted to know.

"Nothing, Cami. We were just so… um… overjoyed at the… um… prospect of what Chaelea was proposing, that the release of nerves…" Jesse attempted to explain, trying hard not to snort. It was not working.

"Please," Breeze said, cutting him off. "Do not say any more. You will only embarrass yourselves further."

Rambo and Jesse tried hard to get serious and not laugh. The effort was bringing tears to their eyes. They were excused from the meeting to get their giggles under control, like naughty children sent to time-out. As they left the assembly and rounded the small hill, an explosion of hearty laughter could be heard by all. Despite the seriousness of the discussion, others caught the infection of laughter and joined in. Chaelea was not pleased but found that she too was grinning at the sound.

When Jesse and Rambo returned to the group, Jesse was hiccupping, and they were not surprised to learn that Chaelea's proposal had been accepted. They never really doubted the outcome.

Chapter Sixteen
Called to Serve

With the strategy of the moon soldiers understood, Zealoc and Martha prepared to leave. They would take twelve soldiers, six each, and travel to Xanthara. Mr Chambers and Cami would accompany them for transport and communication. Jesse truly wanted to go, but then so did many others. Zeela was anxious to join them. She was confident that Nexlucimus would be released, and she desperately wanted to be there. Tommy asked her to remain and help with base operations.

The Keepers who were not part of the leadership were told that they would soon be returned to the mortal world and their homes. Mixed feelings prevailed around the camp. Some of the Keepers were eager to go home, while others were not so sure. Those wanting to stay hoped to see the conclusion unfold in the game world. It was explained to them that they could watch it on their telewaves if they desired. When they learned the main reason for going home was to intercept Tazeron on the other side, they understood the importance.

They were to start social media flash drive events around the world, spreading the word to gamers and others who knew of the 'missing ones', exposing the evils of Tazeron. When the 'missing' returned to their homes, it would hopefully add more fuel to the anti-Tazeron movement.

Going back and spreading the word would not be easy. There would be resistance and doubters. However, as reports from around the world were gathered and linked, more people would accept the truth, or so they hoped. There would always be those who were sceptical about everything. Jesse remembered hearing about the C.A.V.E. people in one of his classes: Citizens Against Virtually Everything.

In today's world, when Tazeron finally did make his appearance, people would either scoff at him and his claims, or want to join him. It was anyone's guess how it would go. So many unanswered questions, and so many possibilities.

Before Zealoc and Martha left for Xanthara, they decided each of the soldiers would duplicate five times. They experimented with one of the soldiers to observe the consequences of replication. They learned that for each replication, the soldier would shrink by approximately one inch in height and one inch in width. No other effect appeared. They did not lose any magic, strength, or ability to reason and learn.

Mr Chambers escorted Martha to Rodashu with her six soldiers. Cami went with Zealoc. This way they all had transportation and communication because of the talismans that Sean and Cami each possessed. At first, Martha was not sure where to place her troops, with so many large buildings. It was the soldiers themselves who helped her decide.

The first soldier that Martha asked to replicate revealed that he and his fellows were sensing danger and violent unrest coming from the vast library. Martha sent them in that direction. The next told Martha that she was feeling menace and grave disturbance in the central marketplace. Once again, Martha sent her and her fellows there. So it went with each of Martha's soldiers.

As soon as they were called into service, they told Martha where they should go. Some of them patrolled the city, searching for conspirators, while most ventured farther out into the surrounding highlands and mountain valleys.

As the last soldier left, Martha and Scan found one of the few vendors with food and drink. They each grabbed two roasted meat sandwiches, some fruit, and a large banana and pickle smoothie. They laughed as they struggled to balance everything to a table. Sean went back for a couple of apple pies that looked delicious but that they could not carry on their first trip.

They ate and talked while waiting for their army to return. They marvelled that they had not seen any Skeedlers. Normally, the happy little scrubbers were the first to greet a returning adventurer. It was just another sign of how deeply Tazeron's evil infection had spread, upsetting the balance of life in this world. First the Refreshing, now the Skeedlers.

Not surprisingly, they discovered that they both enjoyed eating as much as adventuring. This became clear when both returned to the vendor to buy more roasted meat, fresh fruit, and another smoothie, grape this time. Each was astounded that the other could eat as much as they did, but it was true, and being in each other's company as they gobbled down the excellent vendor food was a pleasant experience.

Martha told Sean that one of her favourite pastimes, besides eating, was to go to her secret spot and fish. The blue pinckles were her favourite, not just for catching the marvellous little fighters but for cooking them. They had a delightful lemony flavour, which went well with her noodle cakes and creamed peas. Even though they were starting to get full, Martha's food sounded wonderful to both, and they made plans for a fishing trip together after things settled. Martha promised to cook all the blue pinckles they caught.

When Martha asked Sean how he had become interested in the games, he explained the need to divert his attention from the tragic loss of his wife, Eloise, and daughter, Chloe, Cami's twin. Martha was very sympathetic, and Sean found it easy to talk to her about it. This was something he had never been able to do before.

She mentioned that she, like her brother Zealoc, had never married. She blamed her life as an adventurer and the fact that she would rather travel, visiting other worlds and helping wherever she could, instead of settling in one spot. She had never met a man who wanted that kind of wife. Sean admired her ability to mix her love of adventuring and helping with her love of eating. Time passed as they warmed to each other's easy-going nature and shared love of laughter. At one point, they were laughing so hard that they did not notice a distant rumble until it became a roar.

They had barely finished their roasted meat and grape smoothies when the noise finally became so loud that it commanded their attention. As they turned towards the commotion, they saw a very strange sight approaching at an alarming rate of speed. It was an enormous fuzzy sphere, squirming with arms and legs. To their astonishment, the ball launched itself in their direction, threatening to smash them.

They scrambled out of the way, nearly knocking over the friendly vendor, who stood in shock before survival instincts took over. She soared into the air with blazing red wings. As the mass hit the ground, the fuzzy balls were knocked free, much like the spider babies on the back of a mother wolf spider that had been dropped or had fallen. Just like those spider babies, the fuzzy balls, once knocked off, scrambled back to their mount, or project in this case.

What Martha and Sean discovered during that instant of no Skeedlers was that one of the soldiers had gathered about fifteen foul, smelly ogres. They could only guess at the number, since the soldier had skilfully woven them into a tight knot. Apparently, Skeedlers were so offended by the stinking primitives that they decided to come out of wherever they had been hiding. They worked hard to get their prey tidied up, no easy task considering the way the ogres were intertwined.

Once the ogre pile was scrubbed to the Skeedlers' satisfaction, the little creatures noticed Sean and Martha. It was their turn for a bath. After such a long absence from Xanthara, and with not nearly enough restrooms or bathing facilities, including soap that did not draw flies, the Skeedlers again had their work cut out for them.

After their cleaning, Sean and Martha were the freshest they had been in a long time. While it was embarrassing to have such a public washing, it did feel sensational to smell and look nice again. Their hair was another matter. Martha's impressive braid was clean, unbraided, and all skew-whiff. Her long, vibrant red hair appeared electrically charged, sticking out in every direction.

Mr Chambers had a similar problem. Even though he was not in his game character form, he still had long filthy hair and a tangled beard. Barbers were hard to find in the game. Female barbarians did not have to shave too often, but in that form Sean did have a beautiful long braid, which was now unbraided and, except for the vibrant red colour, would have been as twisted and snarled as Martha's.

While Mr Chambers was not a barbarian just then, the cleaning seemed to reach past his mortal exterior and into the game. They never understood how that worked, but it did. So when they travelled back into the game, he, as well as Martha, would be a much cleaner version of himself, complete with long tangled hair that appeared electrically charged and totally out of control.

Following the Skeedlers' scrubbing, when they got a good look at each other, they forgot all manners and sensitivity and roared with laughter, pointing at one another. Doubled over at the sight, they laughed until their sides hurt and their jaws ached. Without thinking, they reached for each other and hugged as they laughed. The plump little dwarf and the tall skinny maths teacher had found friendship and happiness in a crazy world of dawning hope, and they loved the experience and each other's company.

Before they could completely get their snickers under control, Sean and Martha watched as all the remaining soldiers returned with similar results. Each soldier delivered huge squirming balls of trolls, their arms and legs tangled around one another and their loud mouths gagging, as the Skeedlers happily did the job they were born to do. When all six of Martha's soldiers and their five replications returned with their captives, they had collected almost five hundred prisoners.

The number of Skeedlers needed to clean up the crowd was massive, but before long the squirming balls were ready for delivery to Clay. Transporting the criminals there was easier than expected because of their packaged form. Sean decided to let Master Osuweep figure out how to untangle them.

Martha sent out the soldiers again, while Sean transported the conspirators. This time they returned empty-handed, reporting that there was no more danger or unrest in this part of the world. With

Sean's deliveries completed, they moved to seven other areas, uncovering only one or two more troublemakers.

Reporting their success to base camp, they were told to locate the few remaining Keepers and transport those who could not travel themselves to the main camp. Chaelea would then explain what was happening and send them back to their homes with instructions.

As it turned out, most of the Keepers had already been notified and gathered in common areas. Some could communicate and transport using the talisman, and they helped with transporting the others. After the last of the Keepers had been delivered to the main camp, Martha and Sean returned to the forest of Elves to assist Zealoc if needed. What they found surprised them.

Zealoc was busy helping a large mixed group of trolls and ogres rebuild the healing facility. His face was glowing with a huge grin, barely visible under his very bushy unbraided beard and long tangled hair. Apparently, Skeedlers had discovered this area too.

Cami was somewhere unknown. After a while, she came skipping down the trail leading to the Slaters' house with about fifteen children of mixed races. When Cami saw the two dwarfs and her father, she tried, but failed, to control her laughter. She, on the other hand, had fared much better in her appearance after her bath. No charged hair – hers looked sleek and shiny.

"Not fair," the others whined, with smiles.

Sean and Martha learned that because of the Toulonians' and Ravens' friendly natures, groups of these primitive people had been hidden from the ones affected by Tazeron's influence. The children that Jesse and Rambo had met in the cave had helped open the doors of communication and cooperation. Sean and Cami were delighted to report this finding to the main camp. Jesse and Rambo were ecstatic at the news.

Zealoc's soldiers had not found as many dissenters as Martha's because most had gone to the city of Rodashu and the surrounding area.

That night, when the day's work had settled, Zealoc, Martha, Sean and Cami enjoyed a meal with the trolls, ogres, Ravens and Toulonians. There was singing, dancing and storytelling. Mortals and immortals alike had an enjoyable evening as the soldiers stood guard in a world without danger.

In the morning, the soldiers told them that they had twenty-four hours left to help, and asked what they would like them to do. Zealoc sent them out to cover Xanthara and find any other traitors or troublemakers. They were to bring them back to the forest of Elves as soon as possible before their time was used up. The soldiers assured Zealoc that they could accomplish his wishes within their time limit.

Zealoc and the others were amazed at the ability of these moon soldiers. They truly were an answer to prayer, but it felt as though something was missing. It was almost like waiting for the other shoe to drop before trouble landed again. Perhaps it was simply that they had lived with unrest for so long that turmoil felt normal. Then Sean thought of something that jolted them all. What about portals? Could they still be active?

They sent a message to the main camp to ask, and waited.

While they waited, they shared their experiences working with the moon soldiers. They marvelled at the number of captives each group had gathered, especially Martha's, and how quickly. They laughed about the Skeedlers, how timid they had been at first, and how aggressive they became with each new ball of squirming, filthy bodies.

Zealoc complained that it would take a mortal lifetime to untangle his beard and hair. Martha challenged him to a brush-off, to see who could untangle their hair first. Sean was invited to participate in the brush-off, since his hair had endured the same Skeedler twisting and knots. Sean suggested to a horrified Zealoc and Martha that it might be easier just to shave it all off and start over with new growth. That idea was shouted down immediately.

The soldiers began coming back about dawn. They were haggard but empty-handed. No new dangers were detected, which was a relief. They explained that their worn appearance was due to the service they had performed, not because of anything else.

They had about six more hours of service remaining when the message from the base camp came back. They were to return to camp, but first they were to send the moon soldiers out once more to double-check the capital and all the portals known to them. They stood by for that report.

After about four hours, the moon soldiers informed them that all the portals were either closed or destroyed, and that the capital city was indeed free from any other dangers.

Sean noticed that the soldiers were starting to crack, and pieces of their blue stone flaked away. They gathered with the blue army one last time to give them their sincere thanks for all the service they had performed. The soldiers were then told to combine into one stack and collapse down into a small blue beetle.

Cami picked up the crumbling stone insect and gently placed it in one of her many pockets. As she did so, there was a soft pop. When she removed her hand, a fine blue dust scattered to the wind. She did not wipe the tears that rolled down her face.

Chapter Seventeen
Preparations

After bidding the Ogres, Trolls, Ravens and Toulonians in the Forest of Elves farewell, Cami and Mr Chambers transported Martha and Zealoc back to the main camp. Chaelea and Jesse greeted them, calling an assembly of the encampment.

Before their meeting, Chaelea cast a protective bubble around the gathering as before, to keep spying eyes and ears away from their meeting and exchange of intelligence. She noticed, off in the distance, a magician's infiltrator ball. She alerted Jesse and Rambo to its presence. The orb seemed confused when the bubble was cast, and after searching the area, it appeared to give up and disappeared.

"Welcome back," Chaelea said warmly, as she studied Zealoc and Martha. "It seems that you had a very intense encounter. I am sorry to say, but your appearance is rather alarming, Zealoc and Martha. Sean, yours is not as startling, but then Barbarians were always wild looking."

"Skeedlers, Milady," Martha explained dryly.

"Ah, I see… um," she said, trying to overcome her distraction. Shaking her head for clarity, she continued, "We are eager for your final report. We decided to wait before activating the remaining soldiers until you returned. You surprised us with the number of dissidents the soldiers uncovered. It is shocking how far Tazeron's influence has spread. First, tell us about the mixed group of primitives you found, and what they are doing."

"When we left, the Ogres and Trolls, under the direction of the Toulonians, were discussing the rebuilding of the village."

The gathering tried to listen politely to Zealoc's report, but many found it difficult. His frizzled red mane, cascading over him like a blanket and sticking out in every direction, was a distraction and hard to ignore. Zealoc generally took great pride in his appearance, and this new version of him was shocking, to say the least. Martha had a similar effect on the gathering, and there were muffled giggles peppered throughout the crowd.

"The Toulonians wanted the village to be habitable when the Elves returned," Zealoc told the gathering. "They were hoping that some of the Xantharians still here could return and help in their efforts. I was wondering if some of the guards could be used for that purpose once we released Tazeron. The Ravens were still planning on searching for the missing council members."

"I believe that will be possible, Zealoc," Chaelea said. "Once the Elves learn that their village has been cleansed, I am sure they will want to return. The village will have plenty of leadership and work power once that happens. I am more concerned about the capital and the buildings of leadership. It seems that most of the citizens there will need a helping hand as well. So much destruction and senseless waste. I also want to get seedlings for the Dumplumba and Naqisha trees from another world. Perhaps Zeela's parents will help with that, or maybe Nexlucimus' parents. How did you feel about the attitude of the Ogres and Trolls, Zealoc? I understand that you worked with them in years past. Do you think their willingness to help is sincere?"

"I believe they are as sincere as their kind can be," Zealoc said. "The soldiers detected no malice in them, and I feel as sure as I can possibly be. The Toulonians have ways of discerning dishonesty, and they gave no indication of such in those primitive people. The Ogres and Trolls have always been a peaceful people until Tazeron. Even after many of their clans joined with that evil, these stayed faithful to their previous service. What happened to their people frightened them, and they are anxious to repair any harm done. When this war is over, it is my greatest wish to become an ambassador to those tribes."

"I can vouch for Zealoc on that matter," Jesse told the gathering. "I have heard him talk to my grandmother many times about his desire. In fact, they hoped to serve together."

Chaelea studied the little man with his wild beard and hair and smiled. "I shall keep all of this in mind, Zealoc. May I, at the risk of your embarrassment, suggest a little magical help with your appearance? I would include your sister in my offer, of course, and Sean if he so wishes."

Zealoc was not sure how to react, but Martha had no problem accepting Chaelea's proposal.

"Milady, I would be honoured to accept your generous recommendation, and so would my brother and Sean." She winked at Zealoc and Sean, smiling at their discomfort and reddening cheeks.

"Please stand in front of me, you three. And Zealoc and Sean, it is no dishonour to accept help when it is sorely needed," Chaelea grinned at them. With a wave of her hand, Sean, Zealoc and Martha were fit for a photo session, with neatly braided hair and, in Zealoc's case, an elaborately plaited beard.

"Now, with all of the physical distractions taken care of, shall we proceed with planning Tazeron's release from this world? Zealoc and Martha, we are impressed with your handling of the Moon Soldiers, and we hope that you will help us understand what we should do with the twelve we still have at our service."

The two dwarfs, along with Mr Chambers and Cami, explained how they used the soldiers. All the remaining Keepers and Xantharians gathered round and listened as they described how the replicating worked, how the soldiers knew exactly where they needed to go, and how neatly they packaged their prisoners. Sean explained that it was easy to transport the detainees. He mentioned that Master Osuweep, as always, was a tremendous help. Sean expressed no apprehension in changing three of the soldiers into the Slater children.

"They are easy to programme, Jim. You and Sara will be surprised at how well this will work. I suggest that the three becoming Slaters are not replicated because they will retain their full size. I am sure that Tazeron will be convinced that he has the twins and Caleb. The other soldiers should be told to take on different appearances such as Trolls, Ogres and blood fairies."

"We need to work out all of our plans before we activate the soldiers. We want to be sure to get Tazeron and his minions over to the mortal world before the soldiers run out of time," Cami said.

"Absolutely, Cami. We do not want the soldiers turning to dust just as they are leading Tazeron and his minions to the portals," Chaelea said.

"Indeed," Cami said a little sadly, thinking of the blue dust still in her pocket.

"Do we know if the soldiers can cross over?" Beloe asked.

"We still do not have the answer to that, Beloe," Chaelea replied. "It really does not matter, because even if they can cross, their time would be short, and by then we will have sealed the portals anyway. We plan to seal the entrances as soon as we can after everyone is through."

"When we gathered up the Keepers in Xanthara, the mortal rescuers who came here on their own to help, and others such as Rusty Palmer, we were surprised at the increased passion they all expressed. They have all had life-changing experiences, even the characters that were created in the game world. They are all anxious to continue their service to the people of both worlds and to us. Their continued support, both here and in the mortal world, will be appreciated," Zeela said sincerely.

"Zeela, we feel the same as you. Since most of our troops are being prepared to go home, we seriously need to get ready for the final battle. This is what I propose," Jesse said. "Tommy, you and Cami, along with Jim and Sara, prepare the three soldiers that are to be the Slater children. The DNA in the single drop of blood that they will need contains much of the children's personalities, enough to fool Tazeron at least. They must act the part of scared but brave warriors.

"Dad, you and Ginnea take four of the Moon Warriors and prepare them to be nasty but loyal thugs. Have them be something huge like Trolls or Ogres, which are familiar to Tazeron, and replicate them five times. Be sure that each replication has a different appearance. Find out if they can travel through the portal into the human world. Of course, now that I think of it, Trolls and Ogres would not actually work in our world."

"Jesse, remember that the humans see what we want them to see. So, David, be sure the soldiers, if they can cross over, know that the humans must see them as human people," Rambo advised.

"Will do, Rambo. I sure wish I could go through the portal and help," David said.

"Why can't you?" Ginnea asked. "I understand that you would become an essence, but would that not be a significant benefit? Couldn't you be an effective spy? You could sit on Tazeron's shoulder and whisper sweet enticings in his ear." Ginnea roared with laughter at the vision that conjured.

"That is a fantastic idea, Ginnea," Chaelea said. "I like that idea very much, and why not call on Pearl to do the same thing? How would you feel about becoming an anti-devil spy team with your mother-in-law, David?"

"I don't know, Chaelea. She can be pushy sometimes. OUCH!" David winced, surprised. "See, I told you, she just sucker-punched me. I'm going to have a bruise now," he scowled, rubbing his shoulder.

"Go Gran!" Jesse shouted. "How could she do that?"

"Even though she is an essence, so is David," Rambo explained. "I think we all forget that fact since he is in game form while in this world."

Jesse noticed Zealoc standing off to one side, grinning at the exchange, and he wondered if Gran had said something to him about what she was about to do. The thought made Jesse smile too.

"Ok Jesse, we still have five Moon Soldiers unassigned," Chaelea said, drawing the group's attention back to the planning. "What are your suggestions for them?"

Jesse was just about to give his answer when a surprising thing happened: a message came from Nexlucimus in the form of a one-way telewave.

"My friends, marvellous things are going on here in the capital. The remaining council and I have been freed, and we are assisting the citizens of the city to rebuild. It is like a new beginning. Jesse, I know some of what has been happening to you, Breeze and Rambo. Welcome back, Chaelea. Zeela, my dear, I have a need to counsel with you. Chaelea, might I enjoy the company of my wife for a while? I would also like to retain two of the Moon Soldiers. The Toulonians told me of them, and we here would feel safer knowing that we had them on watch until we are sure that Tazeron is banished from the game world. In the meantime, we have you all in our prayers, and we feel great joy in the plans that you make. Take care."

"Jesse," Chaelea said urgently, "we need to implement our plans immediately. I am not entirely sure that it was Nexlucimus." This shocked everyone.

"What do you mean?" Zeela asked.

"It is more a feeling than actual knowledge, Zeela. Perhaps there is another way. Jesse and Rambo, could you go back to Xanthara using invisibility, taking one of the Moon Soldiers? Search out this Nexlucimus and discover, with the help of the warrior, if he is truly himself or an imposter?"

"Yes, Chaelea, we can do that, and we will leave immediately," Rambo and Jesse both said. Rambo became his smallest dragon form with Jesse mounted under a bubble of invisibility. Jesse transported them first to the cave of the Toulonians.

Landing in the cave was a good idea, as it turned out, because it was empty. This gave Jesse a chance to activate the Moon Soldier and give him his instructions. He was to become a small beetle that could travel in one of Jesse's pockets. The soldier was to alert Jesse and Rambo to any deceitful activity. After the soldier was activated and instructions were given, the three of them became invisible, and Jesse transported them to the Village of Elves.

The soldier announced that he could detect nothing of concern in the community. Jesse and Rambo were amazed at the progress that had been made since their last visit, after it had been burnt. They watched for a few moments as busy workers carried lumber, painted designs on doorways and shopfronts, and vendors prepared their food. Then Jesse saw something that surprised him. It was Heralon, Tommy and Ginnea's father.

"Rambo…"

"I see, Jesse. And look, there is Trusol, another council member. Shall we go to the capital and look for Nexlucimus?"

"I think I want to talk to the Toulonian Chief first and find out where Bob is."

"That might be a good idea. Perhaps he can answer some of Chaelea's concerns for us."

Jesse had the soldier lead them to the Chief's location, and they found Bob there as well, along with the Ape leader and the Cats.

"Jesse and Rambo, how wonderful to see you again," the Chief said as he welcomed them. "What brings you back to Xanthara?"

"Sir, we received a message from Nexlucimus, and we are desirous of finding him. Have any of you seen him?"

"Yes, Jesse, we have seen him, as well as all the remaining council members. They returned to us shortly after Zealoc and his party returned to your camp in the game world. I believe that Nexlucimus was very anxious to visit the capital city and attend to the reconstruction there. Is anything wrong?" the Chief asked, concerned.

"We don't know," Rambo said. "There was some concern in a message we received, and it created questions for Chaelea."

"I detected nothing unusual from any of them, Jesse. They were perhaps tired, and they did seem preoccupied with concerns," the Chief stated.

"Would you like us to go with you?" the great Cat asked Jesse.

"If you are free, then yes, we would appreciate your company. Would you need transport or can you do that yourselves?"

"We will meet you at the great library," Oongo said.

Jesse and Rambo warped to the library, where the Cats and the Ape leader, Molo, were already waiting for them.

"How did you get here so fast?" Jesse wondered.

"Thought travel," Oongo answered.

"Wow, I want some of that," Jesse said, smiling at him.

As they started up the stairs of the building, the Moon Soldier whispered that he was feeling something deceitful and asked if he should go to the location and investigate. Jesse agreed, and the warrior, still in beetle form, left to search for the problem. A few moments later the soldier returned, saying that the problem was indeed Master Nexlucimus, or at least it appeared to be him, but something was different. Jesse and Rambo followed the full-sized soldier to the chamber room. They knocked.

"Enter," came the reply. Nexlucimus stood as they entered.

"Ah, my friends, and Moon Soldiers as well. Where is Zeela, could she not come?"

"Beware, Master Jesse, he is not what he appears. There is a mechanical device that is searching all of us. I feel the pull to persuade me to do its bidding. It is strong, but the magic that protects me is more powerful. Shall I disable it, sir?"

"Yes, immediately."

"You will need to catch Master Nexlucimus, sir. His strength will leave him."

"Master Nexlucimus, have a seat, and we will tell you of Zeela," Jesse said kindly.

As the Elder took a seat, the Moon Soldier stepped behind Nexlucimus and grasped his head, waving his hand over the Elder's face and catching something in his hand. The Elder slumped back into the chair, apparently sleeping, and was wrapped in the chair's warm comfort.

"This, sir, is the object that was implanted into the Elder." The Soldier held a tiny black cylinder with minuscule wires attached. He gave it to Jesse.

"Holy crap," Jesse exclaimed, staring at the object, watching it twitch and jiggle. "What the heck is this thing?"

"A controlling, tracking and listening device, sir. Now that I have felt this one, I can feel others. Eleven to be exact, with the other council members. Shall I disable them, sir?"

"Yes, and while you are at it, please double-check with speed anything else that we might have missed. Let me know if you need additional help of any kind. Rambo and I will remain here with the Elder. And Soldier, thank you. You have been of tremendous help to us this day. Now make haste."

"Oongo and Molo, would you return to the forest and assist the Moon Soldier and the Toulonians if needed?"

"Yes, we will do this," Oongo replied.

"Chaelea was correct in her feelings. Rambo, can you tell her what we have learned and that we are waiting? This is shocking, something out of science fiction, not fantasy. I am wondering if there are more of those things in the heads of some of the people we sent to Clay. Scary thought."

"I will let her know, Jesse. I doubt that the others sent to Clay were infected. This seems new. However, when our Moon Soldier returns, perhaps it would be a good idea to make a short visit to the detention centre and let him check it out."

As Jesse and Rambo sat there watching the Elder, he began to wake. Looking around, apparently confused, Nexlucimus' eyes focused on Rambo and Jesse.

"What happened to me, and how did I get here? Where did you two come from, and where is Zeela?"

The Elder was obviously going to need some help getting his memory back. Jesse and Rambo wondered if the other council members were going to need attention as well. Perhaps this would be a service the Toulonians could help with.

Before returning to the Forest of Elves, Jesse discovered that while he was holding the tiny black tube, the minuscule wires had tried to attach themselves to his hand. Startled, he threw the thing on the floor, but it flew back at him. Jesse yelped, and Rambo swatted it out of the air, sending it crashing into a stone pillar where it shattered. While they watched, the thing began to reform. Both Jesse and Rambo incinerated it with their fire, careful not to breathe in any of the fumes in case they too contained particles of the contraption.

"That must be one of the creepiest things I have ever seen, Rambo," Jesse said, shuddering.

"Indeed, genuinely disturbing. I never was a sci-fi fan," Rambo said.

It was just another moment or two before the Moon Soldier returned with the other squirming black tubes. They could not infect the Warrior, but they were certainly trying.

"Soldier, we need to destroy those things with fire. Can you hold them while we do it?"

"No, sir, but I can crush them against a stone pillar, and before they reform you could incinerate them."

"That would work. While you were out, did you detect anything else that was deceitful or would cause this world to be unsafe for the Elves to return?"

"No, sir."

"Okay, crush those monsters so we can destroy them. Then let us head to Clay to double-check things there, after we deliver the Elder and the other council members to the Toulonians, of course."

Chapter Eighteen
Operation Banishment

Clay was beautiful, so different from Xanthara. Each head Elder and the people of the new worlds of fantasy were free to create a masterpiece of their own design, with the blessing of the gods of course. It had always been like that.

When Rambo landed on Clay along with Jesse, the first thing that happened was an army of Skeedlers greeting them. This was expected, and it did not even faze Jesse anymore. He often thought back to his first encounter with those happy little scrubbers, and instead of a grimace, now he felt only humour at his first reaction. So many memories.

"Master Rambo, Master Jesse, how wonderful to see you again. How can we help you this time?"

"Master Osuweep, we were wondering if we could visit the prisoners that Mr Chambers brought to you from the Forest of Elves. There might be a problem. We brought a Moon Soldier with us to check things out," Jesse told the Elder.

"A Moon Soldier? So, are the Ancients involved now? How astonishing! Yes, I will show you to the detention centre."

Jesse and Rambo were surprised at the size of the building and grounds of the detention centre, but a large facility was needed with the number of inmates there. Jesse wondered how they managed so many detainees and still built such an amazing world, especially since no magic was allowed in the construction. Once Jesse and Rambo were shown the facility, they had the Soldier replicated five times, and all six were sent to scour the area looking for more of the strange black cylinders and any other problems.

While they waited for the return of the Soldiers, Jesse and Rambo, in elf form, walked over to a vendor to get some food. Rambo decided to eat something besides bugs this time, surprising Jesse.

"What, no bugs for you today?"

"Nope, they're starting to give me gas," Rambo smiled at Jesse. "And dragon gas can be a scary thing."

"Are you serious?" Jesse asked, worried. Rambo howled with laughter.

After a while, the Soldiers returned and reported no further problems. There were no more strange black cylinders. They also mentioned that the tangled balls of dissenters were disassembled, and the prisoners were progressing nicely in their rehabilitation. The people of this planet were fantastic in everything that they did. Many of the inmates were eager to repair the damage that Tazeron's influence had caused.

Jesse and Rambo met back with Master Osuweep after the Soldier's sweep of the facility, letting him know that they were pleased with how well things were going at the detention centre and that no other qualms were found. Preparing for transport back to base camp, Jesse had the Soldiers collapse into one tiny beetle, which he placed in a pocket.

Before they left, Rambo and Jesse decided to make a quick visit to Zeela's parents, Amber and Patonious. Jesse asked about replacing the Dumplumba and Naqisha trees. Amber said that she would talk to the head gardener about some tree starts for Xanthara. After that, there was nothing left to do but head back to camp.

Arriving back at camp, Rambo and Jesse were greeted by Breeze and Chaelea, and instead of calling a group meeting, the four of them flew to a quiet place to chat about things. Chaelea and Rambo positioned protective bubbles around them so there would be no eavesdropping. This was pretty much standard procedure now, as there seemed to be an increase in spying from Tazeron's camp with the return of Chaelea.

"So, there was a mechanical device implanted in Nexi and the council?" Chaelea asked, stunned. "Will there be any lasting effects?"

"They were confused when it was removed, but there did not seem to be any lasting effects. We left them with the Toulonians. The Toulonians will perform a healing ritual on each of them to detect any more damage or problems," Rambo said.

"Zeela must be informed. This is truly shocking. Never has anything like this happened before. Tazeron," she sighed, "such evil, and the corruption of so many other souls. It makes me furious,"

Chaelea said, as she stood and paced. "We must finish preparations and banish this evil monster into outer darkness along with all those that continue to willingly serve him."

"Milady, I have been thinking of a possible plan. An illusion," Jesse said, "to completely fool Tazeron, we need to make it look like the dissenters have ravished our camp and defeated our troops, including you and Rambo, and all of the leaders. Tazeron needs to believe that he has complete control of the situation so that once the fake kids are in his clutches, along with the army of pretending rebels, he will create portals and leave. As they leave through the portals, we will close their escape route by sealing and destroying those openings, banishing them to the human world. We must create the rebels and the illusion of our destruction at the same time. This must be done so that it is entirely believable. I, for one, think that our troops won't mind becoming acting troupes." Jesse snickered at the play on words. The others missed the joke, but they understood the idea and loved it.

"In the printed side of stories, I am sure that there are tales of zombies, ghouls and other horrors of the night. Under a shield of protection so that Tazeron cannot see us, we will dress and prepare an army of truly horrible and hideous creatures out of our weak and 'slaughtered' Keepers and Xantharian Soldiers. While we are preparing for our production of a defeated army, the Moon Soldiers will be prepared to steal the fake children and flee to Tazeron to act their part as rebels.

"Then we wait for their escape. I suggest that my dad, David, follow them through the portal, as Ginnea suggested, and meet up with my grandmother, Pearl, to be our eyes and ears with Tazeron and his minions. The timing must be perfect. Chaelea, the bubble of protection must be removed at the precise time that the rebels, with their captives, leave for Tazeron's camp so that they can witness our defeat."

"An ingenious plan, Jesse," Chaelea praised. "Let's see what the rest of the leaders and warriors think of this idea of yours, my son."

Chaelea's praise and calling him her son still felt strange to Jesse, but he said nothing. Instead, he bowed slightly, smiling, as they prepared to return to camp.

Back at camp, Chaelea had Rambo change into a rooster and bugled the troops with his crowing. After the protective bubble was in place and the gathering quietened down, Jesse started explaining the plan of an illusion of destruction and why it was needed.

"The fake children and rebels must not be seen by Tazeron as a trap," Jesse explained.

At first, there was confusion. Then, as they realised what was being proposed, the faces of battle-hardened and weary warriors changed from blank silence to happy smiles, along with laughter, whooping and shouting, with everyone talking at once about what they wanted to look like and become. There were tales of gruesome imaginings, slit throats, gouged eyes, dripping blood, torn clothing, slashed wounds and other fearsome injuries. Magic was amusing at times.

One of the younger Keepers suggested that instead of the bubble of protection just quietly disappearing and the illusion being staged, maybe Chaelea could explode it in a visible eruption like a bomb going off.

"That would make all the injuries appear more reasonable and real. Plus," Peter gushed with excitement, "it would be a heck of a lot of fun."

"That would be totally wicked!" someone in the back shouted. Others echoed their agreement.

The consensus of the gathering was one of total support, and assignments were made for implementing the scam.

The next couple of hours were spent magically changing everyone's appearance into horribly injured players in their scheme against Tazeron. There was almost a party atmosphere. In addition to the costumes they were creating, the camp was trashed, and an explosion was planned. Moon Soldiers were replicated, except for the three that were to be the Slater children, who would be changed at the last minute. The Moon Soldiers that had returned from Xanthara with Rambo and Jesse were sent out to spy on Tazeron and his forces. They reported back that Tazeron was still at the location in the Red Mountain, surrounded by glass spiders and blood fairies. The Soldiers agreed that an explosion of a bomb would be of benefit, as it would alert Tazeron and his camp that something massive had happened at the Keepers' base.

After all the preparations were completed, Zeela approached Chaelea and asked if she could be excused to go and check on Nexlucimus and the other council members. There was some discussion, and it was agreed that her involvement was no longer necessary for the plan's success, now that the injuries had all been applied to the actors. Everyone looked bizarrely horrifying. Zeela's artistic eye had made it all absolutely perfect.

It was also suggested that the Slater children go with Zeela, so if they were seen after the fake children were deployed, there would be no confusion. The Slater children were not sure they agreed with that until they were reminded that the elves would be coming back soon and the troll children were already there. Mary was very excited to see Samalla again, and the boys were excited to see their friends and not have the previous restrictions anymore.

Ammon was told that he too could go if he wished, but he decided to stay with his sister Breeze until the banishment was complete. He, like Breeze, could become invisible in any world, and that ability was sure to be of benefit, especially since they could communicate with each other no matter their location. Ammon was actually intrigued with the scam and expressed a desire and excitement in becoming a victim.

After Zeela and the children had been transported to Xanthara by Jim and Sara Slater, the camp finished Operation Banishment preparations. They were almost ready to launch. People picked out their staging locations and practised playing dead. One creative person wrapped himself around a branch in a tree and dripped blood — fake, of course.

It would be up to the Moon Soldiers to act their part and let Tazeron and his minions see the camp, but not approach it. Not everyone was good at holding their breath. A protective spell was placed on the victims so that a blood fairy or other nasties like glass spiders could not inflict real damage with their darts and poison. Chaelea made sure that spell was undetectable. They were ready. Jim and Sara would remain with their children until given the all clear to return. If the children wanted to come back at that point, they would be allowed, but if all went as planned, there would be no reason. The next battleground for the Keepers and their Xantharaian companions would be the mortal world.

The Moon Soldiers, real and replicated, and the fake Slater children were given final instructions and sent on their way. Ten minutes later, Chaelea blew up the bubble and camp with a tremendous blast that rocked the whole game world. Keepers and Xantharaians alike protected their ears, but they were still tossed around with the force of the explosion, which only made the scene more believable.

"Excellent work, Mum!" Jesse praised. Rambo just snickered.

"You two behave yourselves, and act well your part."

"Cover my mind travels, Mother. I want to check up on Tazeron and his lackeys."

Chaelea chuckled softly but complied with Jesse's request. Jesse sent his mind after the Moon Soldiers as they marched to Tazeron's camp. They looked completely realistic in their modified forms. The imposter children acted scared and yet brave, just as they were supposed to. Jesse was surprised when Rambo's thoughts caught up with him.

"Hey, Dad. I didn't expect you to come too. I'm glad you did, though."

"You didn't think I was going to let you have all the fun, did you?"

"I should have invited you. Sorry."

"No, not necessarily. I was just curious and decided to butt in."

The Soldiers were just reaching the mountains when a large group of people and monsters started pouring out of the caves. Jesse figured it was in response to the remarkable explosion.

The Soldiers stopped marching and stood their ground. The minions froze in their fleeing from the caverns, surprised to see this large group of trolls, ogres, blood fairies and trogs heading toward the mountain. Then they saw the children bound and gagged. One of Tazeron's minions raced back into the cave, and within a few moments, Tazeron himself approached the group.

"Who are you, and what are you doing here with these elves?" Tazeron sneered at the Soldiers.

The leading Soldier approached Tazeron. Two of the guards at Tazeron's side raised their weapons, but Tazeron waved them down.

The Soldier bowed slightly. "We come to serve you, Milord, and we bring these children as an offering of commitment to you and your purpose. We have heard of you and the cause that you seek, and we wish to join our forces with yours. If you do not want our service or need these children anymore, we will leave. But before you decide, we would show you something."

"Why should I believe you?" Tazeron questioned hesitantly.

"Did you not feel the massive explosion? Did you not hear it? Come, follow us, but we caution you to do as we say, unless you wish the same fate."

"How dare you come in here and threaten me. I am Lord of this place." Tazeron hurled a huge fireball at the Soldiers. The Soldiers did not even blink before sending the fireball back at Tazeron, surprising him, burning his robes and frizzing his beard and hair. The fake Mary screamed despite the gag.

"Perfect," whispered Jesse to Rambo.

"Who are you?" Tazeron asked, fearful.

"Come, follow us, and we will tell you."

"You know, Rambo," Jesse whispered, *"those Soldiers could take out Tazeron and his whole camp."*

"That might be true, my son, but that would prove nothing. Tazeron and his followers must be allowed to seal their fate. It is not too late for some of them to repent. Warn your mother that Tazeron approaches."

"Yes, Father," Jesse said, without a sliver of discomfort. *"Milady, prepare yourselves. The Soldiers are returning with Tazeron and his followers."*

"Thank you, Jesse."

"At your service."

"Shall we go, Dad, so we do not miss the fun?"

"Yep, besides I want to check on my body."

"Holy cow, that is right. Let us go."

They followed behind the Soldiers and Tazeron's minions, watching and listening.

"Why do you wish to join us?" Tazeron asked sceptically.

The Soldier acted as though he did not hear. They continued to walk until they topped a hill overlooking the Keepers' camp.

"Did you do this?" Tazeron gasped, taking in the total destruction of his enemy, believing what he saw.

"We did," was the reply.

"How? Why? When all of my planning has not worked, even with the mortal game masters. What did you do? Who are you?" Tazeron stammered.

"We come from a far place. Word of you and your plans reached us, and we were created to meet you and deliver you to the world that you seek. We follow only one person, and that is not you, but we will do what is necessary to fulfil our orders."

Little warning bells were going off in Jesse's mind, and he said this to Rambo, but Rambo replied that he felt no problem.

"You must go now," the Soldier told Tazeron. "Prepare your ritual. We cannot stay long, and when we go, we take the children with us. You do not have any time to delay your decision. Make it now. Do we help you, or do you continue to run in circles?"

Tazeron was speechless, appearing indecisive. He seemed to snap out of his stupor.

"Yes, yes, come, let us hurry. The ritual, we must prepare the ritual."

Tazeron turned so fast to retreat that he stumbled. It did not slow him down. He ran back toward the mountain, calling out orders.

"We must get the knife, the basin, the herbs, the cauldron. Prepare the table. We will create ten portals. It will be glorious. Our arrival will be spectacular. We will be worshipped. We will control the mortal world. The human anti-gods will bow to us."

Tazeron was laughing now, a sick, demented cackle. He was spewing evil, reeking of it. Some of his followers were looking at each other, questioning, unsure of who this man they had followed really was. Jesse saw some of them fall away, stumbling to a stop, watching as the procession progressed forward without them.

"Those are the ones that Chaelea was hoping to save," Jesse said. "What can we do to help them?"

"Nothing now," Rambo replied. "If they are serious, they will find us, or the elves. Without Tazeron's influence, they will wander and perish unless they seek asylum. So we will either see them again or we will not. Either way, they can do no harm once things are sealed to them."

"We need to watch the ritual," Jesse said, not sure that he wanted to, yet knowing it was necessary. "To see where the portals will be, and then make sure that everyone who serves Tazeron passes through."

"Yes, Jesse, it will be hard to watch, but remember, these are not really the Slater children. They will act out their part without flaw, but they cannot in reality feel a blade as it pierces their flesh. You must remember that, my son. This is the best way, the only way. Chaelea was correct, as she always has been."

"Rambo, look to our left, on that hill over there. What do you see?"

Rambo gazed to where Jesse had mentioned.

"Nexlucimus? Who is that with him?"

Jesse stopped too, not seeing a second person with the Elder at first. Then he did.

"The Ancient. It is Matilda. Hurry, Rambo, we must go to them. I feel it."

As Jesse and Rambo approached the Elder and the Ancient, Matilda spoke.

"Well, well, Jesse and Rambo, how are your out-of-body explorings going this day? Before you answer that, seek your mortal father, Jesse. Tell him that I have need of his service. Perhaps it would be a good idea for you to re-enter your lifeless bodies first. Come to me when that is accomplished. Bring Breeze and Chaelea with you. Go now, my children, make haste."

"Chaelea, Milady, we are returning. Tell David that the Ancient, Matilda, has need of his services. Rambo and I will be there shortly. Oh, one more thing, she wants you and Breeze to come back with us after we get our bodies."

Chapter Nineteen
Matilda

Jesse and Rambo pulled their minds back to their bodies and stood up. When they looked around, they were surprised to see everything as it was when they had left, except for three very shocked people: Chaelea, Breeze, and David.

"What is going on, Jesse?" David asked.

"We aren't sure," Jesse replied honestly. "The only thing we know is that Nexlucimus and Matilda are waiting for us on a hill not too far from here."

"Can we return the camp to its former self first, or must we delay?" Chaelea asked.

"I think we had better postpone that for now," Jesse said. Then he shouted to the camp's actors, "Hey, all you dead people, you can get into a more comfortable position, but don't look too alive yet. We need to go check something out. We'll be back soon… I hope."

"I need to pee," shouted Beloe. "Do you think I could do that first?" Everyone chuckled.

"Yeah, that'd probably be all right. But then, as you were, Soldier."

"Aye, aye, Captain."

"Ok, let's get going. We must not keep an Ancient lady waiting," Rambo urged.

The four of them warped to the spot on the hill where Nexlucimus and Matilda were standing. Jesse bowed to the Ancient and addressed her.

"What can we do to help you, Milady?"

She studied him for a moment and then smiled.

"Jesse, you are constantly a joy to me. You always have been, and you always will be. For now, I mostly need the service of David. David, my dear, I want you to stick to that crazy man in the cave like a tick on a dog. Grab him around the neck, and never let go. Whisper discouragement at everything he tries. Plague his dreams.

"I will take away your game body so he will not see you when you go through the portal with him. Pearl will be waiting on the other side; she will help. Between the two of you, the world will not be what Tazeron was hoping for. You two will be his own personal devils."

Matilda laughed at the thought.

"Say your goodbyes quickly. You are needed soon. When this madman is completely destroyed, I will grant you a gift as you wish."

"Yes, Milady. I must return to the camp. I'll be right back."

David warped back to say goodbye to Ginnea. Jesse was sure. He came back quickly and said a hasty farewell to Jesse.

"Take care, Jesse. I will talk to you on the other side. I love you."

David hugged Jesse, and then he was gone, returned to his essence form by Matilda.

"I love you too, Dad," Jesse said sadly. "This is what Ginnea suggested."

"Where do you think I got the idea?" Matilda asked. "I've been watching the Keepers, and so have many others. We, that you call the Ancients, are always watching."

She smiled at the astonished expressions on their faces.

"Chaelea, you of all people should know that. You have spent years in our presence. You just didn't realise who you were with."

She chuckled at their reaction as they realised what she was saying. Then she cleared her throat and addressed them further.

"Rambo, Chaelea, Jesse, and Breeze, the four of you have a rocky road ahead of you. I can say no more, but with David and Pearl as your secret weapons, and all the mortals and immortals who know of Tazeron and his evil ways, you will not be alone.

"Jesse, you have surprised us all. We knew that you would rise to the responsibility, but what you have accomplished makes us glad for our decision to send you here when we knew this problem would arise. I will not say more at this time. You still have much to do.

"Breeze, you are very unique to the gods, and because of this, you will be given special abilities not known to you now. Chaelea and Rambo, because of your suffering and sacrifice, you will be rewarded beyond your understanding. Fear not, the future is bright for you.

"Be kind to your Elders, children. They watch, and they wait, and they deserve your respect. Now go, be wise, and take care. Close those portals. The ritual has been completed, and Tazeron and his minions are preparing their final descent into the world of mortals.

"After you finally seal this world from the human world, Tazeron and those who serve him will never again be able to enter this or any other realm. There will be no rush to follow Tazeron and his minions. Once the portals are sealed, let them fester under the whisperings of David and Pearl, but not for too long."

After saying those final words, Matilda was gone, leaving them as suddenly as she had the first time. Only then did they remember Nexlucimus.

"Master Nexlucimus, I'm sorry, sir. I forgot you were here," Jesse said rather sheepishly.

"That's ok, Jesse, I forgot I was here too," the Elder smiled at them. "Such an amazing woman, Matilda. We will talk more about what she said, but first I want to thank you, Jesse, and Rambo, for rescuing me from the clutches of Tazeron. The other council members express their gratitude as well."

"It was our pleasure, sir. But the Moon Soldier is the one who solved the problem, and Chaelea is the one who sensed that there was a problem in the first place. We all worked together."

"Indeed you did, and that, my friends, is why we will be successful in this quest, even as it moves from this world into the one that we wanted to protect it from. However, since it started in that world, in a way, it only fits that it ends there.

"Now, my friends, I believe that Matilda gave you a directive, and I suggest you follow through with it immediately. I will wait for your return back at your camp with some of the most bizarre-looking soldiers I have ever seen."

As he finished talking to them, Nexlucimus waved farewell and started walking back toward their base, chuckling.

"Jesse, the chain that you wear has the power to seal," Chaelea said. "Use it. Ask it to take you to each portal that has been used and is now silent, and it will take you there. You will know what to do when you get there, since you have done it before.

"We can all go with him in case he needs help. Rambo, my love, might we catch a ride with you?"

"Of course. Welcome aboard," Rambo said, changing into his dragon form.

Once seated on Rambo with the rest, Jesse grasped the chain and asked it to take them to the portals, one at a time, which it did without incident. All of the portals were empty of anyone near them, except for the tenth and last one. There, two of the Moon Soldiers stood at attention, apparently waiting for them.

"How is it that you are still here?" Jesse asked after he sealed the final portal.

"Matilda asked us to linger and wait for you. We are to give a report."

Jesse tried hard to ignore the fact, as he sealed the portals, that each was painted with blue blood. He was glad that he had not witnessed the ritual. Even though Jesse knew it wasn't really the children, it would have seemed real, and that would have haunted him the rest of his life. He was sure Matilda had known that, and that was why she came when she did.

"Thank you, Mother Matilda," Jesse whispered with humility.

"You are welcome, child."

"Thank you, Soldiers. Would it be alright if we take you back to camp and let the rest of our group hear your report as well?"

"Yes, sir, that would be acceptable, and it would be our pleasure."

"Before we return to the camp, I have another question for you. The other soldiers, were they able to travel through the portals with Tazeron?"

"Yes, sir, but their lives will be shortened because of the mortal world."

"Excellent, thank you. Soldiers, tiny blue beetles, collapse," Jesse said, choked with emotion. A tear rolled down his cheek as he picked up the small blue insect.

"Let's get back to camp. There are going to be a bunch of hungry zombies and ghouls when we get there, and they are all going to want to hear this," Jesse said, as he warped them back to the waiting troops.

When they arrived at camp, Jesse removed the little blue beetle and had the two Soldiers reform into their original appearance.

"Rambo, would you call everyone to us, please?" Jesse requested.

"Of course, Jesse," Rambo said, as he changed into his rooster form and bugled the troops.

"Jesse, I feel like I need to return to the city," Nexlucimus said. "I'm not sure why, but it is a strong feeling. I will talk to all of you later. Might I trouble Cami for a ride back?"

"Of course, Nexlucimus," Jesse said. "Cami, hurry back. We will wait until you return for the Soldiers' report."

Cami and Nexlucimus were gone in an instant, and Cami was back just as quickly. In the short time that Cami was away, Jesse had Chaelea and Breeze prepare to restore the troops to their pre-scam appearance. There were groans of disappointment. Apparently, most of the younger members were enjoying their gruesome appearances. Rambo chuckled at their reaction.

"Maybe as a going-away present," Rambo said. "We'll have Zeela chop you up and put you back together like a Picasso painting."

"Can she do that?" one of the Keepers asked. "That would be so awesome. Think of the newspaper headlines if we did that."

"I was kidding, but I am impressed that you even understood the Picasso reference," Rambo said.

"I had an art class in school," the young Keeper responded.

"Actually, Dad, I'm impressed that you knew," Jesse said.

"Pearl had an old art book that I looked through one day. But this just reminds me of how young some of these Keepers are."

"Ok gang, now that Tazeron and his minions are no longer in this world, we need to…"

"Jesse, wait," Rambo interrupted. "Look over there."

Rambo was pointing down into the valley that contained the large lake. Out on the lake, there appeared a ship, and it was flashing light at them like a mirror catching the sun. Stunned, everyone's attention was drawn to the sight. Jesse's first reaction was to call the Moon Soldiers to him.

"Soldiers, how much time do you have left before you leave us?" Jesse asked.

"We have thirty-six hours, sir. What is your wish?"

"I want you to investigate that ship out there and report back."

"Yes, sir."

While they waited and watched for the Soldiers' return, someone suggested that they get food. Beloe and a few of the others left for Xanthara and the vendors.

"What do you think is going on, Chaelea?" Jesse asked her. Rambo and Breeze moved closer to listen.

"I have no idea, Jesse. This is highly unusual. Nothing was ever said about a ship."

"Any of the rest of you have any ideas? Any of the games have landlocked ships in them?"

No one had an answer, and then an even stranger thing happened. The ship sprouted wings and started coming their way.

"Whoa!" Jesse exclaimed, jumping up. "What the heck is going on here?"

"No idea," Rambo said. "Anyone? Tommy, Zealoc, Martha?"

"I wonder," Mr Chamber said. "Isn't there a legend in immortal history about some missing Elves?"

There was a collective gasp at his suggestion. As the ship drew closer, they could see the Moon Soldiers standing on the deck, but they were the only ones visible. When the ship landed near the base, four people walked down a gangplank and approached them. Jesse watched carefully. There was something familiar about them, but what was it?

"Oh my gosh," Jesse exclaimed. Everyone watched, confused, as Jesse slowly walked toward the four people.

"Jesse, we have waited for this chance to meet you. We know that you have many questions, as do all in attendance. The only way that you know us is because of your dreams. You alone know us, and now we have returned to help our people, the Elves."

"Why did you come to me in my dreams, and why are you here now?"

"Because of our heritage, we are bound to you. Matilda called to us, and we were obliged to answer."

"Who are you?"

"Everything will be explained at a later time. For now, tell the audience that we are Shyloanians from the world of Shyloan, coming to assist our people, the Elves. Tell them that Matilda sent us. I am Zeltora, and this is my husband, Rasban. There are twenty others below deck. That is enough for now."

"As you wish, Milady."

"People, it is an honour to present to you Zeltora and her husband, Rasban. They are Shyloanians, from the world of Shyloan, coming to assist their people, the Elves. Matilda has sent them."

The reaction was one of surprise, but not of shock. It seemed that everyone was starting to adjust to strange occurrences. There were questions, of course, but they were told that answers would be given at a later time.

After a brief meal, the Moon Soldiers were asked to give their report, which they did.

"We were told by Mistress Matilda to give a report concerning Tazeron's final moments in this game world," one of the Moon

Soldiers said, addressing the gathering. "After Tazeron witnessed the destroyed base camp of the Keepers, seeing all of the destruction and hideous injuries, he was convinced that the path was clear for him to open portals into the mortal world. The ritual was performed, and the fake children were sacrificed. Tazeron and all who served him passed through to the human world.

"Some of the followers decided to stay behind, but as soon as Tazeron was removed from their presence, they ultimately withdrew all allegiance to him. They will remain in this world until they can prove that they are worthy to be returned to their own people. They are required to clean up all of the areas that were destroyed by Tazeron's army. They must rebuild and replant. When they accomplish that, I am sure that Mistress Matilda will have other projects for them. The plan is to keep them busy here for a very long time. Things will not be as easy for them as they were with the game masters in control."

The gods of both worlds decreed that this world would cease to be a receptacle for online games. The created characters that still lived here would be allowed to remain, serving as caretakers. They would have no further contact with the human world. From now on, all created game creatures would exist only in the imagination of those who created them. They would no longer have a life of their own, and once deleted they would no longer exist. They would cease to be saved to a data bank, cloud, or any other technical device. All of you will return to your world and find you can no longer access this realm. The games have changed.

This world will become a place of exploration and discovery, once the detainees have cleaned and restored it to a sanctuary of peace and beauty. It will stand as a museum of human creativity. No evil will ever be allowed to enter here again. It will be a safe haven for those seeking refuge from the technology of the games. An app will be created that will allow peaceful 3D CGI visits, a virtual reality experience.

There were expressions of excitement from the gathering following this report.

"What a fantastic idea," Jesse whispered. "Is there anything else?" he asked the Moon Soldiers.

"We have a request for you, sir. We would like to go with the Shyloanians and assist them in the time we have remaining. Is that agreeable with you?"

Jesse asked the others if there was any reason why that would be a problem.

"Nope, no problem that I can see," said Rambo. "I would like to go back to Xanthara myself. I believe we are done here. Are you in agreement, Chaelea? I believe that we have a daughter who would like to meet with her mother after so long, and many grandchildren who need to see their grandparents."

"I would also like to return," said Jesse, taking Breeze's hand. "Shall we go before anything else weirdly happens?"

"Indeed," said Breeze and Chaelea, both with smiles.

It was decided that everyone, including the soldiers, would leave for the Forest of Elves. The game world was quiet now, after such a long period of turmoil. It was time to move on. It was time to complete the quest.

Chapter Twenty

Shyloanian's

Returning to the Forest of Elves was enjoyable. The Elves had not returned yet, but the Toulonians hoped that it would not be much longer. With the help of the primitives, returning council members, and the Shyloanian Elves, things were shaping up nicely. Buildings were being rebuilt, plants were growing back, pathways repaved, and most of the painting was done. It looked like a storybook village, which in a way it was. Everyone was excited about the Elves' homecoming.

One of the gifts that the Shyloanians brought with them were two Dumplumba and two Nisqisha trees. They were more than just saplings and began producing fruit as soon as they were planted in the fertile Xantharian soil. The Shyloanians told stories about whole forests of those trees on their world. People wondered if that was true, though not openly of course. Another gift they brought was word of the missing Elves. This was a surprise, because Jesse and the others had thought that the Shyloanians were part of the missing. When this was suggested, the Shyloanians found it humorous.

"Oh no," Rasban laughed. "We are descendants of Elves that split from the known worlds. Only the Ancients would know where the missing are."

Jesse smiled at this idea. Someday he would ask Matilda if he ever saw her again, and somehow Jesse knew that he would.

"Our world has had visits from Elves who claimed to be descendants of the missing. They gave us the knowledge of our flying ships, and how to nourish the healing trees so that they multiply faster and produce stronger, bigger fruit. These trees that we brought you are only two seasons old."

That was a shock to those who heard.

"How could that be?" Zeela wanted to know. "Our trees were only half that size, and they were hundreds of years old. What do you do to make them grow like that?"

"For one thing," Rasban continued, "we noticed that you have spike ants tending trees here. That must be stopped. The missing told us that the spike ants suck the juice from the trees and rob them of their energy and nutrients. Spike ants are better suited to attending the woodier trees and flowers of the forest. We found that our healing herbs thrived better with spike ants cleaning their roots and stems."

This conversation was only mildly interesting to Jesse, and he wandered off to find Breeze, who was visiting with Mary and Samalla down by Lake Os. When he got there, he found Breeze and about twenty children of mixed races playing in the lake and having a picnic. Mary and Samalla had gone to the Troll village to visit Samalla's aunt, Trinzella.

"Jesse, my love, come sit with me. I have been thinking of something," she smiled and patted the blanket next to her.

"And what have you been thinking about?" Jesse asked, smiling back playfully, which made her blush.

"I was thinking perhaps we should travel to your world and see what is going on there with Tazeron. What do you say?"

"Funny that you should have that thought, because I too have been thinking it was time for us to check in on the old boy and find out what kind of mischief he has been stirring up. When we go, I would like Rambo, Chaelea and perhaps Tommy, if he is able, to go with us, just so we have back-up."

"I think that is an excellent plan. Now, do you want to know why I have been thinking thus?" Breeze smiled.

"Ah… sure," Jesse said, suddenly feeling a bit nervous.

"I think that the sooner this war with Tazeron ends, the sooner we can get married and begin our life together. And the sooner we stop Tazeron, the safer all of our worlds will be."

"I am willing. When do you want to leave, Breeze? Now?"

"Not now, perhaps in a day or two. I need to stay with the children until Mary returns and then tend to a few things. Maybe you could talk to Rambo and find out where he and Chaelea are and what they think of the idea."

"I will do that. I think I am going to get something to eat first. Would you like something?"

"No, I am fine. See you soon?"

"Sure," said Jesse, as he gave her a kiss. "Soon."

Jesse decided to visit Nexlucimus in the capital after he had eaten, since Mary still had not returned and Breeze was staying with the children. Walking into the library brought back many memories, but much had changed. The building was not as large as it had been, and the statue of the White Druid was no longer a focal point in the entrance hall. Instead, there were banners with scenes from Xantharian history and upcoming festivals. Chaelea wanted any reference to her removed from the display; she wanted her life to return to as normal as possible. Since returning, Rambo and Chaelea had maintained a low profile, enjoying family life like all the other citizens of Xanthara. After the war with Tazeron was finished, they hoped one day to be part of a splitting and move on to a new chapter in their lives.

Jesse approached the council chamber doors cautiously. For some reason he felt nervous. The fairies at the door waved excitedly at him, and he greeted them with a wave and a smile. It was good to see them again. He knocked.

"Enter," came the reply. Jesse waved the doors open, remembering when he first came here with his dad, David, and how impressed he had been when the Elder had done the same thing. It all seemed so ordinary to Jesse now.

"Welcome, Jesse," Nexlucimus said. "I have been expecting you, or rather, we have been waiting for you."

Out of the shadows walked Zeela, Tommy, Zeltora, Rasban, Matilda, Rambo, and Chaelea. Something was definitely up.

"OK, what is going on?" Jesse asked. "I am feeling sort of ganged up on right now," he added with sarcasm, seeing all of their smiling faces. "Rambo, I wondered where you two went. Breeze and I thought that it was time to see what old evil bucket was up to in the human world."

"Jesse, it is time for us to disclose your actual name and identity," Matilda said.

"Man, you do not beat around the bush, Mistress. I am curious, did you summon me here? Wait a minute, did you just say 'actual name and identity'?" Warning bells were firing off in Jesse's mind, and he staggered.

"Please have a seat, Jesse, as I see you are about to fall down anyway. And yes, I did summon you," Matilda chuckled as she indicated a chair that was sliding away from the table.

Jesse was stunned, and Matilda was correct. His legs felt as if they would buckle at any moment, like the first time he saw Rambo and Brutus at Gran's front door. He sat down heavily in the chair and felt its arms reach up to comfort him. He waved them away.

"What are you talking about? I know my name and my identity. There are some weird things, sure, but everyone has strange stuff in their life."

Then Rambo spoke, "Jesse, you are a human with Red Magic. You can talk to animals, including a knuckle-headed dragon in rooster form, with thought alone. You have had dreams all of your life, dreams of other worlds and elven people, not of the game. Intuition comes naturally to you; you get feelings and impressions that guide you. And Breeze confirmed you a finding," Rambo said with a chuckle. "Tell me, how many of your acquaintances at school could say that without the game?"

Jesse was speechless. Rambo was right.

"From the very beginning, we have all wondered about these things. Even you have wondered, have you not?" Zeela said kindly.

"I have," Jesse peeped out, not sure now if he wanted to know, but as in his early days, curiosity was prodding him. "So, I am assuming that you have the answers, and that is why this meeting?"

"Simply put, yes," Tommy said. "We now know, and that is why this meeting."

"Jesse, ever since you first came to Xanthara, people have been calling you a Prince, Lord of the Prophecy, Chaelea's child, and other things. Or they said they could see Chaelea's kiss on you. Is that not true?" Nexlucimus said.

"Yes," Jesse squeaked as his voice broke. He glanced at Chaelea and saw that she was smiling with tears in her eyes. He was feeling more than a little uncomfortable, and he wished that Breeze was here with him.

Just then there was a soft knock at the door and, at Elder Nexlucimus' invitation, Breeze walked in with a Toulonian escort.

The Toulonian spoke. "We found her by Lake Os, Milady Matilda. Two of our flock are watching her charges so that she might answer your summons. I am Bresheta."

"Thank you, Bresheta, I am pleased with your service," Matilda told the young Toulonian. "Breeze, my dear, please have a seat next to your husband. This concerns you as well as him."

"Are we in trouble, Milady?" Breeze asked, worried. She took Jesse's hand and looked around the room while climbing into the chair next to him.

"Heavens no, child, quite the opposite," Matilda answered. "We gather now to respond to questions, but to do that properly, I must ask Jesse a critical question."

Matilda eyed him carefully. "Jesse, normally what I am about to ask comes much later in a person's life, and usually that person has no choice. You, however, are a special case and as such, you have a choice. May we have access to your memories? The memories I wish to retrieve are the ones of your life before this life."

"What? I do not understand," Jesse said, confused. Breeze, sitting next to him, gave a little gasp. He looked at her and was surprised at the expression of total shock on her face.

"Jesse," Breeze whispered, "say yes."

"But…"

Breeze knelt up in her chair, taking Jesse's face in her hands and looking him full in the face. "Do you trust me?" she asked him.

"Yes, of course, but…"

"No buts. Do you trust me? And if you do, tell Matilda yes."

"Mistress Matilda, yes, you may have access to all my memories. Um… will it hurt? I am sure that I am going to be embarrassed."

"Jesse, most of us have things in our memories that would be embarrassing if shared. It will not hurt, just relax and enjoy the story. Jesse Finch memories, forward," Matilda said, as she waved her hand at the screen. It came alive as the lights dimmed.

The first memory that Jesse had was of darkness. Swirls or ribbons of light-coloured fog or mist pulsated through the dark. Then, as they watched, a hand came into view and a finger began to gently swirl the darkness, streaking the tufts of coloured fog and causing them to clump or cluster into segments. The gentle hand took four of the segments and transferred them into individual crystal tubes or cylinders. Each of the essences floated in its new environment.

Once again Breeze gave a little gasp, but this time she started to sob silently. Jesse wondered at her reaction and put a comforting arm around her. The chair tried to comfort her as well.

After a while, as they continued to watch, a voice softly spoke to the misty substances in their crystal locations. "Little ones, we have a need for your services. Are you willing?" Two of the ribbons of fog glowed bright white, one glowed bright red, the fourth one did nothing and was returned to the darkness.

The essences were released into a softly lit area with pleasant, soothing music. They began to sway to the sound. They seemed to dance with each other. Their movement gradually appeared to become play, and the gentle voice tenderly chuckled at the sight. After a period of time, the voice spoke again. "We are pleased with your learning and how you interact with each other. Next, we will take you into the heavens and allow you to learn from others with more experience."

Jesse saw the next step in the development process and how the swirling mists learned even more as they grew and retained knowledge.

Matilda fast-forwarded Jesse's memories, and again the voice was talking to the mists as they swirled around the hand. "Children, we are pleased with your progress, and we are ready to release you into the heavens, to become Shadow Dreams, carrying our messages to those with bodies."

Now it was Jesse's turn to gasp as he realised what his memories were telling them.

"There will be others that will need your services, such as the Elders of new worlds. You will receive your assignments shortly. Are you still willing?"

Again the essences of light pulsed white and red.

Matilda fast-forwarded the memories once again. Jesse saw the red mist with a little girl about six years old, with golden hair and darkly tanned skin. The dream that the vapour gave her was not revealed. The girl had many visits over the years as she grew into a lovely young woman. Those watching with Jesse recognised her as Chaelea.

At one point she was introduced to her Shadow Dream, as Jesse had been to Breeze. They became close as she received her dreams of help and comfort through her trials. There were times when they visited, as Jesse and Breeze had done.

Jesse watched as Chaelea escaped with Rambo from her imprisoned life. She and Rambo fell in love and married. Jesse saw the red mist pulse with happiness for them. He watched as Chaelea blew the essence a kiss and petitioned the gods to allow him to be born to her and Rambo as their son.

The gods refused. She was told in a dream that he was to be born to mortal parents. Even though it was unheard of for a Shadow Dream to be born as a human, it was necessary in his case. He would have unique skills and abilities that were needed for a quest that was soon to come to the mortal and immortal peoples.

Chaelea was sad and she cried much for her loss. Later, a child was born to Chaelea and Rambo, a girl, but Chaelea and their child were taken by the evil people that craved her wisdom and healing skills. Rambo was banished.

Jesse witnessed the sadness of Rambo and his anguished pleadings with the gods for their help. The gods, seeing Rambo's great suffering and the enslavement of Chaelea, took Chaelea and the child to themselves. The child was later sent to live with her maternal grandparents, but Chaelea remained in the presence and service of the gods. Jesse witnessed Rambo's transformation into a shapeshifter and his calling from the gods on the mortal world.

Jesse saw the red essence placed into the body of a developing mortal child. The boy was born to loving parents who cared for him deeply. Jesse watched as the child grew. One scene showed him sitting by himself, feeling alone and friendless. Jesse remembered the feelings of being different and separated by that difference from other children his age. He saw the tormenting teasing from bullies. He saw himself finding friendship with Cami and the terrible pain caused by the death of his mortal father and the subsequent remarriage of his mother. So many memories and emotions.

Matilda stopped the memories.

"Jesse, are you ok?" Breeze asked, concerned.

"I'm not sure. It's an awful lot to process. How could I possibly have been a Shadow Dream? And why do I not remember, even now after seeing these memories? I feel like screaming at the thought. Please tell me how this could have happened, and why it happened. My mind feels on the verge of a complete emotional overloaded breakdown."

"Jesse, you cannot remember any of this because of your human body. Mortals come to their bodies innocent, without memories. Even though you have the essence of an Elf, you have the body of a human. That makes you an heir of both realms. Breeze and other immortal Shadow Dreams retain their memories," Matilda explained.

"Jesse, as soon as Mistress Matilda said she wanted to show memories from your life before this life, I knew," Breeze said lovingly. "And I was shocked. As I watched, however, I realised the wisdom of the gods. Elven children live differently. The gods needed someone with your abilities who was both Elven and human to head this quest. The Slater children also have that heritage, but in reverse. Your essence is Elven, and your body is human. Their souls are human while their bodies are Elven. Do you remember the riddle that Tazeron was so obsessed with? He needed their blood to pass through the portals, but remember the part that said 'Beware the heir will eat you'? It makes sense now. You, my love, are that heir."

Jesse was so stunned he had no words. Indeed, his shock was so sincere he sat there for what felt like a long time before any words came to him. They watched him, waiting.

"Why me? Why me?" was all Jesse could squeak out.

"Why not you?" Matilda asked. "We needed someone like you, Elven soul, human heart and strength. Even the bullying you had as a child and the loneliness added fibre to your being, making you stronger and more able to fulfil your future foreordained mission to the two worlds that you call home.

"Jesse, if you had not been chosen for this mission, you probably would have been born to Chaelea and Rambo, but even they agree that no one else could do what will be required of you as you hunt down Tazeron in the mortal world and discover what will be needed to send him into outer darkness. You know the human world, and you understand the magic. It has always been a part of you. Your intelligence, the ribbons of light you saw, glowed with the magic that you possess now. The magic needed to be powerful enough to challenge Tazeron. You needed to be sufficiently tough, and you are, you have proven that. Now you need to continue in your quest. It will not be easy, and we can't see the ending because it hasn't been written yet, but we have high hopes for success. Do you have any other questions?" Matilda asked.

"Are you serious? Do I have questions?" Jesse asked incredulously. "Yes ma'am, a boatload of them. The first one is, do you have a personal mobile number? Because I want it if you do. Next, what part do the Shyloanians have in this, and why are you telling me all of this now?"

Matilda laughed. "Jesse, the Shyloanians, Zeltora and Rasban, are your soulmates, as the Earth people would say. You were Shadow Dreams together. They have been friends to you through the years as you struggled with the strange world to which you were born. In reality, the mortal life you lived was very different from what your essence prepared you for. Zeltora and Rasban have brought you comfort in your dreams, have they not? They were the other two ribbons of light that you shared the eternities with, that you learned with and played with. And even though you don't remember, they were your friends.

"I am telling you this now, and not at the end, because even though it is overwhelming, it is also strengthening. Have peace, child, and know that in every way you are a Prince, a Lord of the Prophecy. Chaelea's hand has been in your travels here for a reason. She was taken to be with the gods because of Rambo's pleadings and to protect her, but also so she could influence you and your path, just as a mother would do while raising her child. You are very unique, and as Nexlucimus once told you, a pivotal player in this drama. Now go. Act well your part. We will meet again on the other side, in the life to come." With those words, Matilda again departed.

"Wait!" Jesse shouted, but it was too late. Matilda was gone. "What about my actual name? And what is the purpose of that name?" Jesse quietly asked the gathering.

"That I can answer for you, Jesse," Chaelea said, with a sad little smile. "I gave you a name when you were my Shadow Dream, and that name is the one that I always called to you as my child. I will tell you in private, but not now. Now come, my son, for you truly are my son in spirit and no mother could love you more. We, together with the other Keepers, must finish this battle with Tazeron."

Jesse was overwhelmed. He couldn't move for a while as the strangeness of this meeting sank in and he absorbed what he had learned.

As Chaelea finished speaking, Nexlucimus watched Jesse a moment before addressing him. "Jesse, you, from the beginning of this quest, have been a leader, a beacon to those around you. Now it is time for your empowered self to finish this task. We, who must remain behind, pray for you and those that go with you. Take care, my friend, and 'give them hell' as another warrior once told you." Nexlucimus and Zeela stood and bowed to Jesse before leaving the room.

"Jesse, it is time to go to the mortal world and rid it of Tazeron once and for all. We advise you not to mention this meeting to anyone not here now. We are so glad to once again be in your company, and we look forward to visiting when this is over," Rasban said, smiling.

"Perhaps you will even remember us then," Zeltora chuckled. "Take care, our dear friend. The gods are cheering you on." She then gave Jesse a hug, and she and Rasban left for the Forest of Elves.

Jesse, in his dazed state of mind, knew that it would take time for this meeting to be completely absorbed into his consciousness. He thought back to his years in mortal school when teachers or his human parents would ask him, *what do you want to be when you grow up?* He honestly could never come up with an answer for them.

Now he knew why. Never in many lifetimes would he ever have thought of what this life was giving him. Strange, so very strange.

"I hope that you will understand that I need a little time to digest all of this," Jesse said to Rambo, Chaelea and Tommy. "I will call a meeting in an hour or so. Please excuse me for now."

Jesse stood and took Breeze's hand, walking out of the chamber. He could feel them watching him and Breeze as they left. Once outside, Jesse warped them to Lake O's, where they sat on a log enjoying the peaceful scene and the quiet.

"Breeze, I am so glad that I have you. You are perhaps the only person in both worlds who will ever understand me and who I am. I'm not sure that I even comprehend a part of what I was shown."

"Jesse, perhaps this is why I was so attracted to you from the beginning. The gods have known both of us from the time before time, and because of this, we were chosen for each other for this very reason. We could have decided otherwise, but we both felt the attraction and knew that it was right. I believe that right now some of our future children are serving the gods as Shadow Dreams. Perhaps we even knew them and each other from the beginning."

"An interesting idea. I can't wait until I have my full memory back. Right now I feel that I am at a disadvantage. As a previous Shadow Dream, are there things that I should know that might help this quest? Such as being immune to magical interference."

"There are a couple of things, yes. As you know, and as Ammon has told you, becoming invisible is a trait. You just have to think it. Also, communication should never be a problem with another Shadow Dream. However, because you are also human, there might be a difference there. I don't know. I would like to chat with Chaelea and find out more about that chain you wear. I feel like there is more to it than what you know at this time. Perhaps there are skills imbued into that chain that will help us in this quest. We must find out. For now, my love, we should return and get this final book of our journey against Tazeron started."

"Yes, I agree," Jesse said as he stood and pulled Breeze to him, giving her a hug before he warped them back to the forest.

Jesse contacted the remaining members of the Keepers who were still on Xanthara. They would have one more meeting in this world before they headed to the mortal world and the final battle with Tazeron. The Keepers were all glad for the news, feeling that they had been sitting around far too long. Zealoc especially was anxious, as were Mr Chambers and Cami.

Jim would be staying with Sarah and the children in the forest. He was asked to be an ambassador to the primitive people, since he was still in game form as an Ogre. He was excited by the calling. It was decided that the children could not travel into the human world until Tazeron was completely gone. It would be too dangerous for them, even though Tazeron thought them dead, just in case someone recognised them.

Jim asked his daughter, Mary, to assist him with the sometimes shy, aboriginal people to whom Mary had developed such strong, even loving, feelings. She was very excited about the prospect.

That night, as Jesse met with the Keepers, there was a sense of hope mixed with uncertainty among them all. As Jesse and his captains made final plans, there were many questions. It would be a long night, one that they were anxious to begin as they planned for a new tomorrow.

Chapter Twenty One
Return to Earth

The thought of returning to Earth seemed strange to Jesse. Going to Clay would have felt more normal. When he originally left at the beginning of the quest, he had been almost sixteen, a different person, and the mortal world had been a different place. Even with billions of individuals, it seemed empty to him now. Gran was dead, and he had matured. Most of the people he had known as a mortal had either gone to college or worked elsewhere. Mom and Bill were still in Germany, and Jim and Sarah, with their three children, now lived with the Elves on Xanthara. Nothing was the same. Even Rusty Palmer, his ex-nemesis, had changed and now considered himself Jesse's good friend. Something about being imprisoned in a cage changes how you see the world and others.

Part of the plan when the team returned was to contact David and Pearl, but for some reason David and Pearl hadn't responded. When Jesse consulted the chain he wore, it let him know that his dad and Gran were doing fine with their assignment to plague Tazeron. That puzzled Jesse. If they were fine, why didn't they answer? Jesse, and maybe the rest of the party, had expected to hit the road running. Not knowing what was going on was annoying.

With nothing else to do, Jesse, Breeze, Rambo and Chaelea busied themselves getting settled into Gran's house. It was bizarre having Rambo and Chaelea in Gran's old room, and Breeze in the guest room. There was no food in the house, but that wasn't a problem; they either conjured something or returned to Xanthara to visit the vendors. Jesse wasn't sure if he would ever get used to the idea that he, Jesse, could conjure his own snacks whenever he wanted. Mr Chambers and Cami went to their house with Tommy and Ginnea. Brutus went to the Chambers' house with Cami. Zealoc, Beloe and Martha took up residence at Jim and Sarah's place.

After about three days Jesse was restless to do something, anything. He was bored, an odd feeling after so long. Breeze suggested they visit Jesse's mom in Germany so that she could meet Sally and Bill. He thought that was a terrific idea, but just as they were getting ready to teleport to Germany, Jesse received a surprise message from Cami.

"Jesse, turn the TV to channel 9 news, and hurry!"

Jesse turned the TV to the news channel and paused the broadcast until Rambo and Chaelea could join him and Breeze.

The paused news commentator was standing in front of the camera with a shocked expression on his face. When they were all gathered, Jesse pressed play, and they heard blaring alarms on the channel and a banner flashing: *'Breaking News. War imminent. Multiple missile attacks launched around the world. Stay tuned for details.'*

"No missiles have landed in the Americas or Canada at this time," the British reporter announced, "but Europe, Russia, Asia and Africa have received multiple hits each. The reports we are receiving from our resources indicate that there are several launch sites located on tiny, previously unknown islands throughout the oceans of the world. Disturbing allegations of responsibility have been claimed by various terrorist groups, including a billionaire and his organisation. Only one known photo exists of this man."

They showed a picture of the person in question, wearing reflective sunglasses, a bushy beard and a ponytail. He was dressed in jungle-print fatigues, waving a fat cigar and grinning at the camera. The caption said that the man's name was Tazeroni Xanzerie, and that he had an empire worth over one hundred billion US dollars, or so he claimed.

"No one knows Tazeroni's location. In fact, there is no reliable information about him," the commentator added. "He seems to have appeared out of nowhere. All of this leads to speculation and grave doubts as to his legitimacy. The other known groups claiming responsibility are well known for their activities throughout the world and are, as such, a more plausible threat. Although there are doubts as to whether these groups have the ability to stage something of this magnitude. Never before, to our knowledge, have rival groups fought over claiming responsibility for something like this."

Jesse groaned at this news and where it seemed to be headed.

With the disguise of the beard and sunglasses, it was hard to know what the man actually looked like, but with that name Jesse and the rest knew who he had to be. Obviously, Tazeron had advanced teams working on this side of the Shield, preparing for when he would arrive on Earth. This could get complicated. As Jesse watched the news report with its sketchy details, he felt his gut drop to his toes.

"Wow, it didn't take Tazeron long to get into the action. I kind of expected him to be here stumbling around, not sure what to think of all the modern technology. I have to admit, firing missiles at the world is a good way to get everyone's attention," Jesse said to the group. "Now I understand why Dad and Gran haven't answered back. Apparently, Tazeron already had an organisation here, and there has been a lot going on. I think we need to rethink our plans. Chaelea, could you have Cami and Mr Chambers contact as many of the Keepers with talismans as they can? Tell them that we are going to have a meeting here to regroup.

"Rambo, my friend, let's pay that old troublemaker a visit to check things out. Breeze, I would like you to come along too. Chaelea, when the troops start arriving, would you initiate the meeting? We won't take too long. I just want to get a close-up look."

"Of course, Jesse. Be safe," Chaelea said, giving Rambo a quick kiss before he became his smallest dragon.

After Jesse and Breeze climbed on board, Rambo placed invisibility on them. Jesse, holding the chain and touching the talisman with his mind, warped them to Tazeron's location.

What they found surprised Jesse. He was expecting a large compound. There were only five people besides Tazeron walking around the tiny island, which was barely broad enough to accommodate the launch pad, rockets and people.

"This would be hard to locate as tiny as it is, and so far out in the ocean. It would appear like a pinpoint on a map. If it was even mappable," Jesse said to the other two.

"Indeed," was the only response they gave back.

The island was completely barren, not even a blade of grass. The entire space was composed of lava rock, black against the dark blue waters of the ocean, and hard to walk on. Waves constantly crashed against the rocky shore, which was high enough to avoid constant flooding. How they could have built something like this in the middle of nowhere was puzzling. Another mystery was where Tazeron had got all of his money to build this and the other launch sites.

"Hi Jesse dear," Gran whispered in Jesse's ear, making him jump and startling Breeze and Rambo. Jesse had to bite his tongue to keep from yelling.

"Gran, where are you, and why didn't you answer when I called to you two days ago? Is Dad here too?"

"Jesse, is there a problem?" Breeze asked quietly.

"No, at least I don't think so. Gran just contacted me," Jesse whispered back.

"Ah, OK. You just surprised me when you jumped. I'll let you get back to your mind talking," Breeze chuckled softly. Jesse gave her a hug, which was easy to do since she sat in front of him on Rambo. Jesse waited to hear if his dad was there too.

"Yep, sure am," David responded. "And we couldn't respond before because Tazeron has been in hyper mode, and things have been happening so fast that there wasn't time. He's planning to visit each of his launch sites in the next day or two and to launch one more volley before hitting the States, Canada, South America and perhaps China. Pearl and I have been yelling at him and his followers non-stop, but they're so focused on their plans that they don't seem to hear us."

"How did he accomplish so much in the short time since leaving the game world?" Jesse wanted to know.

"He has had his Game Masters working around the clock. Apparently, he recruited them for this side too. Remember his supporters that were sent through the portals one way? Well, they had just enough magic in them before they disappeared, or whatever happened when they couldn't go back, that they created these small islands and conjured these buildings. I'm not sure about the launchers and missiles, but one thing that is still holding unchanged is that they can do no harm. So the weapons aren't nuclear or anything like that; they are mostly a scare tactic, and it's working. His primary goal is to control with fear right now, and if possible he would love it if the humans completely destroyed each other. That would prove that he was right all along about their destructive nature and that the gods were wrong for not letting him work his plan in the first place."

"We have to reroute his plans," Pearl said. "We could just expose him, but that might add extra people to his payroll people are so motivated by money, and he has a ton of it. We haven't discovered where his money is coming from or if he really has any. I doubt he's listed on any database unless his Game Masters have access to that too. I wonder if we could curse his resources so their monies disappear like leprechaun gold." Pearl snickered at the thought.

"Jesse, we need to move. I'm sensing detection. Tell David and Pearl to contact us. We must go now," Breeze said urgently.

"We have to go; Breeze is sensing detection. Contact us with GPS on this and the other islands. I have an idea. Love you two."

Just as Jesse started to warp them back to Gran's, they felt a tracker spell and had a harder-than-usual time warping out.

"That was odd," Rambo said as they landed back in Gran's old computer room. Chaelea was there when they landed. They could hear loud talking and laughter coming from the rest of the house.

"What was odd?" Chaelea asked as she closed the door for more privacy.

"A powerful tractor spell that almost trapped us. If Breeze hadn't sensed detection, we might have been discovered," Jesse said.

Chaelea got an amused look on her face. "What is wrong, Chae?" Rambo asked. "Did that spark some kind of alarm in your beautiful head?" Rambo said, smiling and giving her a kiss.

"As a matter of fact, it did. Jesse, there is no way that you and Breeze could have been trapped by a tractor beam. It's just not possible to magically catch a previous Shadow Dream. I think, Rambo, that the tractor beam was targeting you and that's just funny. Perhaps you should let them find you sometime while you are invisible and then, when they come to check out their trap, remove your concealment and fry them," Chaelea burst into gales of laughter.

"That makes me want to go back and try it out," Rambo laughed.

"Since we are the ones with the stronger magic and the Game Masters can't create Blood Fairies or anything else, it would be hilarious to see the reaction. Ooh, I would so love to torment Tazeron and his minions for a long time before we destroy them," Jesse said. "I could even call them through mind control to a particular area. Or better yet and this is something I've wanted to do ever since I learned that I could mind control I would love to give them an itch that they couldn't scratch. Oh, the possibilities are endless." Jesse roared with the hilarity of it.

"That raises another question," Breeze said. "What purpose do the Game Masters serve now? They really would have no purpose, would they, since they can no longer control the surroundings and have no magic?"

"I'm thinking that they are being used as guides only. They know this world, whereas Tazeron and his non-mortal followers don't know it, and that could work to our benefit. Perhaps we could eliminate the GMs," Jesse said. They let those thoughts sink in as they prepared to meet with the rest of the gathering.

As Jesse, Breeze and Rambo opened the door to the rest of the house, they saw that they had returned to a house packed with Keepers. Some were sitting outside on the front porch swing and in the yard. Jesse was surprised at the numbers but glad to see them. Because of the size of the group, everyone gathered outside. Most sat on the grass; others conjured blankets, chairs or couches to sit on. Jesse called the meeting to order.

"Welcome, everyone. One question to start: has everyone seen the news report about the missile attacks around the world?" Jesse asked. Some had seen the news and others had not. Jesse tried to fill everyone in with the help of those who knew about it. There were many questions. Jesse also described what he, Breeze and Rambo saw at the small launch site.

"It was just a tiny volcanic island, barely big enough to house their launcher and a few people. We don't know where Tazeron, or Tazeroni as he's calling himself here, is getting his financing," Jesse said. "David and Pearl didn't know either. It seems that Tazeron has been building a network of support on this side of the Shield that only surfaced after the attacks and that he claimed responsibility. So far no previous knowledge of him has surfaced. Our job will be to make the connection between this Tazeroni and the Tazeron of the game. The people that were sucked into the game will need to step up and describe what happened to them. This isn't going to be an easy sell because probably 99.5% of the general population won't understand or believe what we are telling them. I'm afraid the outside world is going to group us with every other alien-abduction theorist out there. So we are going to have to come up with creative ideas as to how we can convince them that the problem is real and then turn them against this Tazeroni in a comprehensive manner. Right now Tazeron is on a campaign to build fear in the people and in some ways it's working. The world is trying to figure out who he is, where he came from and how to stop him. We can help them with that."

"I don't see any problem with throwing everything we can into the pot, including our magic," Rambo added. "We won't have as much magical flexibility as we did in the game, but with the Xantharaian Keepers at our aid we could make a dent in the world's scepticism."

"I think one way to make a foothold is to organise ambassadors to go to the leaders of the world," Zealoc said. "If we can unite them before Tazeron establishes a larger group of terrorists behind him, that might be a good idea."

"Let's think on that, Zealoc," Jesse said. "If we were on Xanthara that could work. On this planet, however, I'm afraid that unifying the world leaders and people would be a very difficult task and would take a long time time that we just don't have. We need to be creative with our approach and convince the people and leaders out there that stopping this Tazeroni would benefit them. While there are many good people in the world who would embrace getting rid of this evil man, there are many others who, because of greed, would embrace his ideas of control and power. People in this world love their money and power. We already know that this world has plenty of so-called terrorists as it is. I'm hoping they will resist Tazeron's plan to take over. They all have their motives for terror and they all want their glory. My hope is that they won't want to share in the glory. They could be sorely tempted by all the money he waves in their faces, however.

"What might happen and this is a possibility is that they will try to outdo each other, and that must not occur. That would be devastating to the innocent people out there. We've already seen in the news reports that various groups are claiming responsibility for these bombings."

As Jesse was addressing the group, he received a surprising message from his dad.

"Jesse, we just had a very unexpected development here. Guess who just showed up?"

Jesse, of course, had no idea, so David told him. "Heala, Shosho, Tonic and Sheela have been called into service by Matilda. They have been given the same assignment as Pearl and me. Tazeron now has more ticks to annoy him." At this David roared with laughter.

"Dad, is that possible because they are essences like you and Gran?"

"Yep. I'm not sure how it's going to work, but we'll figure it out. Any suggestions that you and the others might have would be appreciated. Maybe with more of us yelling at Tazeron he will finally start listening we can hope. Well, gotta go, son. Take care. Love you."

"Wow…" Jesse said, stunned, which caused concern among the group.

"Jesse, what happened just now? You got a far-away look and kind of staggered," Rambo said, worried.

"I just got a message from my dad. Listen up, people we just got an unexpected boost to our army. Remember Heala, Sheela, Shosho and Tonic? Well, Matilda has called them into service on this side of the Shield. Because they are essences, they will be helping David and Pearl in their efforts to snarl up Tazeron's plans."

There was surprise at this announcement and excitement because of what it could mean for their efforts to break up Tazeron's power.

"Now that we are all gathered here, and we know of the essences that are also helping in our quest, we need to set up some serious plans and get them working. Chaelea, what is our head count?" Jesse asked.

"We have thirty-two Keepers here now; twenty-one of them have the talisman. There will be approximately ten to fifteen Xantharians arriving in a few days and, another thing the cats will also be helping." There was astonishment at the announcement of the cats joining, and with their mind travelling, magic abilities and shapeshifting they could be anywhere the Keepers needed help.

"That's excellent news, Chaelea. Now we need to put it all together and come up with a plan. I have some thoughts on this; let me know what you think. First of all, Tazeron has caused tremendous damage to many souls and to the world of Xanthara. For those reasons alone I would like to see him stripped of all his associates and resources in this world. I would like him to be completely alone of any mortal help when he is finally bound up and sent into outer darkness. He has caused so much pain and grief because of his selfish desires and plans. He was willing to kill the Slater children and anyone else who got in his way. He hopes to destroy this world and all its people because they wouldn't bow down and embrace his suggestions and goals. He does this for pride. I want to strip him of all his pride and show all the people who follow him for greed and power that wickedness never was happiness."

"How do you propose we start, Jesse?" Tommy asked.

"Well, because we now have six essences helping us, plus when they get here the two cats, I suggest we have them track Tazeron and his minions. When they get a solid feel for how large his organisation really is, we will have a better idea of what we need to do. I want to get as many of the gamers out there who know of Tazeron and the 'missing' involved. A few have been returned and, as more are brought back, perhaps they will be willing to help us also. The world is still pretty clueless to his evil power and influence even with his attacks; we need to educate them to the danger Tazeron brings."

"Jesse, I would like to go into the schools throughout this country and talk to kids about the problem and see if they know any of the missing. I would be very pleased if Miss Martha would come with me on this adventure," Mr Chambers said, winking at Martha, who blushed.

"I would be honoured to help you in this adventure, Sean." She went to stand by his side and actually took his hand, smiling up at him.

Cami stared at her dad, then grinned as he understood. Here was someone who shared his love of adventure and believed in the quest as strongly as he did. He finally had someone who once again brought happiness into his life and with whom he would have a purpose. Zealoc looked like he wanted to say something to his sister, but then realised, as he watched Martha with the skinny ex-math teacher turned adventurer, that if she could finally find happiness, like he had with Pearl, then he would support her and not tease.

Cami gave her dad and Martha big hugs and charged each of them to keep the other safe. "We will, Cami," Sean told his daughter as he gave Martha a tight squeeze around her shoulders.

"We will," she said, smiling up at him.

"And, Dad," Cami said, "remember that I'm only a talisman away. Keep in touch."

Sean could only nod as emotion overcame his voice. After they said goodbye to the gathering, Sean and Martha warped from the group.

Several others had ideas that they shared with the group. Peter, Julia, Ginger, Savana, Jeremy and a few others wanted to travel to different countries in Europe and South America. Others volunteered to help them. They wanted to talk with the youth and organise them into support groups for online addiction, similar to what Bill and Sally were organising with the military. Jesse suggested that they meet with his mum and stepdad to find out exactly what they were doing and how it was working.

Rusty Palmer also wanted to travel to Germany to meet Sally and Bill. He wanted to do something in memory of his own father, who had been killed in Iraq the year before David. This surprised Jesse. He didn't really know much about Rusty's past. All he knew for sure was that Rusty's mum had died when he was little and that he too had lived with his grandmother. She, however, didn't play the games or understand them.

Better understanding Rusty's past helped Jesse make sense of the anger and grief that Rusty had acted out with his bullying. Grief and loneliness can create depression, anger and mental illness. When people isolate themselves from the community that surrounds them, as Rusty had when he spent hours on the game, it can validate those feelings of grief and loneliness, and that can increase the anger, bullying and depression. Jesse felt like he was gaining better insight not only into Rusty, but also into all the others out there who were suffering from mental illness and addiction in one form or another.

The group agreed to meet the next day and travel together. Jesse and Breeze would go with them. Breeze was excited to finally meet her future in-laws.

Tanze, Flowergirl, Leapin, Pumpkin, Dropdead and Wisdom, who were all Asian, wanted to go to the Asian people, especially the youth. Online gaming was very popular in all parts of Asia, and they wanted to get the word out and help in any way they could. Rykan wanted to go with them. He had always had a fascination with Asian people and culture and was excited to finally go to Asia with people who spoke the language.

Paylag and Mesola, who were from the African continent, wanted to travel together spreading the word about the dangers of Tazeron. While online gaming wasn't a common problem there, it was important to them to help their own people. Tazeron had, after all, targeted Africa with one of his missiles.

These groups and others would be able to travel with the ease of talismans, and as Keepers they could choose targets for their service. They prepared to leave with wishes of safety from all.

At the end of the day Jesse, Breeze, Rambo, Chaelea, Cami, Tommy, Ginnea and Zealoc were pleased with how the division had gone. Tomorrow they would contact David, Pearl and the other essences and decide what their plan should be. In a few days, the Xantharians would be arriving, and they needed to be ready for them. They felt like it was a good start, and it was, but then David sent them an urgent message.

Chapter Twenty Two
Complication

"What's up, Dad?" Jesse asked David.

"Well, remember that part about how the people of Xanthara, when they came to this world, could do no harm?"

"Yes," Jesse said, fearing what he might hear. "Has something changed?"

"Indeed, it has. Tazeron has formed a partnership with another group of evildoers that can launch a loaded missile."

"What! When did that happen?"

"It just did. Jesse, he's going to start loading his rockets with nerve gas."

"NO, that cannot happen! It just can't. Dad, who are these people? When do they plan to start and where are they going to launch them from?"

"Jesse, warp to me now. Use invisible and bring Rambo and Breeze with you. See you soon, son."

"Jesse, what just happened?" Breeze asked, concerned. Everyone was watching him.

"Dad just sent me a message that Tazeron has made a partnership with another evil group. They're going to start launching loaded missiles."

"Loaded with what, Jesse?" Cami wanted to know.

"Nerve gas."

"Wait a minute," said Zealoc. "Can he do that? Doesn't it go against the Xantharaian code of behaviour? Chaelea, is it possible?"

"It is not possible for Tazeron to do it. However, someone from the mortal world could," Chaelea looked pensive. "And if Tazeron has contracted with them and paid them a ton of money, which he says he can do, he would finance their objectives, accomplishing his own in the process. This cannot happen; it must not happen." She angrily slapped her hand on the table next to her and got up, pacing the floor.

"Dad wanted me, Rambo and Breeze to warp to him under invisibility," Jesse said. "We will go and find out what's going on. Cami, I will send you a message once we find out and you can pass it on."

"I will do that, Jesse. You guys be careful."

"Rambo, Breeze, let's go find out what this is all about."

After Breeze and Jesse settled on Rambo and became invisible, Jesse held the chain and mind-linked with the talisman. They warped to David's location. This place was more tropical and bigger, but it was still a missile launch site.

"Dad, we're here."

"I can see you guys, Jesse, but others cannot."

"Jesse, I can feel the tracker beam. What do you want to do with it?"

"Dad, did you hear Breeze? She says that she can feel a tracker beam. Tell us quickly what you have learned and what can be done about it."

"Jesse, did Chaelea say that you and Breeze aren't trackable?" David asked.

"Yes, only Rambo is trackable."

"Ok, Rambo, let them track you. They won't be able to see you unless you want them to. Jesse, you and Breeze stay here with me. You can cast invisible, Breeze, correct?"

"Yes, David."

"Good. Rambo, I want you to stay invisible and play cat and mouse with that tracker beam. I will show Jesse and Breeze what's going on here and you will listen to it. Ok?"

"Yep, got it."

Rambo took off while David gave Jesse and Breeze a tour and explanation. Jesse and Breeze could both cast invisible on themselves, but David didn't know that yet, so they were double covered as David warped them to the other side of the small island.

What David showed them was an ammunition plant, and Tazeron was walking around inside it talking to a tall, fierce-looking, skinny man with brilliant red hair and gold teeth.

"And you say you can make me four hundred kilos?" they heard Tazeron ask.

"We can do that."

"I will also need you to load the missiles and launch them. I will pay what you asked. Half now, and the rest on delivery, agreed?"

"Yes, that is agreeable. You understand of course that we will accept payment in gold or silver only. No paper money," the tall gold-toothed man said, smiling at Tazeron.

"I understand. We can have the first half to you later today."

"That is acceptable, and we can deliver the rest by boat to this location in four days. Is that satisfactory?"

"It is. As soon as we use the first shipment, we will most likely contract another."

"I look forward to your continued business, Mr Xanzerie."

The man shook Tazeron's hand and left the building. The excited look on the man's face matched Tazeron's, and that made Jesse's skin crawl. So much greed and corruption, all for money and power. Jesse realised something else: Tazeron's desire to make the evil ones of this world his slaves was working. It just wasn't happening how Jesse had imagined. Tazeron was buying their devotion.

Tazeron walked around the plant with a big grin on his face for a while, then a messenger ran in.

"We have located an invader, master," the little man said, bowing slightly.

"Where?" Tazeron asked.

"On the other side of the island, near the far bay. What are your instructions, sir?" The little man waited for Tazeron's response.

"I will handle this. Show me exactly where."

"Yes sir, this way." The messenger left for the location with Tazeron following.

David, Jesse and Breeze followed them.

"Rambo, did you hear what was said just now with Tazeron?"

"Yes, Jesse, you and the others are coming through loud and clear. It must be the talismans. What would you like me to do with this motley group that are chasing me with their pathetic searching devices?" The hilarity of the situation passed through Rambo's mind and they all could feel the humour of it.

"I think it would be appropriate to let them see what they caught in their snare. Tazeron is on his way there now with a messenger waiting for them to arrive. We will be right behind them," Jesse said. "Then full battle form, sir. And Rambo, feel free to blast everyone but Tazeron and the evil dude with the gold teeth. Then, my friend, there's an ammo plant over here that needs to be removed from the planet. After the cleanup, we need to have a little chat with mister nasty and his partner. We will be watching the performance."

Rambo was an excellent player. He paraded around the field that they had 'trapped' him in, still under invisible. After Tazeron and the messenger arrived, Tazeron consulted with his minions. They knew there was something there, they just didn't know what. Then

Rambo, in full battle size, dropped his invisible. The scene was something out of a very cheesy monster movie. The fifteen to twenty minions tried to run in terrified panic as the huge dragon came into view. Falling over their own feet and others that got in the way, very few made it very far.

"Rambo, I've changed my mind," Jesse said to his friend. "Don't kill anyone right now. Channel that tracker beam back to them and round them all up into a neat little package. Breeze and I will be right there to talk to them. I want Tazeron and mister gold teeth included in that, please."

"As you wish, Jesse."

Rambo needed very little effort to round up his captives and Tazeron. The surprise of seeing a huge talking dragon shocked them all into submission.

"Rambo," Tazeron spat out when he saw the huge dragon, "that means that…"

"That I am here too, Tazeron?" Jesse said, as he and Breeze walked out into the clearing where Rambo had contained Tazeron and his minions. "Yes, and do you want to tell all your 'friends' here who I am and how you know me? Or should I fill them in with all the gory details?"

"So, are you going to kill us now?" Tazeron laughed at his words.

"No," Jesse said, as he calmly walked around the shivering, grovelling, frightened prisoners that surrounded Tazeron, who alone faced Jesse, standing tall and defiant as Jesse circled the group.

"We aren't going to destroy you, Tazeron. We are going to let you do that. You will soon be free to go, and you can take as many of these pathetic excuses for humans, who wish to follow you, into outer darkness and destruction. But before we release you, I am going to explain to this assembly who you really are, and what happens to the ones that follow you.

"So, you see, Tazeron, as you once told me, *'I am your worst nightmare'*. I also remember promising you that I would send your black, demented heart back into that abyss that you crawled out of so long ago. I can do that, you know. But you still have a little time to repent and serve your punishment, or you can continue to destroy yourself and all those who choose to travel in your wake. I will now tell these people here with you, that you will destroy them in the end, like everyone and everything else you have ever touched."

Tazeron was no longer sneering at Jesse. He had visibly paled and stood with his teeth clenched and fists balled tightly.

"You can't destroy me, mortal," Tazeron sneered. "I am all-powerful, and I will control this planet, and you are the one that will suffer just as you did on the island."

"Oh, but Tazeron, I conquered that island, and you. Do you remember the animals? Do you remember your singed butt?"

"Oongo, come to me now, bring your wife. I want you to appear to these pathetic captives in your full glory."

"As you wish, Jesse," the big cats replied.

To the horror of the captives, including Tazeron, two huge cats, obviously not of the mortal world, appeared and flanked Jesse. Jesse scratched their ears. The two cats each purred loudly.

"I see that you do remember, Tazeron."

"Who are you?" Tazeron asked, his voice cracking.

"I already told you; I am your worst nightmare. Now I will ask all of you who are trapped with Tazeron, do you wish to continue with him?"

Everyone, including the gold-toothed man that was captured, yelled a hearty "NO!"

"It seems you have no one to stand with you here, Tazeron. But we know that you have other followers across the world. You are free to go to them after you see our last demonstration."

All the prisoners marched up a small hill and through the jungle to another higher hill where they could witness the demonstration. Before he started, Jesse had Breeze place shackles on Tazeron and the gold-tooth man, who was not as fierce-looking anymore. Jesse had her bring them forward and face the ammo compound.

"Rambo, shall we give these gentlemen a small sample of what we can do?"

"I think that is an excellent idea, Jesse."

"On the count of three. One… two… three."

Jesse and Rambo released their fire toward the ammunition depot and, just like the shimmering mountains of long ago, they destroyed it in a giant explosion.

"I have one more thing to show you, Tazeron, and you too, mister 'gold teeth'.

"Chaelea, could you come to our location and bring the others with you? Cami, your talisman knows where we are."

"Yes, and Jesse, I must say, I am impressed with your power and technique, my son," Chaelea said, a smile in her voice with just a touch of pride.

"Like mother and father… Milady."

Within seconds, and much to the added horror of the gathered prisoners, a beautiful, very large white dragon arrived with four passengers.

"Chaelea…" groaned Tazeron as he collapsed to his knees.

"Yes, Tazeron, and there are two others with me that you know."

Tommy and Ginnea stepped forward. "Hello, brother," they both said, grimacing at the word *brother* and the nasty taste it formed in their mouths.

"Why are you doing this?" Tazeron asked, more a whisper this time. "Why not just destroy me? That is what you want to do. Why not just get it done?"

"Because, Tazeron, as Jesse has said, there is still time for you to save your immortal soul. You would need to go back to Xanthara and face the gods, accepting your sins and taking whatever punishment they would give you," Chaelea said solemnly.

"I will not do that," Tazeron mocked. "I would rather face total death."

"As you wish, Tazeron, so be it. You are free to go, but remember we and the gods will be watching, and when you are fully ripe, you will die utterly," Chaelea said, as she turned her back on him and waved her right wing in his direction.

Tazeron disappeared. The remaining prisoners, including the gold-toothed man, gasped in shock at the spot where Tazeron had been. All of them were panicked and pleading for mercy.

Jesse turned to the remaining prisoners. "You have seen a truly wicked man and yet you chose to serve him. We will give you your freedom now, but beware there are many ways that evil can manifest, and if you choose to follow that path it is between you and your gods and the laws of your countries. As mortals, your lives are short. It is better that you serve and help each other. Find ways to do that. Wickedness never was happiness. Now think of a place that we can send you to, and you will go there."

After a few moments, Chaelea again waved her right wing and all but the gold-toothed man vanished.

"Mr Gold Tooth, what shall we do with you?" Jesse asked.

"I suppose if I said I was a changed man you wouldn't believe me, would you?" the man said, sounding hopeful but visibly shaking.

"No, I don't suppose we would," Jesse said. "So, what do you suggest we do with you? We can't have you selling nerve gas to demented people now, can we?"

"No, I guess not," the man whispered, thoroughly fearful now after witnessing the disappearance of everyone else.

"Is there anywhere we can send you?"

"I've always been curious about the far north country where my ancestors came from. I'd need warmer clothing."

"That can be arranged, and if you run short of cash you could always sell your teeth," Jesse said, as he turned the tall, skinny man over to Chaelea, who dressed him warmly and then waved him into the far northern regions of the world, far away from civilisation.

"Somehow I can't think of a better prison for him," Cami said to the group after it had been disclosed what had happened.

"I don't know about all of you, but I'm hungry," Zealoc said.

"I agree," said Rambo. "Running around in circles can make a person hungry. Chaelea, my dear, one question. Where did you send Tazeron?"

To their surprise, she burst out laughing. "I sent him back into the game world. I figured that would be a good place for him to rethink things. We will visit him in a couple of days after we have rested and regrouped. Sometimes when you are fighting a war, it's nice to get a jump start."

"But is that safe? Has it been completely sealed so he can't escape?" Tommy wanted to know, worried.

"Yes, Tommy, it is completely safe. He will have no portals, no magic, no loyal followers, not even any food, and there are still wild things there that must be avoided. Tazeron will not know that world without his Game Masters and slaves. He is alone and friendless in a foreign world. I sense that there is something that still bothers you. Can you express yourself?"

"I'm not sure what it is, just a feeling, I guess. Something doesn't feel right."

"I will check with Matilda, but she said it was completely sealed and returned to its original purity," Chaelea said.

"Thank you, Chaelea. Perhaps my feelings come from… I don't know, but I will trust you."

"Oongo and Purja, my friends," Chaelea acknowledged the two cats. "It is so good to see you again. Would you mind tracking the rest of Tazeron's followers that came through the portal with him and then report back to us with what you find."

"Of course, Mistress, we are here to serve you and the Keepers. We will see all of you again soon."

"Pearl, I would have you join us here, please," Chaelea said to Pearl, and yet all heard it, including Zealoc, who squealed with delight. When Zealoc realised what he had done, he turned beet red.

"Um… guess I got a little excited there," Zealoc said sheepishly.

No one laughed, but they did snicker a little. When Pearl arrived, Chaelea had a surprise for her. But first, she assumed her Elfin form, and she had Rambo do the same.

"It has been whispered to my mind that I am to give you a blessing for your faithful service. David, this is for you too. Would you please join Pearl. This gift is to be used now and in the hereafter as you serve the gods. Rambo, would you assist me, please?"

"Of course, Chaelea," Rambo said, as he stood by his wife and held her hand.

"Children, because of your faithful service we bless you to be joined with your mortal bodies into immortality. Because of the talismans that you wear, this is made possible. You will still retain the ability to fade from mortal sight and become invisible. I want you to know that this is a gift to you, promised by Matilda and sanctioned by the gods. It is not a gift from Rambo and me. We are messengers only, because of our years in service to the gods. You will continue as if you had not died, only know this, you can never die again. So it is, so it is given."

As the previous essences became immortal in their bodies, there was another squeal of delight, but this time it was from Ginnea, not

Zealoc, as she charged David and embraced him by giving him a kiss right in front of everyone. Pearl was likewise greeted by Zealoc, and they all noticed something else. She was a little shorter than him, just like on the game. Pearl smiled at Chaelea and Rambo, and they both winked at her.

"Before we go get something to eat and celebrate," Zealoc said, "I have something to say. It is something I have thought long on." Zealoc took both of Pearl's hands in his, looking her full in the face with tears in his eyes. "Will you marry me, Pearl Smith? After the quest, of course."

Very surprised, but joyful beyond measure, Pearl responded, "YES! I don't ever want to have another moment without you." She then kissed him through their happy tears.

"Well," said David, as he stood in front of Ginnea and knelt on one knee. Ginnea looked very surprised.

"Miss Silverrod, would you do me the honour of becoming my wife, after this quest is ended of course?"

Again, Ginnea squealed as she almost leapt at David, hugging him so tightly that she knocked him off balance, and they both fell to the ground.

"Um… I'm hoping that was a yes," David said, as he and Ginnea lay in the dirt laughing.

"Not just yes, but YES, YES, YES, you great big wonderful…" but the last of her response was lost as David leaned over and kissed her.

Everyone cheered and congratulated the two happy couples before warping to the forest of elves for food, celebration, and more surprises.

Chapter Twenty Three
Baby Steps Forward

Chaelea asked David and Ginnea to check on Tazeron before they went to the forest of elves. She asked the cats to go with them and she didn't care if they were using invisibility or not.

"It really won't matter since you will be the ones in control. With the cats' magic and David's talisman there won't be much Tazeron will be able to do, especially without his minions. But be safe, there are still wild things there to be avoided."

"We will be careful," Ginnea told Chaelea. "As you said, with David's talisman we should be able to track Tazeron, and with the cats' magic he can be controlled."

David and Ginnea bid farewell as they warped into the world that used to be games. Rambo, Chaelea, Cami, Tommy, Jesse, Breeze, Zealoc and Pearl prepared to visit the elves back on Xanthara. The other Keepers, including the Xantharaians that had joined them, had their assignments on the mortal world and would not be going back to the forest at this time.

Chaelea sent a message to Nexlucimus alerting him that their group would be arriving soon, and she wanted to have a meeting. They were excited to see all their friends, and Breeze and Tommy were especially anxious to see their families.

Returning to Xanthara and the forest of elves was a wonderful idea, a much-needed diversion. Jesse didn't even mind the skeedlers that greeted them as soon as they arrived. Seeing the village fully restored was amazing. It was beautiful, like a fairytale. The thought made Jesse smile as he gave his beautiful fairy a squeeze.

"I love you," Jesse whispered to Breeze.

"I know, and I love you as well," she whispered back. He kissed her.

"There is only one thing troubling me right now," Jesse said to the group. "Where is everyone?"

"I was just wondering the same thing," Pearl said, and the rest, especially Breeze and Tommy, agreed. This was concerning. Then they saw Nexlucimus and Zeela approaching. Zeela carried a small bundle in her arms.

"Welcome back, our dear friends. It is indeed good to see you all," Nexlucimus said, smiling widely. "Especially you, Pearl. We were told of your immortality. How wonderful for you and David. This will help the quest, we are sure."

"Thank you, Nexlucimus. As a happy result, Zealoc and I will be married as soon as this quest is completed." She grinned at the Elder's surprise. "If we had commitment rings, we would be wearing them now, as would David and Ginnea. It has been a joyful day all around."

"Indeed, and perhaps as a small gift to you and Zealoc I can help with the commitment rings," the Elder said, looking over to his wife with a big smile as he waved his hand in Pearl's and Zealoc's direction. "You have our blessing, and well wishes that this quest will end soon so that you can continue your next life together."

The happy couple noticed that they now wore gold rings. They were surprised at the generous gift and very happy to display the token of their love and devotion.

Cami noticed that the bundle Zeela carried was a baby. "Zeela, whose child do you carry?" Cami asked.

"She is ours," Zeela said, and her eyes shone with a joy they had never seen there before.

"Oh, Zeela!" Cami, Chaelea and Pearl exclaimed as one. "May we see her? What is she called?"

Jesse, Tommy, Rambo and Zealoc leaned in for a peek at the tiny bundle, perhaps not as enthusiastically as the females in the group.

"She's beautiful," Breeze enthused, giving Zeela and then Jesse a radiant smile and a wink. This made Jesse edgy. He knew that Breeze wanted many children, but he hoped she wasn't getting baby-hungry just yet. There was still much to do in their quest with Tazeron.

"She was quite a surprise," Nexlucimus said, with just as much joy in his eyes as Zeela had shown. "A great blessing from the gods since we thought that we were destined to be childless."

"I didn't know that being childless could happen on this world," Pearl said, concern in her voice as she glanced at Zealoc. "I am hoping that Zealoc and I can have many children together," she said, her cheeks pinking slightly.

Zealoc stepped closer to her, smiling, but could only answer, "Aye."

"It does happen here, but it is very rare," Zeela said. "Not being able to have children on a world with so many happy families has been our greatest sorrow. Because of the war with Tazeron these many seasons and working with the Keepers, we didn't have time to think much on our empty home. Now that things have changed, we have been blessed to open our lives and hearts with this little one. We hope that many more are to come."

Zeela bent forward and gave her child a kiss on the top of the tiny one's head.

"What do you call her?" Cami wanted to know.

"We call her Maiya."

"She is adorable. Might I hold her?" Cami asked.

"Of course," Zeela responded happily as she carefully transferred the now squirming bundle to Cami, who walked over to a shady spot and sat in the grass.

"Nexlucimus, we were all wondering why it seems so empty here. Where is everyone? Where are our families?" Tommy asked. Everyone listened intently, except Cami who was busy cooing to the baby.

"I knew you would be wondering about that," the Elder sighed. "It is almost mealtime. Everyone please get something to eat. We will sit in the shade of this tree at that table over there," he pointed to a larger round table that had chairs. "And I will tell you all that has happened. It isn't anything bad," he said, seeing the stricken looks on Tommy and Breeze's faces. "Just very unusual. Never in all of history... well, go get some food. Then we will talk."

After a few moments, Zealoc and Jesse both returned from the vendors looking like they were in a contest to see who could carry the most food back to the table.

"Did you save anything for anyone else?" Pearl asked when she saw them balancing their stacks of sandwiches, pies and smoothies.

"There might have been a few scraps left," Jesse said, taking a huge bite out of his first sandwich.

Breeze just stared at him as she nibbled on a piece of fruit. Tommy sat next to Breeze; he didn't have anything to eat in front of him.

"Aren't you hungry, Tommy?" Pearl asked, as she sat next to Zealoc, who was already eating his second sandwich and finishing off his first smoothie.

"Not really, I'm worried about my family. I guess it's a habit after so many years of tribulation and anxiety. I just want to be sure that they are safe and happy now that the quest has cooled some. I know that there is still much to do, but it seems like we are doing a lot of sitting around and waiting for something else to happen," Tommy said sadly.

Jesse was feeling a little guilty about being so hungry when there were things to be concerned about, but he figured that he could process the concerns better if his stomach wasn't rumbling and stabbing him for want of food.

After a while, Chaelea, Rambo and Nexlucimus joined them. Zeela returned after a while holding Maiya, who had started crying while with Cami but was now quiet. Cami had gone to the vendor to get something to eat. After a few moments, a rather large, astonishingly purple skeedler swung down from the tree and landed next to Zeela.

"There you are, Vokkey," Zeela said to the furry creature. "I just fed Maiya, but she will need changing before you put her to bed."

The skeedler squeaked softly, taking the baby from Zeela. Vokkey didn't seem to have hands but was still able to carefully put the baby into a hidden pouch, like a marsupial, before popping out of sight.

"Um… Zeela," Cami said, having seen the skeedler whisk off with Maiya. "Is Vokkey Maiya's nanny skeedler? And how can she… it is a she, isn't it? How can she handle Maiya without any hands?"

Breeze chuckled softly to herself as Zeela answered Cami's questions.

"Vokkey is female. All female children have a female skeedler and all male children have a male skeedler. They can handle and tend to the children using their own form of magic. It's more a thinking magic than a physical magic. All children born on Xanthara and the other worlds of magic are given a nanny skeedler when they are born. The skeedlers care for them like mortal nannies do until the children can take care of their own needs. When their charges can care for themselves, the nannies join the other skeedlers that care for their world. As the children grow, they can still have contact with their skeedler if they wish. They are never assigned to anyone else."

"Wow, what a cool idea," Cami said. "That way no child is ever neglected or left unattended."

"I'm sorry to interrupt, but Nexlucimus, could you explain what's going on with the elves, and more especially with mine and Breeze's families?" Tommy pleaded.

"Of course, Tommy. It seems that some of the elves and others that were with them have decided to relocate. For now."

"You mean they never want to come back here? But why?"

"Not never, Tommy," Nexlucimus said. "Just for now, and not all of them. The majority are planning to come back to the forest soon. They are still healing. Don't worry about them, my young nephew. They are enjoying their work on the new mortal planet next to Clay. I'm thinking that there was just too much heartache here for some of them. And even though the forest and village have been restored as before the war, there are still many traumatic memories."

"But where are the ones that have returned? The forest seems deserted. Are we missing something? Where are the Slaters, and Wolfa and Heralon, and Breeze's parents?" Jesse asked, but they all wanted to know.

"The Slaters are living with the Ogres and Trolls for now, rebuilding that community with the Toulonians, and it is progressing nicely," Nexlucimus said. "Wolfa, Heralon, Dalaron and Miranda are on a special assignment. I'm sorry, but I can't say any more right now. I can tell you this," he paused, gathering his thoughts. "The ancients are involved."

There was a collective gasp.

"Does this have anything to do with the quest with Tazeron?" Zealoc asked, coming up for breath before devouring his fourth sandwich and second smoothie. Pearl sat there speechless, watching him.

"No, Zealoc, this has nothing to do with Tazeron. Well… I guess you could say it does. When Chaelea stepped in and rescued the whole village from the ravages of Tazeron's fury, she took them to Clay. While they weren't part of the splitting, they were treated as if they had been. They were transferred to the new mortal world to help with the young ones starting their mortal lives there while the people of Clay continued to build up the facilities on Clay.

"The large number of prisoners being delivered by the Keepers to the holding facility on Clay, and others being sent there by the Moon Soldiers, have overwhelmed those of the splitting, and they needed the help. The arriving elves were willing to provide that help. That made it temporarily impossible for them to return to their forest. The Shyloanians, assisted by Toulonians, were able to finish the work needed to complete this magnificent village that we see before us. A few returning elves and Toulonians are here to maintain the Elven village until the main body of elves feel comfortable returning, or the people of Clay can perform all their duties and the elves are no longer needed on the new world. That time is approaching soon, I am sure. The remaining Shyloanians have returned to their home world."

"But what about our parents?" Breeze and Tommy wanted to know.

"Your parents," Nexlucimus said, "are on a special assignment from the gods, one that I am not at liberty to talk about. I will tell you this: the ancients are helping, and something of this magnitude has never been done in all our history. As residents of Xanthara, they were requested for this special assignment because of their skills and previous service to the gods."

"Uncle Nexi, are you just going to leave us hanging like that? Why tell us anything if you can't finish what you were saying?"

Tommy asked, but then he smiled. "You know, after working with Matilda, I can understand how your mouth is shut on this matter. I suppose it is enough to know that they are safe, and I am sure that they are happy working in the presence of the gods. I guess I am just jealous."

"I feel the same, Tommy, and I can't wait until I can sit them all down and find out what is going on. I just hope that Jesse and I don't have to postpone our wedding until after this assignment is over and he is a very old man," Breeze sighed.

"It will be as the gods wish it, Breeze, but I don't think it will be that long a wait," Nexlucimus smiled at her.

"All things are in the hands of the gods, a very lovely and clever fairy lady once told me," Jesse smiled at Breeze.

"You catch on pretty fast for a mortal," she laughed as Jesse tickled her.

"Hey, I think all of you had better come over here to the game world. You have got to see this!" David said in a group message.

"On our way," Jesse replied.

"Well Tommy, didn't you say that you were tired of sitting around waiting for something else to happen? Looks like you're going to get your wish," Rambo said, as he and Chaelea changed into their dragon forms. "All aboard…"

"Now I wish I'd eaten something," Tommy said.

"No worries, my friend, I grabbed an extra sandwich for you," Jesse said, handing Tommy a foot-long meat and cheese sandwich.

"And I grabbed a pie," Zealoc added. "You'll have to get the milk for it in the game." Zealoc roared with laughter. "Oh, wait, there aren't any inns there anymore, oops!" Everyone laughed, even Tommy.

Tommy didn't have time to eat the food that Jesse and Zealoc had brought for him. Cami conjured a storage bag that would shrink and keep it cold. He attached it to his belt, saving it for later.

Arriving in the game world was totally different from what they remembered. It was lush and humid, with tropical plants that hadn't existed in the previous game world where Tazeron had been trapped. There had been jungles and forests in that other game world, but these looked more prehistoric. Then Jesse remembered one such area from his game. It had dinosaurs, spiders, huge insects, wicked-looking birds, and plants that would try to eat you. Jesse looked around nervously.

Off in the distance they heard roaring unlike anything they had experienced before. Jesse was tempted to mind search to check what was making all the racket but thought better of it.

They were surprised to be dropped off at this location and that David and Ginnea weren't there to greet them, since they had set their talismans to David's location. The cats appeared after a short moment and said that the group was to follow them, using invisibility and stealth. David and Ginnea were in a nearby village.

Jesse guessed that this part of the story world had reverted to everything Jurassic with a touch of Palaeo, and that was strange.

I guess sometimes you have to take a few steps backward before moving baby steps forward. We'll see, Jesse thought with a shrug as they followed the two cats deeper into the jungle.

Chapter Twenty Four
Holy Flintstones, Batman

"Oongo, my friend, it is good to see you. We were expecting to meet up with David and Ginnea," Jesse said to the big cat. "Is there a problem?"

"That depends on what you consider a problem," Oongo grinned, or at least Jesse thought it was a grin. It was hard to tell on a cat. "I suggest that you all reapply invisible and follow me stealthily."

Jesse turned to the others. "Did you all hear what Oongo just told me?"

They all said that they did. Apparently the talismans communicated mind talking to all in the group, including Tommy and Zealoc if they were touching someone with a talisman. Cami touched Tommy and Pearl held Zealoc's hand as soon as they realised that Oongo was mind talking with Jesse and that it was something they all needed to hear. Breeze and Chaelea were linked with Jesse and Rambo, so they could hear through them.

"Ok, Oongo, lead on and we will be as quiet as possible. Is it far?" Zealoc asked.

"No, it is close. You have probably already heard some of the residents talking to each other."

"That roaring was the residents?" Cami asked, worried.

"Indeed. You will see. Come, follow me."

Jesse and the others exchanged nervous glances before becoming invisible. Oongo was telling the truth when he said it wasn't far. It was less than ten yards before they broke through the jungle flora and were shocked by what greeted their eyes. They were met with one of the most unusual sights any of them had ever seen, except for Pearl, who remembered the old cartoons of the nineteen-sixties.

"What is this place?" Cami whispered through the talisman.

"It isn't anything like what the games offered. What's going on here?" Jesse quietly asked.

"Follow me, and remember, stealthily," Oongo reminded. "We don't want to excite the residents any more than has already happened." Again, a tiger's chuckle, more like a croaky cough.

Oongo guided them through a large compound and they were all glad to be invisible. The residents were dinosaurs of every description and size. Mixed in with the dinosaurs were Neanderthal-looking people, but they had wings. Their wings were connected from their ankles and shoulders to their wrists and all the way down their sides, looking like bat wings. All the bat-winged people wore a kind of one-piece toga that draped between their legs and was tied at the shoulders.

"*Holy Flintstones, Batman,*" Pearl whispered through the talisman to everyone. Jesse had to stuff his fist into his mouth to keep from laughing as he remembered the old cartoons. He sent a picture of the cartoon reference through the talisman so that everyone would know what Gran was talking about.

"Is this part of the hard copy stories' side of this planet?" Zealoc asked as he held Pearl's hand so that his thoughts would travel through her talisman.

"We think so," said David, surprising them.

"Where are you two?" Jesse asked.

"We are in the small building to the left after you cross over the piazza. Oongo, my friend, thanks for guiding them to us. We'll tell what we know when you get here."

Since they were almost to David and Ginnea's location, everyone held their questions until they arrived there.

"So," said David, when they got to their location, "what do you think of the natives?"

"Interesting," said Chaelea. "Are they friendly? On second thought, I guess if they were, we wouldn't need invisible and stealth, correct?"

"Maybe you should ask Tazeron that question. And Jesse, I think you're going to enjoy this," Ginnea snickered.

"You'll see in a moment," David said, keeping his voice low, "but first, I'm sure you have questions."

"Did the talisman bring you right here, David?" Pearl asked.

"No, but we did land near Tazeron. Then we followed him for two game days, keeping to the shadows so he wouldn't see us. It's a good thing we did, because he triggered one of the traps that the people you saw out there had set for game animals. They were shocked to see someone like him in their trap. I'm not sure what this place is, but we are pretty sure it's part of the storybook side."

"We were glad that he landed in a place that was meaner than he was," Ginnea said. "Just imagine what would have happened if he'd landed in something tamer, or perhaps worse."

"I didn't even think of the book side of the world when I sent him here," Chaelea said. "It makes me shudder when I think of what could have happened. I was only thinking of the games. No wonder you were concerned, Tommy."

"Where is Tazeron, by the way?" Rambo asked.

"He's out back. Just wait until you see what the natives do with their captives, or perhaps their food."

David had everyone reapply invisible, and then he and Ginnea led the group around to the back of the little building. There they were surprised to see Tazeron spread-eagle and nailed by his clothes to a small platform. He was sunburnt and covered in what looked like old spoiled fruit that was semi-dried. It smelt horrible. Fairly large ants, flies, and other insects were enjoying a tasty meal on their evil elf dinnerware.

Just about the time Jesse thought about talking to Tazeron, a group of what looked like children—more lizard than the other humanoids and less dinosaur than the big residents—came around the corner with a fresh bucket of rotten fruit. One of the larger children emptied the bucket all over Tazeron before they ran away laughing. Tazeron tried to lick some of the disgusting fruit off himself but couldn't reach it with his tongue. He started to whimper.

Jesse dropped invisible and walked up to Tazeron. "I wonder what you are thinking now, Tazeron? Still feeling all-powerful? Still want to rule the world? I would be interested in hearing your reply."

"Go ahead and mock me, Jesse Finch. I am still more powerful than you, despite my present circumstances. I would still rather die than face the gods. Kill me, Jesse Finch. Release my body so that I can continue as an essence. I will still control you and all the other mortals of your world." At that, Tazeron laughed, a fiendish, demented laugh that sent chills up Jesse's spine. Jesse felt tainted, as he had when Tazeron had controlled his mind back on the island and when he, Jesse, had felt so lost and alone before the Toulonians cleansed him.

Tommy, who was holding Cami's hand, squeezed it so tightly that she yelped.

"Who is here with you, Jesse? Do you bring your friends so that you feel protected?" Tazeron laughed.

"No, Tazeron," Chaelea said, as she dropped invisible. "Jesse doesn't need our protection, but it looks like you might."

Tazeron tried to spit on Chaelea, but his mouth was so dry it wasn't possible. Off in the distance it sounded like others were approaching. Chaelea made a split-second decision and told everyone to warp back to Earth. She and Rambo would take care of Tazeron. What that meant they would find out later. The cats were also told to leave.

Back at Gran's house the group sat around the table talking about their trip into the game world as they enjoyed a large vendor meal that Jesse, David, Tommy and Zealoc had got shortly after they arrived back at the house.

The cats decided to warp to Xanthara and check on their kittens. They would rejoin the group in a couple of days unless they were needed before then. Cami was very interested in the fact that the cats had kittens. She was invited by Purja to go back with them to visit the four little ones. Cami also said she was going to visit Zeela to see the new baby while she was there. Breeze asked if she could tag along, and Cami was delighted to have her company. Jesse wasn't sure if it was a good idea, but the only reason he could come up with was that babies made him nervous.

"Well then, it's good that you aren't going with us," Breeze teased. "But you better get over that, because..."

"I know, I know, you want lots," Jesse sighed. "Just be careful, Breeze, you can't get too baby hungry yet. You need to at least wait until this quest is completed and we have that huge wedding your parents are planning."

"Oh, if this quest would only end!" Breeze moaned, and she actually stomped her foot and pouted.

Jesse couldn't resist. He gathered her up in his arms and kissed her. "Don't be too long, Breeze, I'm going to miss you."

After the girls and the cats were gone, the house felt empty even though Gran, Zealoc, David, Ginnea and Tommy were still there. Just to have something to do, Jesse warped to the lake that he and Rambo had flown through before the quest. While he was sitting on the beach of the lake a large dragon landed next to him.

"Hey Rambo, welcome back. What did you and Chaelea do with Tazeron?"

"We warped him back to Earth to one of his strongholds so that he could complete his destruction. It was really our only option. If he were separated from his body, his essence would still be free to roam, but if he continues to rot his essence with evil doings while it's still attached to his body, then his destruction will be complete. We still must allow him to work his demise for a while longer. Our job will be to protect the mortals while permitting his wickedness to play out. And despite all the heartache he has caused, he needs to continue to prove his evil tendencies until the gods say, *'it is enough'* and he gets cast into outer darkness and is no more."

"It seems hard to believe that there is anything left worth saving in him, but I guess that isn't our decision. I'm wondering how long it will take him to make the headlines. In the meantime, I'll send word to the others with a talisman to let them know what is happening, and maybe they can spread the word around the world. Hopefully we can alert enough people to the cause of the quest. I'm thinking it's going to be mostly kids in the forefront of this war."

"That may be true. I was wondering something, Jesse," Rambo said pensively.

"What's that, Dad?" Jesse smiled at his friend, but Rambo didn't seem to notice as he looked out over the lake.

"What would you think if we visited some of the other places around the world where our Keepers are trying to spread the word of Tazeron? Have you ever been to Asia or Africa?"

"I'm not sure how to answer that question, Rambo. As a baby and younger child our family moved around a lot as my dad was transferred to different locations. I remember some things about Europe. If we did make it to those places, I don't remember them. What are you thinking?"

"Well, Chaelea and I were thinking of paying a little visit to countries that had a stronger history with dragons and magic. If we were to appear to them, there is a better chance of convincing them of the problem. If we appeared anywhere else as a dragon, the governments would bring in the big guns and start shooting before we had time to explain what was going on. We could go in our true form, but why would they take us seriously even if we concealed the fact that we were elves? Elves, like dragons, aren't supposed to exist in this world, and unless you have fame or money not very many people will even listen to you. I'm sure that's why Tazeron got as far as he did when he first came here. Money, lots and lots of money."

"You know, Rambo, what you say makes sense. Who would you want to come with us on this trip?"

"We, Chaelea and I, were thinking that a small party would probably be best. Maybe just you, me, Breeze and Chaelea. What do you think? The others could filter out to either help the other groups or do their own thing for a while. They all know the quest and its importance. There really isn't any reason to keep having meetings and making plans. Everyone is a seasoned warrior and capable of making their own path to help the mortals."

"I guess that this would be the ultimate delegation of authority," Jesse sighed. "I would still like to keep tabs on everyone, perhaps divide into groups with a captain that they reported to every so often. That way if there is a problem, they can contact members or the whole team if necessary. I like this idea, Rambo. Shall we get started? I for one am anxious to help Tazeron closer to his destruction."

But then Jesse had another thought.

"Rambo, what if we helped Tazeron? What if by helping him, we push him closer to his goal, and by doing so we move him closer to his destruction?" The idea so excited Jesse that he whooped before Rambo could respond. "We wouldn't really be helping him, but he would think that we were because he wouldn't know who we were. It would be like the Moon Soldiers when they appeared as supporters that delivered the twins who really weren't the twins. What do you think?"

Rambo just sat there a moment and stared at Jesse while he processed what Jesse had suggested. "You know, Jesse, it might just work. It would be better than sitting around waiting for Tazeron to set fires that we rushed in and put out. What if we didn't put out the fires, but instead we fanned them?"

"I just remember how much fun everyone had faking the camp destruction when Zeela turned everyone into gory dead people," Jesse laughed.

"Yep, and I'm sure they would love pretending to be the bad guys, but they would have to be very careful and convincing," Rambo cautioned.

"True, very true. Shall we call a meeting to discuss this, or just assign captains to choose their teams and then let them plan their own attack while we reintroduce dragons to Asia?"

"Assigning captains to choose teams sounds good to me, Jesse. You want to walk back to the house or take a little flight into the lake for old times?"

"I don't walk much anymore, Rambo, but I would never pass up an opportunity to fly through a lake with you."

The lake hadn't changed that much while they'd been away, except the building seemed more deteriorated. The fish seemed excited to see Rambo and engaged in a lively game of chase and tag with him. They flew through the lake, playing with the fish and exploring for a while, but Jesse was feeling anxious to get back.

"Rambo, this has been enjoyable, but I feel like we should get back to the house."

"I was just thinking the same thing."

As they headed back to the house, Jesse was reminded of the first trip he'd made through the lake and how they had hurried to return home so Gran wouldn't worry because it was getting late. He then remembered her reaction to Rambo giving Jesse a ride and then demanding one for herself. He remembered having to spray Rambo down afterwards. All the happy memories made Jesse feel a bit melancholy.

"Rambo, do you ever miss things before we left for the quest?"

"I saw your thoughts, Jesse, and yes, I do miss those times. But I'm happier to have Chaelea back with me, and I know that Pearl and Zealoc are very happy as well. Looking back to the past is pleasant sometimes, but it's not good to spend too much time there. Think on happier memories, Jesse. Breeze, for instance."

Jesse laughed. "You know, Pops, I enjoy these father and son moments, but you can sure spoil a good pity party with wisdom and common sense. Love you, Dad."

"Pops? Where did that come from? I'm not sure I like that title. I may have to ground you for that one. Love you too, son."

"Oh, please, please, please ground me. Send me to my room, take away all my responsibilities and problems, but leave me the beautiful fairy and all my new friends."

"Wouldn't it be nice if we could pick and choose our problems?" Rambo sighed.

"Yes, it would be, but I'm starting to realise that we are given exactly what we can handle. Maybe in our previous life we did pick and choose our problems," Jesse said pensively.

"Interesting thought," Rambo said.

When they landed at the house, Brutus was asleep on his porch pillow in little dog form. Cami and Tommy were sitting on the porch swing talking. Breeze and Chaelea were picking flowers in the garden, and Zealoc and Pearl were in the kitchen baking cookies. David and Ginnea were in the family room watching TV.

Everything seemed so normal. Too bad it wasn't.

Chapter Twenty Five
Let's Rock 'n Roll

"Hey Rambo, come here a second," Jesse called to his friend from the computer room.

"What's up?" Rambo said as he walked into the room.

"After talking to you earlier, when you said that maybe we should go to Asia or Africa because they had more knowledge of dragons, I decided to do some research and look at this. Pages and pages of information on dragons all the way back to ancient times, and look at this. There were actual sightings in Europe and Asia as late as the late eighteenth century. I had no idea."

"Did you think dragons were myths or imaginations?"

"Well, yeah, sort of," Jesse said, embarrassed now. "That is until you shocked me into reality that day you and Brutus showed up on Gran's doorstep. How come there aren't any live ones now? Except for you and the others of fantasy, of course."

"Sadly, most of the dragons that were on this world weren't as friendly as the ones of fantasy or even other planets. It was an experiment that went bad. Dragons of this world were allowed to go extinct either through natural causes or extermination. Most of them were hard to live around. They weren't very good neighbours, that's putting it mildly.

"Most of the time the smaller ones were nocturnal, but the bigger ones weren't always. They came and went and ate what they wanted, including the local humans. That is why I always covered my dragon appearance with dog, or goose, or whatever camouflaged me the best. Modern mortals don't really appreciate live dragons. I'm glad I have myself back."

"What do you mean they were an experiment?" Jesse asked.

"Most of the dragons or dinosaurs were, um… genetically modified. They were supposed to become beasts of burden like oxen or horses, but it didn't work out so well. Anyway, the humans tried to tame them and train them, but most of the time it had a tragic ending for the people. So, they raised the smaller ones for eggs and novelty, and a few of the bigger ones for hides. Eventually, when the novelty wore off and the danger became a huge issue, they started killing them.

"There are many books, legends, collections of bones, paintings and even fossil tracks that document their existence. Even the mortal Christian Bible talks about dragons and flying fiery serpents. Many of the mortals think of those stories as allegorical, but the dragons really did exist. It was supposed to work like we saw on the story side of the game world where we found Tazeron. I must admit, however, I have never seen bat-winged people before."

"Interesting, I didn't realise that there was so much history with real dragons. So, do you still want to head over to Asia and Africa?" Jesse asked.

"It might be a good idea to at least check on things around the world," Rambo said, as he thought about the idea. "The news has been quiet lately. I liked the idea you had about fanning the fires, but so far we haven't heard of any fires. I was thinking that Heala, Sheela, Shosho and Tonic would be logical choices to do the fire fanning, since they can warp anywhere, are invisible as essences and, of course, they can't be killed. They would be the perfect undercover agents.

"You, Breeze, Chaelea and me on the other hand," Rambo chuckled, "we need to work incognito and always under invisible. Especially when we are around Tazeron. It would be fun to assist those four." Rambo laughed. "I've never been a troublemaker before. Might be fun to do something different."

They both laughed.

"What are you two cooking up in here?" Chaelea and Breeze wanted to know as they walked into the computer room.

"Well," Rambo stated a bit sheepishly, "I was just thinking how much fun it would be to start fanning Tazeron's fires."

"What do you mean by that?" Breeze wanted to know.

"Perhaps you should ask Jesse. It was, after all, his idea," Rambo smirked at Jesse, who groaned when he saw the expressions on Chaelea and Breeze's faces.

"What were you talking about, Jesse?" Chaelea asked.

"Thanks, Dad," Jesse mumbled, as he punched Rambo's shoulder. "And the fire fanning was your idea," he muttered.

"Ouch! That hurts now when you punch me, so watch it," Rambo smiled as he started to punch Jesse back, but then thought better of it, seeing Chaelea's expression.

"Do you two think you could be serious for a moment while you explain what you were talking about, please?" Breeze said, and Chaelea echoed with a "Yes, please."

"Ok, I will explain what we were talking about," Jesse said, and he explained the idea of instead of following Tazeron around putting down the trouble that Tazeron and his minions caused, perhaps they could fan their trouble a little bit with Heala, Sheela, Shosho and Tonic. Jesse mentioned the idea of following the exploit and maybe contributing to the deed. They would, of course, make sure that no innocents were injured in the process.

To Jesse's and Rambo's surprise the two girls loved the idea and wanted to start planning right away. Chaelea thought that they should involve Oongo alone, since Purja would be busy with their new kittens. Breeze brought up the idea of travelling around the world to visit the other Keepers.

"I know that we can contact them with the talismans, but in person we can better see their individual situations. We could then perhaps suggest to them that they come up with their own plans to start trouble for Tazeron," Breeze proposed.

They spent so much time discussing the idea that the rest of the party at the house became curious as to what they were doing for so long. So, they explained to the others what they had in mind, and everyone thought it was an excellent idea. They liked the idea of visiting the various groups around the country and world, and they liked the idea of starting their own fires in the name of Tazeron. The plan was to get people watching for Tazeron and his followers.

The details of all these plans would be worked out as they met up with the other groups. Right now, it was just in the talking and planning stage, and each of them decided to do some of their own private brainstorming and wandered off to different parts of the house and yard.

Later that night, as they watched the news, they learned that Tazeroni had once again made an appearance in the world.

"You know something, we should probably enjoy the down times when we get them," Jesse said to the group as they watched the breaking news and the lady reporter.

"Once again the citizens of the world are stunned by the velocity of the madman Tazeroni and the damage he has again inflicted."

The lady reporting appeared to be in disbelief. Jesse and the others didn't understand what she was saying because she spoke in Spanish, but they learned what was happening through closed captions. They were given a view of the destruction she talked about as the camera showed the surroundings. It looked like either a bomb or a very powerful earthquake had struck the village that she spoke from.

Apparently, the reporter wasn't sure what had happened, but she said that there had been a message delivered to her station demanding airtime for the villain. He was to address the world at 9 p.m. Uruguay time.

"I wonder if we should track Tazeron to his location with the talisman using invisibility," Tommy asked. "It would be interesting to interrupt his broadcast."

"Let's see what he has to say first," Chaelea suggested. "After we know better what his plans are, we can make our own plans accordingly."

"I think both of your suggestions are good ones. However, I am thinking a little worldwide panic might work to our advantage."

"What are you thinking, Jesse? How is panic going to help our efforts?" Cami wanted to know.

"Well, we will know better if panic is going to work for us or against us after we hear what he has to say and how the world reacts to it," Jesse said. "We know that he is aware of us and the fact that we are watching him. We also know that he understands that we have our magic, and I'm sure that he has considered the fact that the gods are on our side and taking notes. Perhaps he has even considered the idea that the more evil and chaos he distributes, the sooner he can have control of the easily manipulated humans. For now, I think we wait until we know more."

"That is probably a good idea," Zealoc said. "However, after we have the information we need, I say we interfere with everything he tries to do as best we can."

"I just don't want to see any more suffering if we can prevent it. Intimidating is one thing, panicking is part of the frightening part, but maiming, killing, torturing, destroying life and property, I have a problem with those," Pearl added.

"Unfortunately, Pearl, those are all part of war, and this is war," David said. "You are a very kind-hearted person. Not that the rest of us are hard-hearted jerks, but we are fighting one, and difficult things are going to happen before we come to the end of this."

"What time is it in Uruguay where this is being broadcast from?" Breeze and Ginnea wanted to know.

"I think that they are four hours ahead of us, and since it is 4 pm here, that means we have another hour before the world hears from the old scumbag," Jesse told them. "I'm going to send out a message to all the Keepers with talismans and let them know about the broadcast so they can watch it. The internet will probably be everyone's best option. I'm sure that all of the news channels will be covering it and replaying it, especially tonight and tomorrow."

"I think Pearl and I are going to get something to eat. Do any of you want to come with us, or would you like us to bring back something?" Zealoc asked the group.

Cami, Tommy, David and Ginnea decided to go. Tommy and David wanted to talk to Nexlucimus.

Later, after they had all regrouped and eaten, they turned on the news channel and waited for the broadcast to begin. It was about fifteen minutes late because, as the newscaster explained, the power in the city was weakened by all the people wanting to watch. When it finally did get reconnected, the picture was dark and very fuzzy. The volume was scratchy, making it hard to hear and understand. Closed captions helped.

"People of the world," Tazeroni said in his opening statement. "We will not discontinue our aggression on your countries, homes, towns, cities, governments and people. We will destroy everyone and everything if it is necessary to get what we want. What do we want, you ask? We only want your unfailing devotion to the cause of peace and brotherhood."

There were gasps and snorts from the group as they watched.

"It is necessary at times to cause destruction to weed out the weak, the old, the infirm and the rebellious. We must have complete allegiance for success. If we cannot convince you how serious we are by this announcement, then we will commence our attacks in earnest. If you can realise the beauty of what we propose, we invite you to join our cause and help us weed out the ones that do not. And unless the people of the world bow to me, I will continue to point my missiles at the greater populations of all nations. This is your only warning, your only chance to join us or suffer the consequences. We will be sending examples of our power shortly."

With those few words, the airing ended.

"He's insane," Ginnea said with a shudder.

"Did he just open the floodgates of Hell?" David and Pearl wanted to know.

"I am thinking that we are going to see some serious panic if we don't step in and at least try to temper his words," Rambo sighed.

Jesse pointed out that before this, Tazeron had aimed his missiles at the world, causing no real damage or injury since he had targeted open country. But the populations were frightened, and he was becoming more brazen and dangerous. He had sent a stronger message and made demands. They needed to do something, and quickly.

"Ok gang, enough sitting around. It's time to rock 'n' roll. Tazeron just lit the world on fire. Let's go fan the flames and explain to the world exactly who and what this idiot is," David said. "Ginnea, let's go track this bozo brother of yours down and nail his butt to another plank after we scare up some mischief of our own where he lives. Jesse, we will keep in touch. Take care, everyone."

With those words, David took Ginnea's hand, cast invisible on them both, and warped to unknown locations.

"I always liked David," Chaelea said with a big grin on her face. "Shall we follow his and Ginnea's lead and *rock 'n' roll*?"

"I love that idea, Chae," Rambo said.

"Me too," Jesse said. "Shall we pay a visit to Heala and his group before we do anything else?"

"That's a great idea," Breeze said. "What about you, Pearl and Zealoc, and you, Tommy and Cami?"

"I think I want to go back to the forest and see how things are going there first." Tommy paused, and then hopefully he turned to Cami. "I would enjoy having you along, if you don't object."

"I would like that, Tommy, but first I want to check on my dad and Martha. Would you come with me to them first?" She smiled at him.

"Of course," Tommy said, as he walked to Cami's side and took her hand. Cami warped them to Sean and Martha's location.

"I think I want to go to Europe, Jesse, and see how your mum and Bill are doing and what is working for them," Pearl said. Zealoc agreed, and she took his hand and warped them to Germany.

As the different groups were warping to their various locations, they failed to notice one little problem. A magician's detector ball was hovering in the shadows of the room like an undetected spider. They might have missed it because it was much smaller than any other seen before. After everyone had warped, the ball made a quick search of the house. Its master was taking mental notes. While nothing could be heard, what the magician saw was enough to show that the Keepers were still active and dangerous to their cause. Something needed to be done to eliminate them.

Before the ball could return to its master, Chaelea walked into the house.

"I thought I felt something wrong," she said to the ball, but before she could do anything to it, it popped out of existence. Chaelea ran out to the others and told them what she had discovered. An immediate change to their plans was in order, and they quickly mounted onto Rambo. Under an invisibility bubble they warped to Tazeron's location.

What they saw when they landed sickened them. It was a scene out of a horror movie, and Jesse had to swallow hard to keep from losing his dinner. There were bodies everywhere, and the people had died in the most horrific ways. The smell was gut-twisting and the screams were deafening, but the worst thing was Tazeron and his demonic laugh. He was enjoying himself.

"This is what happens to those that try to fight me. This is what the world needs to understand. I am serious."

Breeze muffled a sob as she said, "Everyone, look over to your right. What do you see?"

It was a camera crew; they were filming this.

"What are they doing? Do you think it's a direct feed, or are they making a film of what they are doing here to be released later?" Jesse asked. "How much worse does he have to get before the gods say that it's enough?"

Everyone was stunned. Jesse had an idea. "Heala, bring the other three and meet us outside Tazeron's camp. Warp to our location. Rambo, take us out of here. I don't want to see any more."

Rambo flew them a few miles away from the horrible scene and, within a few minutes, Heala and the other three joined them.

"Have you seen what is happening at this camp, Heala?"

"No, we haven't, Jesse, we've been busy at a couple of other camps. What are you referring to?"

"Tazeron is slaughtering people," Jesse told them.

"That same thing seems to be happening in other camps. We chanced on one as they lined up people for a firing squad. We tried to interfere, but it was pointless, they were determined in what they had planned. It appeared to be local villagers, Jesse, even children. It was horrible. We warped to several other camps and the same thing was happening there too. It seems like Tazeron has upped his force to get people to act like sheep or cattle. What can we do? We must do something. This is getting way out of hand. Why can't the world find him and his minions?"

"I have an idea that the world will listen to us now," Jesse said. "Rambo, we are going back to Tazeron's camp, and this time I want to incinerate the whole camp, and I want everyone there to see who is doing it. We will ride in on Rambo under invisible and, as soon as we get there, Rambo, drop invisible. Both you and Chaelea, change into full battle dragons. Breeze, I want you to confuse Tazeron with one of your darts. He needs to remain alive. After we do this camp, we will follow you, Heala, and the other three. I want you four to split up and guide us into other camps."

"Jesse, that will get rid of this immediate problem, but what about long term?" Heala asked, concerned.

"Heala, because we can track Tazeron with our talismans, we can lead the world to where Tazeron is, but first we have to get the world to believe us," Jesse said.

"Jesse, do you remember right before we left for here, I said there was something I needed to check on and went back into the house?" Chaelea asked.

"Yes, I remember," Jesse responded. "You said that you found a magician spying orb snooping around, only this one was the smallest you had ever seen."

"I wasn't able to destroy it before it warped out," Chaelea said.

"So, they have been spying on us, and we didn't know it?" Rambo asked.

"Yes, and I am sure that they can track us like we can track them. I just don't understand how they are doing it."

"From now on, Chaelea," Jesse said, "please put up a cloak of concealment so that they can't follow and spy on us. Up to this point they have not been able to hear what we have been planning, correct?"

"Yes, but who knows what they are capable of now."

"I wonder," Jesse said, thinking out loud. "Should we rush in and put out this fire? Or should we allow it to burn a little longer? Maybe what we need to do instead is convince the world leaders of what we can do to help them in a permanent way. We were talking of fanning the fires, but maybe what we need to do is let them burn themselves out."

"But Jesse, the innocents, the women and children, and even some of the men. What about them?" Breeze asked, worried.

"As hard as it is, Breeze, sometimes evil men need to prove just how evil they are. Think of Hitler or Mussolini in World War II, or think of all the modern-day evil men and terrorists. We haven't always rushed in to put out their fires, but when we were finally able to corral them and destroy them, they were indeed ripe for destruction. We know how evil Tazeron is, but he needs to prove it to this world before we can corral him and send him into outer darkness, where he will be no more, along with all the other truly wicked men."

"Ok, Jesse, what do we do now then?" Heala wanted to know.

"I think we wait until all of this makes its way to the world. As hard as it is," Jesse said, as Breeze started to protest. He continued, "as hard as it is, we need to give this fire some time to ignite the world on fire so that when we offer them our solution, they will be ready to listen."

"And what is our solution?" Breeze said, with a sob in her voice and tears streaming down her face.

"Breeze, my love, we are the only ones that can save this world from that madman down there. We have the power to take him out now, but the gods haven't told us to do it yet. We must patiently wait on their command. If we don't wait until the gods tell us to get rid of Tazeron, then we risk the chance of losing our souls also. As much as we know that this is our quest, they have drawn the battle lines, and we must follow their lead, their counsel, and their commands so that we serve them properly. There is order in this madness, there must be."

"Another thing we must all remember, Breeze," Chaelea said, taking Breeze's hand. "All of those innocent victims are taken immediately to their gods. They are safe. It is the same for all innocent victims around this world or anywhere else that suffer or die needlessly."

"I just want to add something to what Chaelea said," Heala said solemnly. "When I was murdered by Faber, my spirit went to a place where I was greeted by people I knew in this life, my mother and father, a sister and friends, but also by a glorious being. He was everything that I remember from my early years at Sunday School. I can't say that I was a believer before then, but I am a believer now. Not one soul is lost unless they choose a path of evil like Tazeron has done. As hard as this is, it must run its course. This is an end game dungeon. It takes planning and failing and falling on our faces, but we will win. We will win, that is the only ending possible."

"We too were greeted by people we knew and a loving personage that radiated light. It was a shadowless world, full of love," Sheela, Shosho and Tonic all testified.

"You know," Chaelea said to the group. "I'm not sure that we should be completely comfortable with this situation even with the assurance that these innocents are saved after death. Why can't they have a normal, fear-free life if we can do something to make it happen for them? I guess what I'm saying is, instead of fanning the fires or even letting them burn out, what if we stepped in and took out Tazeron's camps around the world, and let the world see who was doing it? All the mortal bad guys can deal with their gods after death, but it's better to take out the few to save the many.

"Tazeron is another matter. I think when we released him into this world, we underestimated his ability to connect with evil on this side that would support his agenda. If we can locate his support team and camps, then that's what we need to do. But Tazeron must not be killed until the gods command it, and then Jesse, you will be the one to do it."

"Me? Why me? And how am I supposed to do it?"

"The chain you wear, Jesse. It can separate Tazeron's body from his essence. I don't remember all the details of how it's done. That information will be given to you when the time is right. For now, Jesse, we need to concentrate on eliminating as many of Tazeron's mortal followers as possible. Tazeron's immortal followers must be removed the same way as Tazeron, through the chain."

"Jesse," David spoke to Jesse's mind, but all of them heard it. "Jesse, Ginnea and I just discovered where Tazeron's financing is coming from. It's coming through an underground website called NYTEVIZON. They have unlimited funds, and they are completely untraceable. We happened to stumble onto that information. Jesse, they can set up anything, anywhere. It has completely outgrown its creators and has taken on a life of its own. Ginnea and I happened to overhear a conversation in one of Tazeron's camps. It's scary what they were talking about. Even the creators have been forced into hiding.

"We need to do something more than fan the fires, Jesse, we need to put them out, and we need to do it yesterday. This world is in danger as this thing grows, and it will. We can do many things under the cover of invisible, but we need to come in with both cannons blazing. Rambo, old man, this is something for you and your wife. Gotta go now, we will keep you updated. It's time to Rock 'n Roll for real!"

Chapter Twenty Six
We're Stuck on the Ceiling

"Holy cow," Jesse said, as he collapsed onto a conjured chair that Shosho quickly placed behind him. She had noticed him wobbling.

"Hi Jesse," Pearl said to Jesse, but the group heard. "Apparently David's message was in broadcast format because everyone here heard it too, and I'm sure we aren't the only ones. Zealoc and I had an idea. What if you used the immortal Keepers and all the others that have invisible and warp, including the four essence? Put them to work hunting down these fiends and don't forget the cats. Anyway, it was an idea. All of you, take care, and Jesse, your mum says hi. Bye for now."

"This just keeps getting weirder and weirder," Jesse said, to no one in particular, but everyone heard him just the same.

"Jesse, your chain can find these people, whoever they are," Chaelea said urgently. "Use it like you did when you found the portals. When you locate them, Rambo and I can come to you and do what's needed. We need to hit Tazeron in his wallet, but not just him. If this is as big as David was saying, then they could very well be financing other terrorist groups out there. I'm sure that there is plenty of profit for an organisation like that."

"I think that's a good place to start, Chaelea," Jesse said. "I would feel safer if you and Rambo came with me, but if Breeze and I go alone under invisible then we aren't traceable. You and Rambo, on the other hand, would be tripping detectors. I'm sure that if these people can make themselves untraceable to the outside world, they'll have sensors to pick up on invaders or spies. Breeze, are you willing to fly into the hornet's nest with me?"

"Absolutely, Jesse," Breeze said enthusiastically. "Anything that we can do to stop Tazeron's minions from killing more innocents. Let's go!"

Jesse took a moment to send out a broadcast to the Keepers and the cats. He wanted an accurate count of all Tazeron's base camps and how many people were in them. For safety's sake, everyone was to use invisible, and those with talismans were to partner up with those that didn't. As soon as totals were calculated, everyone was to report back to Chaelea and Rambo. No one was to engage until they reported back and a plan was set in motion.

"Nice delegation, son. You two be careful out there," Rambo said, chuckling. "You're finally starting to get this Prince Leadership thing down."

"Gee, thanks, Pops. I did have an amazing teacher," Jesse said honestly, but with a chuckle.

"You did have a good teacher, didn't you, and don't call me Pops! Be safe," Rambo responded.

"Will do…"

Jesse and Breeze cast invisible and then, holding hands while Jesse clutched the chain, he connected mentally with the talisman, and they warped to a location unknown, hopefully to learn the untraceable location of a mysterious terrorist financier.

What happened then was not what they were expecting. They ended up inside a small cupboard or a box with vent slots that they could see out of. They could tell that it was very dark wherever they were, because they couldn't see clearly or very far, and that was strange because they both had night vision. There didn't appear to be people there, but they couldn't tell for sure. Jesse warped them just outside of their location and they discovered that, in the process of travelling to this place, they had shrunk down to roughly two inches in height. At least it felt like two inches. Either that, or the people in this facility were huge. The room was sparsely furnished. They could only see what looked like tables and a few large crates.

"Jesse, I'm going to fly around and check out the room while you wait here, ok?"

"Good idea," Jesse said, feeling like a bug in a jar. "Don't take too long, Breeze, this place is creeping me out."

"You should see this, Jesse. These tables are covered with big rocks. I wonder what they are doing. I wonder if we are even in the right place. There's really nothing else up here. I'm coming down. Wait a minute, what's that? Wow! Jesse, this is amazing! Come up here, hurry!"

Jesse warped to the top of the table, but it really wasn't a table. It seemed to be a conveyor belt and the rocks were slowly moving toward an opening in the wall. Jesse and Breeze were small enough that they could ride one of the big rocks through the hole. On the other side, there seemed to be a processing centre where the rocks were crushed. There was just enough light that they could see that the rocks were gold.

For such an enormous operation it was very quiet. They hadn't heard anything until they were right inside the room. They decided to return to the original room and wait to see who was bringing in the rocks.

"I guess we now know where all the money is coming from," Jesse said, amazed. "Tons and tons of gold would finance anything."

Hearing a chirping sound coming in their direction, they stepped into the shadows with invisible on and waited. What they saw surprised even these two experienced

adventurers.

"I don't understand, Jesse. Where are we, did we go back into the games?" Breeze asked to Jesse's mind through the talisman, since they were still holding hands.

"That's a very good question, Breeze," Jesse answered, "and I don't know how to answer that right now."

"What are they, Jesse? And will our invisible hold against them?" Breeze managed to think, through her shock at what she was seeing.

"Good questions, but my answer is the same. I don't know," Jesse answered, stumped.

"They look like fat glowing ants," Breeze said. "What are they carrying? Is that more gold?"

"It could be, that would explain why they have so much money to throw at the terrorists. But that doesn't explain where we are and why they are so big. I'm going to try something, Breeze. I'm not sure what will happen or where we might end up. I'm going to warp us out of this building. If we end up someplace dangerous, I'll take us back to the house," Jesse said.

"Ok… I'm ready," Breeze answered.

The only problem with that plan was that they didn't go out of the building. What happened? They ended up on the ceiling, or what seemed like the ceiling. It was dirt, frozen dirt, and they stuck to it like flypaper, or people paper in this case. It was very tacky. The action of the warp separated them from each other. Jesse attempted to scoot over to Breeze but discovered that he couldn't move. They were both going to be popsicles if they didn't figure something out very soon.

While they tried to wiggle free from their situation, they watched the ants drop their rocks and retreat into the shadows.

"I can't move, Breeze, can you?" Jesse whispered, his teeth starting to chatter.

"No, Jesse, I can't. I'm stuck so tight I can barely breathe."

"We've got to do something or we're going to die here like flies stuck in molasses. I'm going to see if I can talk to Rambo through the talisman."

Jesse tried the talisman and thankfully it worked.

"Rambo, I need you to come to me. Breeze and I are currently stuck on a ceiling. It's not funny. I can hear you laughing at me. This is serious. Tell Chaelea that if we don't come back soon, she needs to be aware of the situation and to send someone else that has a talisman."

"OK…" Rambo attempted. "Are you sure I can't laugh at this, because I really want to. My sides hurt from holding it in."

"No, it's not OK. Now get your armoured butt here, pronto, or you are forever going to be known as Pops. Hurry! We're freezing!" Jesse shouted to Rambo's mind, his teeth chattering now.

"OK… OK, I'm on my way," Rambo said with difficulty. While he was concerned, just the mental picture of Breeze and Jesse stuck on a ceiling had him roaring with laughter as he headed toward their location.

Jesse felt, along with everything else, that Rambo's huge burst of laughter was going to give him a headache. That did it. Rambo's new name was going to be *Pops*.

It took forever for Rambo to get to them, according to the clock in Jesse's head, but Rambo finally made it. The strange thing was that Rambo wasn't tiny like Jesse and Breeze were. What was up with that? Rambo seemed even bigger than normal, his head nearly scraping the ceiling that Jesse and Breeze were stuck on. The huge ants were still gone, which was lucky for them, because Rambo would have squashed them. Maybe that wouldn't be so bad, Jesse thought.

After getting his snickers under control once he saw them, Rambo carefully scraped Breeze and Jesse off the ceiling. Sometimes claws do come in handy.

"Why are you two so small?" Rambo wanted to know.

"No idea," Jesse said. "Why are you so big?"

"Obviously so I could scrape you two off the ceiling," Rambo broke into another round of laughter.

"OK, I get it, enough with the laughing. You big clown, you're going to alert the workers in here. Can you shrink and fly?" Jesse asked.

"Yes, Jesse, I can fly in here and reduce in size. That's how I got to you two. Well, that and invisible. There are some evil-looking ants out there."

The chirping started again, and the ants returned. The problem was, the ants entered the room so fast they didn't have time to reapply invisible, and they were spotted. The chirping intensified, and twenty or thirty ants poured into the room. Jesse warped them home. It was good that Rambo had at least reduced in size.

When they got back to the house Jesse said, "Oh man, I wish we'd put on invisible to find out if they could see through it."

"Let me pop back over there and test it," Rambo said, and he was gone. Probably ten seconds passed before he was back. "No problem, but man, those are some huge ants!"

"Rambo, how can you do that?"

"Do what?" Rambo asked.

"Pop in and out like that, and why have you never done it before?" Jesse questioned.

"Good question. I don't know. I didn't think about it, I just did it. Chae… come in here a second, please!" Rambo yelled, and then grinned at Jesse. "We need to have a meeting anyway."

"You bellowed, my love… Oh, hi Jesse and Breeze. When did you get back?"

"We just did, Chaelea," Breeze said before Jesse could. "We have some questions for you."

"OK, how did your investigating go?" Chaelea asked. It was obvious that she knew nothing about the ceiling incident, and Jesse hoped to keep it that way, but with Rambo, it was guaranteed to get out. Jesse wanted to ask her about it anyway, so it really didn't matter.

"Chaelea, when we first landed, wherever it was, Breeze and I were in a box or a small cupboard."

"A box? And you didn't know where you were?"

"Just wait, Chae… it gets better," Rambo added, trying not to snicker, but not successfully.

"What else happened?" Chaelea asked as she watched Rambo. "Did you see anyone or overhear any conversations?"

"When we got out of the box, we were about two inches tall."

"Four. I think you were closer to four inches," Rambo added, with a snort.

"Rambo… please let them tell it. OK?"

"How tall do you think those ants were, Rambo?" Breeze wanted to know.

"As tall as me in my full battle dragon size, probably eighteen feet at least."

"Oh my goodness," Chaelea said. "And you were only four inches? What happened then?"

"We don't know. I tried to warp us out of the building or wherever we were and only accomplished getting us stuck on the ceiling instead. Neither of us could move and we were separated. The ceiling was frozen and sticky, almost like a resin. I called Rambo to our location. I told him to tell you before coming just in case there was a problem, but I guess he didn't," Jesse added, and then enjoyed watching Rambo squirm under Chaelea's scrutiny.

"Go on, Jesse," Chaelea said, watching her husband.

"By the time Rambo got there, the ants had stepped out. Rambo carefully scraped us off the ceiling just in time for the ants to return. Because none of us remembered to reapply invisible, they saw us and chirped for reinforcements. There must have been thirty of them, all different sizes. Thank goodness warp worked better getting us back here. Then Rambo said he would go back and test invisible to find out if they could see through it, which he did, and the ants couldn't see through it."

"Question for you," Chaelea said. "Did these ants use lights? Headlamps, torches, nightlights, skylights or anything like that?"

"There were no lights that we could see, Chaelea, but the ants seemed to give off a soft glow, kind of like a firefly. Why do you ask?" Breeze wanted to know.

"Well, real ants find their way by scent, underground and above, through their feet," Chaelea told them. "There are several things about this situation that cause me concern. Why were you, Jesse, and Breeze so small, why did the ants not detect your presence through scent, why was Rambo able to warp there, why did you get stuck on the ceiling, and why was the dirt frozen? I think we need some help with this."

"Actually, Chaelea, now that I know what is there, I think Rambo and I can go back and investigate this alone. In fact, that's what I want to do. Rambo, are you with me?"

"The only problem with that, Jesse," Rambo said, "is if they have tracer alarms, I might set them off. But then again, no alarms went off when I got there, and I travelled down their tunnels to find you."

"We can't really learn much if we set off alarms, and that's always a possibility, even if we didn't this first time. I wonder if my dad and Ginnea would investigate for us if I led them to the spot? That way they would have the flight path, if it works that way here," Jesse said pensively.

"There's also the cats, Jesse," Breeze said. "Remember that they can mind-travel and shapeshift."

"That might be a better option, Jesse, because as cats, they won't smell the same as a human. Also, Rambo, you might have slipped past their alarms because of invisible, or because you were in dragon form and wouldn't smell like a human to them either," Chaelea added.

"That's a good point. OK, I'll talk to Oongo and Purja. I'm sure they will be happy to do it. Maybe Zeela can kitten-sit for a while." Jesse smiled at the idea of Zeela and little Maiya playing with the tiny balls of fluff.

Chapter Twenty Seven
What to do…what to do

Jesse contacted Oongo and Purja and they were more than happy to help with the investigation. They told Jesse that there was no need for anyone to kitten-sit, because Purja's mother was staying with them, visiting her grandkittens.

Jesse warped to the outside of the hidden facility and was surprised to find that it appeared to be at the South Pole. He was very glad that he had worn warm clothing, but he was still freezing. It only took a moment for the two cats to join him at the spot. He was surprised to see that the cats needed no additional clothing.

"The magic protects us, Prince Jesse," Purja told him as they changed into very large white bats that blended into the surrounding blizzard. Jesse was glad to leave and warp back to the warm house, where he informed the others that he'd discovered the location.

"That would explain why the ground of the ceiling was frozen. Being underground would also explain why it was so dark in there without lights. The only reason we could see at all was because of your earlier blessing, Chaelea," Jesse said to the group.

"That's probably why you were so small too — the chain was protecting you from detection," Rambo said.

The chain warmed at that suggestion and Jesse smiled.

"I wonder if the stickiness of the ceiling was some kind of protection against detection?" Breeze mused. "Perhaps signals could get in, but the tackiness would keep them from getting back out. That's just a thought."

"That's a good thought, since we don't know the capabilities of these creatures at this point," Jesse said. "I'm still perplexed at the idea that large ants would not only have the intelligence but also the ability to produce such advanced technology. I understand their capability to dig out gold and even move mountains, but the rest makes no sense at all. Hopefully the two cats can find out more information for us soon.

"Change of subject," Jesse added as he rubbed his growling stomach. "I don't know about the rest of you, but I'm hungry. I'm going to go get something to eat."

The rest of the group decided to make a brief trip to Xanthara for food. As soon as they got back Oongo contacted them.

"Child of Chaelea, we have some information for you," Oongo said to Jesse, and Jesse linked it to the others.

"Do you remember the black cylinders that were placed in the minds of Elder Nexlucimus and the other council?"

"Yes, Oongo, I do," Jesse said, stunned. "Are they related?"

"Yes, sire. These creatures were created by the same group. It started as an experiment with the Xantharaian elders, but when they were removed the creators tried other creatures such as these ants and found that the longer the devices remained, the more changes took place in the hosts. The appliances morphed on their own from simply a controlling device to a form of artificial intelligence, much more sophisticated than the cylinders. If the black cylinders on Xanthara had not been discovered and left in place, the people they were placed in would have grown into similar beings, only in a more anthropoid form. These appliances have grown beyond what they were ever intended to be. So much so that the creators lost control of them and have since gone into hiding. It seems that the devices are always searching for new hosts. It is a mystery how these new invaders can control them and not be affected themselves. When the aliens saw what was happening and then discovered that they could control the devices, they saw their chance to work their plan here for possession."

"Whoa, wait a minute," Jesse stammered. "Are you saying that if the Moon Soldiers hadn't discovered those cylinders in the minds of Nexlucimus and the others, they would have morphed into something like those big ants?"

"Yes, that is what we are saying, but they would have resembled themselves, not giant ants. These poor creatures have been invaded by those who wished to control them to dig out the gold that you saw. Since ants normally hibernate in frozen conditions it was necessary to change them into what you saw. They are now more machine than insect. They can work nonstop, require no food, will never break down and require no monitoring. They dig and process the gold, turning it into pure gold bricks. It is picked up by those in control and transported where needed."

"Who is in control, Oongo?" Jesse asked, astonished and not sure he wanted to know.

"Jesse, they are not from your world, nor are they from fantasy. They come from far away; their world is dying or perhaps already dead. They have been living on their ships for a very long time and have lost contact with their home planet. They needed a new place to live and this one, out of all those of similar design that they explored, met their needs. They are trying to possess. They have watched humans for millennia in their search for a new home. They know human weaknesses; they sense that humans are easy to control."

"Is there any possible way to get rid of them, Oongo, before it's too late?" Rambo asked, concerned for all of them.

"The workers we spoke to did not have an answer, but I have a suggestion: fire. That is the only way. These aliens cannot tolerate fire or heat of any kind. That is what was killing the planet they came from. That is why they are at not only the South Pole but the North as well, and deep beneath the oceans. Do you and Rambo remember how you incinerated the black cylinders? That is the only answer here as well, but trust me, Jesse, that will call down the aliens that control them. We must be ready for them."

"Oongo," Jesse said, "is there any way to discover how these aliens control those creatures and not become infected yourselves?"

"I'm not sure, Jesse, since the aliens spend most of their time aboard their ships, which they can dock here under the ice cap. I might have Purja return to Xanthara to be with our family while I continue here and engage the help of one or two of the essences. I believe both Heala and Sheela have computer experience. What did you have in mind, Jesse?"

"I'm not really sure it's just a thought right now. But thanks, Oongo. Keep me posted," Jesse said.

"I will do that, Jesse."

"Oongo, how did you get so much information so quickly?" Chaelea wanted to know.

"A couple of the younger workers," Oongo said. "I was able to understand their speech pattern; it is one of my gifts. They are very sad about what has happened to their kind and what they are being forced to do. They know that it is too late for them and the others that are going through the change. These younger ones are still in their own minds and they wish to see the cruelty to their colony stopped. If you fly over that location you will see a large hole going down into the ice and snow; it is the opening to their colony. It is deep within the permafrost and a perfect location for the controllers. The controllers can fly their ships through the opening, where there is plenty of flat space to land them. They have built a small compound here, but it looks very technical. They seem to live on their ships and work in the compound. I'm not sure, but they might be powering everything with their ships.

"The ants are foreigners to this region; they were brought here against their will. It is because of the huge gold deposits that they were imported from a much warmer climate. They were transformed to withstand it there. These aliens are untraceable because of the magnetism of the poles, and the fact that their ships transmit on a different frequency than is possible with earthly technology. They can blend in and communicate with humans, but when humans try to trace the transmissions it is scrambled before detection is possible."

"But why this planet?" Jesse asked. "The two poles are small and anywhere else underground isn't as cold. In fact, some places are very hot. There wouldn't be that much space."

"They have the technology to change the climate. They needed this planet because of its oxygen levels and environmental water content. They can actually increase the snow and ice levels of the area they are occupying," Purja told them.

"Wow. I do remember how those little black cylinders on Xanthara tried to work into my hand. What to do… what to do?" Jesse asked, to everyone and no one in particular.

"Oongo, Purja, thank you so very much. No one could have served us and the quest with this information like you two have, because of your gifts and skills. We all owe you a great debt. This is truly horrifying news, but it is better to have it now while there still might be a chance to change things. Tazeron seems like a small problem next to this discovery," Chaelea said, shaken.

"It has been our pleasure, as always, to serve the Keepers," Purja said to the group.

"I don't understand, Chaelea," Jesse said. "How could this have slipped past the gods?"

"Perhaps I can answer that for all of you, young ones." Surprised, they turned to discover that Matilda had joined them.

"Please, all of you, have a seat and I will answer all of your questions," Matilda told them with a sad smile.

Before Matilda could begin her discussion with the group, they started receiving information from around the world about Tazeron's camps. After tallying up the numbers they discovered that there were about one hundred and twenty-four camps with a few hundred followers at each camp. Not all of them were as aggressive in their destruction of life as the ones they had first discovered, but many were. It appeared that the more destructive camps were ruled over by immortal followers of Tazeron. Jesse sent out a return message, thanking the field members for their information with orders to destroy those camps that were slaughtering people, except for any innocent victims that might still be there. All the immortal followers that they might find were to be taken to Tazeron's base camp and left there. Jesse wished they could destroy the evil immortals, but the gods hadn't sanctioned that yet. Jesse looked toward Matilda as he gave those orders and she approved with a simple head nod and a sad expression. The talismans would be a tremendous help in this assignment, since all the Keepers with talismans were paired with those that didn't.

Jesse sat down hard on a chair and sighed deeply. "Ok, Mistress Matilda, what news do you have for us?"

Matilda watched Jesse for a few moments and then addressed him and the rest of them.

"Children, especially you, Jesse, all of us that you call Ancients are watching this with great sadness. As each mortal world nears its end, it seems evil and corruption increase significantly. This has been the case since the time before time. Some worlds are more wicked than others and this world is one of the worse. But it also has some of the most talented and valiant of all the worlds. That was necessary for balance. However, with the advent of Tazeron and this new invasion, the good are being overrun by the evil. They are losing ground and hope. You have all tested well, but the end is still not yet. Because of this new development that you have discovered you feel that the odds have been greatly stacked against you. I assure you that they have not."

Jesse started to object but thought better of it. "Mistress Matilda, what are you saying? How did this slip past all of those that advised us to release Tazeron into this world? How are we to protect and destroy at the same time? There's just too much, especially with this new threat that's feeding the situation."

"Jesse, did you think that there was only this problem out there in the great beyond? Did you think that there were only two sets of gods, one mortal and one immortal? While the gods of this world are all-seeing and all-knowing, they are not controllers; they love, encourage and bless. As other beings of other worlds expand their own vision, they explore. They do this for knowledge, survival, expansion and, yes, control. The ones that are invading here now are coming for two of those reasons: survival and control. They searched the innumerable galaxies for a new home and their gods let them go. Just as the mortals of this world take ideas and develop them to suit their own purposes, so do the mortals of other worlds, not of your gods. But there, too, are similarities. Those mortals, like you mortals and you immortals, are being tested for their gods. The ones that are invading here have proven themselves in the wrong way and, as hard as it might seem at this point, they are not our problem.

"Your primary concern currently is protecting the innocents of this world and allowing Tazeron to ripen to his destruction. Then, if the gods of those other worlds want you to contend with their mortals, the foreign invaders, we will let you know. Do what you need to do without engaging the new arrivals; that is important. Do you have any other questions not related to the new aliens?"

"Matilda," Chaelea addressed the Ancient, "what advice can you give us? How much longer must we play with this wicked man, Tazeron? It seems to us that he must be ripe for destruction with all the innocents that have died thus far. Please give us some guidance."

"You are correct, he is close, but he is not there yet. I will do one more thing. I will give you a gift."

"A gift?" Rambo asked.

"Yes, a gift. Use it wisely. There will be no more until the end, and Jesse, you will be the only one that can finish Tazeron. He must not be killed until 'it is enough' and then the chain will tell you what to do. You are on the right path, children. Talk to your troops, keep strong, have faith and never give up hope." With those words Matilda handed Jesse a small blue sack with a drawstring at the top. "They activate with sunlight. Take care, young ones." Matilda blew them all a kiss as she faded out.

"What's in the bag, Jesse?" Breeze wanted to know.

Jesse carefully opened the bag and peeked in. "Moon Soldiers!" he said excitedly. "She said that they activate with sunlight. I have no idea how many are in this bag, but this is an amazing gift. Thank you, Mother Matilda!" They all echoed the sentiment.

"You are welcome, children; we are watching with pride."

"Well, I vote we go check out some of Tazeron's sites and see what kind of mischief we can cause that old slimeball," Rambo said.

"I think that's an excellent idea, Pops," Jesse grinned at Rambo. He was feeling much better after Matilda's visit. Just knowing that he had a bag full of Moon Soldiers elevated everyone's mood. "Where should we start? Any ideas?" Jesse asked the group.